Tomaree

letters lost...

letters found...

Debbie Robson

Trellech Press

Tomaree   letters lost ... letters found ...
Debbie Robson

First published in 2008 by Trellech Press
Lake Macquarie, NSW, Australia

Reprinted in September 2008, January 2009

Cover design & re-layout by Matthew Ward, Mockfrog Design

Front cover photograph © Mikhail Matsonashvi, 2008.
Image from BigStockPhoto.com.
Back cover photograph © the author.

Printed in Australia by BPA Print Group, Burwood, Victoria

A CIP catalogue record for this book is available from the
National Library of Australia

ISBN 978 0 646 48629 1

Disclaimer: The HMAS Assault Naval Base at Fly Point, the
Joint Overseas Operational Training School based at Shoal Bay
and the encampment of the Darwin Infantry Battalion at Gan
Gan are all part of the World War II history of Port Stephens.
Please note that although real names of local people have been
used with permission, the main characters are purely fictitious.

To my Mother and in memory of my

Father and our Shoal Bay holidays

There are very few human beings who receive the truth, complete and staggering, by instant illumination. Most of us acquire it fragment by fragment, on a small scale, by successive developments, cellularly, like a labourious mosaic.

Anaïs Nin

Prologue

Mostly we get it wrong – the past. We think we are remembering a day, a night the way it happened but we aren't. We bring our own sensibilities, the so-called 'wisdom' of another twenty, thirty, even fifty years on earth, all of which just distorts and misrepresents. We mustn't add layers to understand the past: we must subtract – the mortgage, the marriage, the fights, the jobs, even the holidays and the honeymoon (if there was one).

We must strip away our world-weariness, our angst especially our cynicism until we are at the beginning. Of course that will leave naivety, gaucheness and a fair amount of recklessness, but there will be a sense of wonder. That all-important part of ourselves we leave behind very quickly. Far too quickly.

I discovered all this and much more in one month. Ingenuously I thought my journey was over when my plane touched down and my suitcase was stored away. But that's when my voyage really began.

Regrets

The plane trip was a nightmare. All I could think about was not being there for my mother. She was dead. She had died alone and all the old regrets resurfaced. Twenty six years ago my decision to leave Australia had seemed the only way out of a very awkward situation, the only way to cope with my difficult mother. But now, of course, I was facing the repercussions: a crushing sense of guilt, my mother's funeral and the daunting task of picking up a life I had left behind as a young bride. *Oh God*, I told myself as the plane began to descend: *If only I had been with her!*

From the moment the plane touched down in Sydney I felt better. There were things to do, a hire car to organise. An LC Holden Torana as it turned out – a little box of a thing. I surveyed it with suspicion but was assured it would be fine, and arrangements were made so that I could drop it off in Newcastle the following Monday.

Back again after five years. While I drove, I recalled my mood during the last visit: 1967 and the war in Vietnam was raging. Now it was over – at least for the Australian troops. They had been withdrawn for months now, thank God.

I remember feeling grateful back in 1967 that we only had a daughter. No son to worry about. But then with a jolt I remembered I had been worried about Sarah. Very worried. Two young friends of hers were drafted around that time and just a month before I flew out, Sarah moved away to attend college. Not surprisingly, it hadn't been an easy trip. Mum and I had struggled to get on and a lot of the time my thoughts had been elsewhere. It was an awkward visit for both of us and nothing was resolved.

To think that was five years ago. In truth it feels more like ten. So much has happened but I can't think about that now. I can only accept the fact that this might be the start of a new life back in

Nelson Bay, my childhood home, and if I do decide to stay, then I will have come full circle. I can almost hear Mum say: *Back again, are you?* The thought made me smile. *Yes, I'm back again, Mum.*

After more than five hours of driving, including some on the new freeway, the sun had finally cleared a low-lying bank of clouds and was now illuminating the flat landscape in front of me. It was gentle, the surrounding scenery, nothing spectacular but tinged nevertheless by what I knew lay beyond. Ahead was the turnoff to Port Stephens.

How many times had I imagined this trip with Tom at my side? Me saying things like: *Here's the turnoff remember? Yes, the road is better. And Tilligerry Bridge is not such a boneshaker anymore.* Twice hoping he would be by my side. In 1950 and in 1967. And now in 1972 there was no hope left. And with that realisation it felt as if a hundred years separated me from my seventeen year old self, a silly gauche young girl.

As I drove I imagined my child hood friend Betsy sitting in the passenger seat, the two of us back after years away and with so much to talk about. I paused in my fantasy. Would we have lots to talk about or would there be just an awful gaping silence? I had no idea. I shook my head to clear my thoughts.

How my mind runs away from me. Sighing, I put my right indicator on, wishing as I crossed the Pacific Highway that Betsy and I hadn't lost contact. As it turned out we could have been a comfort to each other but there we are, as Mrs Davies, my mother's Welsh neighbour would say. *There we are.*

By this time I had reached Bobs Farm and the tall grasses by the side of the road brought back a vivid flash of soldiers half hidden from view. In the war years the troops had trained here as well as on the beaches. I recalled Mum telling me that a woman who sometimes helped out at the ladies auxiliary had got the fright of her life when passing a field near here. Forty or so troops had suddenly materialised from behind trees or stood up after crouching in the long grass. In an instant they were just there, all covered in twigs and bush, she said, nearly thirty years ago. Where were they now? A lot of them dead, of course. I gripped the steering wheel hard and tried to think of something else.

I studied the landscape again. I'd forgotten how blue the sky was here. The intermittent trees, the sand hills all seemed like props, moving backwards and forwards across the centre of the stage, my windscreen. Departing. Arriving. Suggesting something more. Something waiting. The feeling was so palpable. I knew what lay beyond this landscape, only to reveal itself at the last moment. The sea. Always beyond reach until the final dip down into Nelson Bay. The sea, teasing and tantalising. *Here I am. I've always been here. You just couldn't see me.*

Yes, it was the sea waiting for me, telling me: *I'm here. I never left. You left.* Waiting to wrap around me, waiting to wrap around everything where the shoreline tapered to a dramatic end at Shoal Bay. Those wonderful headlands rearing up like something out of Michener's *Tales of the South Pacific*, the book a birthday present from my husband in the early years of our marriage.

Tom. I couldn't think about him now. Instead the sea was calling. *Come play with me.* If I keep driving long enough perhaps I will end up in the deep blue sea, my yellow hire car slipping gently below the surface. No bubbles. Nothing. Just a stray dolphin to nudge at the windows and a mystery for the locals to speculate over. *Whatever happened to Helen Ashburn's daughter? Thought she was expected back last week for the funeral. Joan Davies was watching out for her. Weren't you, Joan?*

The reality of Joan cheered me. Her plump cheerfulness. She *was* watching out for me and had probably bought a few things for the fridge. I hoped so as the thought of facing well meant condolences from the local shopkeepers terrified me. Maybe on Saturday, after the funeral but I had the house to face today.

Twenty minutes later I turned into Magnus Street. As I brought the car to a halt, I glanced back at the suitcase. It could stay there for a little while. It sat there enormous, battered and bulging, complacent yet knowing. It had been with me on all my travels. But no more. It would have to be happy on the top of the wardrobe, at least until I took a holiday. I slammed the door to clear my head and took the short flight of steps to the porch. There was the key, as always, in the pink fuchsia pot. With the door opened, Joan Davies came up behind me. I didn't turn around.

'Oh there you are, Peggy. Terrible long flight I expect.'

'Yes, it was.'

'And no amount of wishing could make it shorter.'

As she spoke I could hear Joan following me inside the house. So no enduring this in private, I thought. 'No,' I said finally.

Blinking through tears I surveyed the small lounge room and the kitchen beyond where the table was spread with one of Mum's brightly coloured tablecloths, gay against the rest of the subdued furnishings. I swerved away from the yellow check and walked towards my old room. Looking across the house I saw with relief that the door to Mum's was closed. I put my handbag down on the bed.

The room was simply furnished. Stripped back of my youthful paraphernalia 25 odd years ago, it was merely a spare bedroom now. I had been so hurt on the first visit back that I had never considered buying anything to claim this room. Maybe Mother had been hurt by the omission. A picture, a quilt would have been nice. The bed covering was plain white, a sort of terry towelling with fringes. No pictures on the walls just a white enamel mirror, an old oak bedside table and wardrobe and that was it.

Fighting for composure I walked back into the lounge room. Joan was in the kitchen.

'A cup of tea is it and you'll feel much better.'

It appeared I was to have tea too. I sat down trying not to look at the tablecloth. With a sharp flick of her wrist Joan turned off the stove.

'I'll be back in a jiffy, love.'

Alone, I had a little cry over the yellow tablecloth and its predecessors, the only bright colours my mother had allowed into her life, except for some of my clothes as a child. She had always been so hard on herself, choosing half tones to hide behind but she had loved her bright tablecloths.

I heard Joan's screen door slam and taking deep breaths I wiped my eyes with the back of my hands. I couldn't just sit here like an idiot. I got up, lit the stove and replaced the kettle. It boiled quickly. I poured hot water into the pot as Joan came back in.

Smiling at me she removed the tablecloth and replaced it with a beige one, trimmed with crotchet. The crotchet was probably Mum's, I realised, feeling tears pricking behind my eyes again. I looked at the new tablecloth, wondering if I had actually spoken aloud about the yellow one.

'Should have thought to do that before,' she remarked, as if answering my thoughts.

'And the tea cosy, the rocking chair, her geraniums and fuchsias and everything in her bedroom.'

I was sobbing again. This time Joan's arms were about me, and with the comfort her embrace gave me, I let go. All the pent up feelings, the grief and anger were in those tears. When I had cried myself out, I felt better. Not great but a little better.

Joan handed me a handkerchief and while I wiped my eyes yet again she remarked. 'Stewed, I expect it will be.'

'What?'

'The tea, love. I'll just make another.'

Sighing, I watched all of Joan's movements. How nice it was to have someone to do things for you. The cup of tea was placed in front of me and Joan sat down. It wasn't until then I noticed the cake.

'Was it there before or am I going mad?'

'I brought it in with the tablecloth, Peggy.'

We both laughed. 'Your seed cake. How sweet of you. It was Mum's favourite.' I put my slice down, choking back tears again.

After an awkward silence, Joan said, 'I'm driving you to the service on Friday, love, and I'll help you with your mother's room.'

'Thank you, Joan. I think I will need moral support. As for my mother's room, I thought I'd leave it for a week or so. I just want to spend the next few days quietly.'

'Walking is always good to the clear the head. At least that's what my mother always said. She was a great walker my mother. Always up the mountain whenever she had a minute. And you were too when you were young I hear, although a different mountain of course.'

'"Gallivanting around", as Mum would say.' There I had mentioned her and this time I felt better. Would Joan change the subject?

'I can just hear her saying that.'

I smiled in thank you. 'It's so good to see you again, Joan. I'm sorry I should have said that when I arrived.'

'Don't you worry about that.' Joan made to stand and collect our plates.

'Do you have to go just yet? It's nice to have someone to talk to.' I really didn't want to be alone.

'Of course I don't, love. Arthur won't be home for hours,' Joan said, sitting down again.

'How is that mad sister of yours?' I asked, relieved that Joan seemed happy to stay for a little while longer.

'As well as ever and your interest in her hasn't waned, I see. Your mother would often beg news of Angharad for her letters to you. She worried, you see, that you would find her letters boring. She didn't have much news of her own. Only enough to fill half a page, she would often say.'

'So Angharad helped fill the rest,' I said. I took a deep breath. 'So what is she up to now? Still a part of that welfare group helping sick and injured foxes?'

'Oh ay and the rest.' Joan paused. 'You remind me of her.'

'Me?' I was a little shocked but tried to hide it. Angharad was sixty and weighed over 15 stone. But the moment the idea had formed, I knew that physical appearance wasn't what Joan was referring to. I waited for her reply.

'The energy of two people. I don't know where she gets it. And determination as well. She's getting ready to go on a little trip. Visiting home and lots of towns roundabout.'

'Oh, that sounds nice.'

'I'll lend you her last letter. She's a good one for describing places, you know. And she loves to look up all the old history. She's been talking for a while now about recapturing the past. Not quite sure what she means by that. Maybe she just wants to get everything right in her head. She's thinking about writing her memoir. Her quest, she calls it.'

'A quest?'

'Oh ay. Her quest. But I don't know that you can ever go back. Seems she needs to though. How about I bring that letter over tomorrow? You need some peace and quiet now.'

'I would love that, Joan,' I assured her. 'Ten o'clock?'

'Lovely,' Joan replied.

I gave her a quick hug and thanked her for the seed cake. Joan had reached the door when she turned abruptly around and said,

'You did hear about Sarah Linden, didn't you? It's five months ago now. I know she was like a second mother to you.'

'She was and I had heard.'

'She was a lovely woman,' Joan said as she walked down the steps.

Brushing away more tears, I simply waved goodbye to Joan and closed the front door. It wasn't until after I had cleared the table and done the dishes that I looked in the fridge and discovered a bounty of food: a casserole for tonight, eggs, milk, butter and cream, even some chops. I moved back to the kitchen bench and checked the bread bin. Bread too. All this food and I hadn't thanked her. But I could thank her tomorrow morning I realised and felt relieved. She would have to accept money for all this. Maybe I could buy her some flowers before she comes, I decided.

After a little while of sitting down and staring into space I got up and looked around the house, searching for something to read to fill in the time. There was only a few readers digest, magazines and one or two Mills and Boons. Not a decent book in the house. Mum had never been much of a reader and I had been too distressed when packing to worry about bringing a few of my own to read. TV it would have to be tonight. I could look forward to buying a book to read tomorrow and going over Angharad's letter.

Still feeling lost in my childhood home, I walked to the porch and glanced out over Magnus Street and beyond. We were on the high side of the street, looking north across the road to the bay spread out like a gift. Tomaree, the headland I had once climbed as a twelve year old was out of sight to the east. With the afternoon wearing on, the sun had shifted across the bay and would soon set beyond Soldiers Point. *I'm here now,* I told the glittering bay. *Better late than never.*

A walk would have been nice but I decided against it. I was too tired and drained. I also thought too of writing to Betsy. Did she know that my mother had died and Sarah too? The question brought another stab of grief. Probably Nancy, her mother, had written. Yes, I should write to her and say: *Let bygones be bygones. We were young. It was the war years. There was so much going on. We're older now. Wiser.* Wiser? I didn't feel any wiser.

Yes I should write but the task of actually beginning such a correspondence again loomed too large for me at the moment, like so many things. I had faced the house (well, all but my mother's room) and coped with seeing Joan again. Tomorrow or the next few days was soon enough to write to Betsy, visit the solicitors and begin to go through my mother's house.

I decided instead on a long walk early tomorrow morning, maybe as far as Shoal Bay. That I could do. Each day I must give myself something to look forward to as a respite from things I must do. That was the only way to get through this next month or so. The only way.

After dinner while watching Division 4 on TV I realised that Joan had never explained why I reminded her of her sister. She had mentioned Joan's quest, her energy and determination. At this point in my life I had neither energy nor determination although I did have lots of things to sort through and perhaps was in the middle of a life change. But that couldn't be considered a quest, not by any stretch of the imagination. There was one question uppermost in my mind though, that needed answering. It had reared its ugly head these last few months and refused to go away:

Whatever was I thinking saying yes that long ago day in May, 1943?

Christmas Bush

On Thursday, 3rd September 1942 Peggy struggled with the sheets of the bed in number five, the last one she had to strip. It wasn't yet past eight o'clock. Too early to be doing this she decided, as with one last tug the bottom sheet came loose. Although she had been working at Ocean View Guest House, for close to six months it often felt like she would never get accustomed to the early starts. She was definitely a night person but other than that it was a good job and Mr Roche nice to work for. From 11.00 am every day the time was her own. Well, usually. Except today. For some reason she was finishing at 1.00 o'clock. Mr Roche had asked her to work back. Extra beds were to be made up.

Ten minutes before finishing up, whilst she was tidying up the laundry, she heard voices. Excited voices. Mrs Hartley had called in and was speaking to Mr Roche in a high pitched rush of words. Peggy walked back in to the guest house to listen.

'It is here, Mr Roche, I tell you. The Queen Mary.'

'Here in Port Stephens? I don't think so, Mrs Hartley.'

'Why not in Port Stephens? Aren't we worth visiting?'

'I don't think Nelson Bay would exactly be on the itinerary of such a ship.'

'It's not in Nelson Bay, it's anchored in Salamander.'

'And from that distance you can tell it's the Queen Mary?'

'Of course it is. It must have simply called in on its way down to Sydney don't you think?'

Peggy could tell by the stunned silence that Mr Roche was obviously too flabbergasted to reply and there was no arguing with Mrs Hartley.

When he didn't answer, Mrs Hartley went on, 'It's long enough to be the Queen Mary and except for the Queen Elizabeth, what other ship could it possibly be?'

'There is a war on, Mrs Hartley.'

'What would the navy want with Port Stephens, Mr Roche? You can see the Queen Mary from just beyond the church, so I've been told. Why don't you go and take a look?'

Peggy didn't hear his reply; she was too busy thinking. She could run there now. It would only take her a minute. Perhaps if she asked, Mr Roche would let her off early. Shaking his head at Mrs Hartley and with a bemused expression on his face he encountered Peggy standing in the hall.

He raised his hand as she began to speak. 'I need that last room swept out Peggy. It won't take you long.'

'Did you know that...'

'Ah now Peggy, don't ask me that. Just a lucky guess. Go on, get your skates on. You'll be finished in a few minutes.'

In fifteen she was off up the hill, past the white timbered Methodist Church and on to a track that skirted through the bush on the escarpment above Dutchmans Beach. She stopped where the trees thinned a little and peered through the scrub, but there was no view of Salamander Bay, let alone any ships anchored there. Mrs Hartley, or her informant, was sadly mistaken. You couldn't see anything from here. Peggy began walking again, ferns brushing against her ankles and her tennis shoes covered now in black sand.

Above her the canopy of leaves became thicker, sunlight barely filtering through. The landscape was hushed as if holding its breath. She felt something soft brush her legs and looked down to a sea of Christmas bush. As she descended the small valley she was enveloped by it. The white flowers, foam and sea spray all in one, moving above her and all around as she scrambled down.

Peggy stood for a moment and let the flowers encircle her. She was drowning in the sight and feel of them. This was one of her favourite spots and she had forgotten about it! Completely forgotten. September was always the time to come here. Ever since Easter when she started work she had forgotten about a lot of her old haunts, but not the strange, comforting feelings they gave her. While sitting alone on Zenith Beach, climbing Tomaree or even just standing looking at a small valley full of Christmas bush it seemed to Peggy as if she was with someone. Someone kind, watchful, breathing through her breath, seeing with her eyes.

She had told no one, of course, about these feelings. Mostly people thought she was such a wanderer because of her mother. She was sure that's what Betsy and Emily thought and she hadn't bothered to convince them otherwise. In truth it was partly to get away from her mother but the other reason was to feel that watchful presence and to be surrounded by beauty. And here it was below: catching her unawares and robbing her of breath but then after a little while, calming her. For a few moments she let herself slip below the surface and block out everything but her view of the flowers. Silently she let the unknown presence merge with her own.

Stretching like a cat, to rouse herself, Peggy began moving again. She was still a little light-headed as if walking under water. Perhaps she was a bit odd but she didn't care. It didn't matter what other people thought of her. She wasn't giving up her time alone for anybody. Now for this ship! She began to look around to gain her bearings when she heard a voice above her head, an American voice say, 'I have never seen anything so beautiful in my life.'

The gentle timbre of his words created a riot of butterflies in her stomach. With a careful movement she turned, her mind stretching the moment out, willing him to be reasonably good looking. He didn't have to be Gary Cooper, her favourite actor. Pleasant would do. But when she encountered him she couldn't see his face. He was above her, looking down with the sun at his back. All she could take in was the pale khaki of his uniform.

As she squinted to make out his features, he walked down the slope towards her. He stood right in front of her now, in the shadows. Looking at his face, she had no idea what to say to him. In fact she stared at him dumbstruck. He had the nicest, most gentle face she had seen in a long time, an intelligent face with blonde hair and dark brown eyes. He waited. She looked about her and was finally able to say. 'Yes, it is beautiful here. It's one of my favourite places.'

'Aren't you lucky to have such a beautiful place to come to?'

The words were spoken without condescension. She studied

his expression. It was serious, his gaze alert. No hint of amusement in his dark brown eyes. She was always on the lookout for both, had been for a long time now. It was a habit she couldn't break, even if she didn't care any more what people thought of her, especially her mother. And all because she loved to climb, and often preferred her own company.

Just when she was about to speak he smiled and Peggy felt like she did when she gazed out into the bay. 'Don't they have places like this back where you come from?' Her tone was teasing but he didn't seem to mind.

He took up her tone and gave it back to her. 'What in Wyoming?'

'No?' she asked sympathetically.

'No,' he said, turning away to gaze around him again. There was silence for a little while but it wasn't awkward. 'Maybe in the Rockies. As beautiful but different. I've never seen flowers like these.'

'It's Christmas bush,' she told him.

'Hey, but it's September!' He was laughing.

'Of course it's September but by December the flowers have turned red and we pick them for decoration, you know.'

'That's swell. I'll make sure I come back in December.'

'You're going again?'

'No, not yet. I'll be here for a while with a few others from my country.'

'Looking after us?'

'Something like that.'

It seemed the time to go but she no longer wanted to see the ship. He was obviously off the ship and much more interesting. 'You're off the Queen Mary?'

His laughter rang through the bush. 'The Queen Mary. Well I'll be damned!'

Peggy spoke quickly to hide her embarrassment, 'That's what somebody was saying. I never thought it was though. Why would it bother coming here?'

'Exactly. Not that this isn't a swell place,' he remarked gazing at her this time instead of the landscape.

Feeling uneasy under such cheerful scrutiny, Peggy stepped

back a little. 'I should be going.'

'To see the Queen Mary?' he asked.

'Whatever it's called. No, I'll go tomorrow.' She smiled at him and walked back up the slope. When she reached the top of the incline and gazed back, he was still looking after her. He waved and she waved back, her head spinning with white Christmas bush and dark brown eyes.

The next day, Peggy set off to walk to Salamander, her mother's suspicions following her every step. Lunch had been awkward. She hadn't said anything direct of course but the inference was there with remarks such as: 'You're off with the fairies, Peg. I hope you weren't this vague with Mr Roche. Lots of strange people about with the Queen Mary here in Port Stephens. Lots of Americans too. You keep away from them do you hear?'

'Yes, Mum. I'm going for a walk this afternoon.'

'Not to see the Queen Mary?'

'It's not the Queen Mary, Mum. It's just a ship.'

'I don't like the idea of you walking so far.'

'I'll be fine, Mum.'

'Don't speak to any of those Americans.'

'Yes, Mum.'

'I only say this for your own protection. I've heard some things about those Americans. They're terribly fast with women for one thing. All please and thank you but fast just the same.'

More likely they were just lonely, being so far from home Peggy thought now as she walked along Dutchmans Beach, passing the Lobsterman's tent, painted a bright red. The garishness of it against the more subdued colours of the other beach shacks and surrounding trees normally lifted her spirits, but not today. She still felt tense from the conversation with her mother. She had been surprised her mother hadn't prevented the walk somehow but she had appeared strangely resigned today. Not her usual self at all.

On the way Peggy had hurried through the Christmas bush trying not to think about him, but it was useless. She hadn't been able to sleep for thinking of him, and she didn't even know his name! Why hadn't he introduced himself? She had asked her pillow the question numerous times last night. Down amongst the Christmas bush it hadn't seemed necessary. But now she wondered if perhaps he had been breaking some rule by speaking to her.

He hadn't seemed nervous though. Not at all. He was in awe of the beauty around him just as she was. It had led him to speak and she had been immediately attracted to him, to a man who was so affected by the spring landscape. Not that other men wouldn't have noticed. Some anyway, but most wouldn't have responded quite like he did. Peggy told herself this over and over.

No matter which way she looked at their meeting, how many times she went over it in her mind, it was his words and the silence just before he spoke which seemed to linger with her and make her feel light-headed. She could still hear him say it. 'I have never seen anything more beautiful in my life.' His words were like an echo of her feelings when she came upon the view. In that instant there had been someone feeling something as deeply as herself and the realisation was as disturbing as it was comforting.

Peggy walked on carrying her sandals, the pale white sand at her feet, beginning to cover her bare toes. The clear blue day lifted her mood. The bay was so beautiful this afternoon she longed to show it off to someone.

Maybe this was the way he came yesterday before she met him. Perhaps he had walked the small beach today, early this morning, restless like she was. Or had he rowed ashore? What did he do all day? What was his job? She had every afternoon off during the week and Wednesday completely. He probably had barely any time at all to himself. But what did they do, these Americans? They were probably very busy, but doing what? How to find out? She would somehow. She wanted to know everything about him.

At the end of the beach she came to the rocks, shining and brown in the sunlight, forming a point out into the bay. She clambered over them and up to a small grassy ledge. Slowly Peggy looked back along the shoreline. From this distance Yacaaba, the northern headland, seemed to merge with Fly Point while Tomaree had disappeared completely. The opening of the bay had gone. There was no great stretch of water just a semi-circle of land on the horizon to the northeast. The ship had come through the headlands sometime yesterday. Suddenly it was just there with no warning and no official declaration by anyone. And were there other ships with it? Surely there must be. Maybe she would be able to tell from Sandy Point but that depended on how far in they were anchored. To the west stretched Bagnalls.

She always forgot what a long walk it was along Bagnalls Beach. The sun was beating down on her. How hot it was for September! Peggy glanced to her left at the heavily wooded shoreline. Of course she knew there wasn't a house in sight but unwittingly she checked before pulling her white blouse free from the waistband of her skirt. She shook it up and down to cool her but she still felt damp.

Sweat was tricking down between her breasts. To let the air on her skin, she unbuttoned her blouse and flapped it across her chest. She stood for a few minutes facing the west with the wind blowing her hair. Her skin was tingling and the breeze was stroking her gently like fingertips. Well at least what she imagined a man's fingertips would feel like. Finally her blouse was a little drier and with lethargic movements she buttoned it up and tucked it in.

Feeling tired but happy she walked on. What if she met him now? What on earth would she say to him? Would he set her at ease like he had yesterday? Yes, he would. He was that sort of person. Peggy felt a smile break involuntarily. Yes, he was that sort of person.

At the eastern end of Sandy Point the small weekenders came into view. Peggy stopped on a sandy strip near the water and looked towards Salamander Bay. She could just make out a larger blob of ship and then smaller ones grouped around it. That must be it, but she would have to walk around the bluff to get a better view. When she rounded the square shaped headland would she find a hundred men on the beach? How exciting but no, that was greedy. One would do nicely.

She walked to the other end of Sandy Point and stood for a little while trying to make out the shapes but with the sun shining in her eyes it was useless. The bay glittered under the sun and the trees on the steep bluff to the west obscured her vision. Green merged with the blue of the ocean and the blue of the sky till her head ached. She was standing on a deserted beach like an idiot giving herself a headache. Rubbing her forehead, she turned back towards Bagnalls. In the distance a man was walking towards her.

It was him! She was sure of it, even though from this far away it could have been anyone. Blue shirt and dark blue pants, against the white sand encircled by the blue of the ocean. Her first impulse was to run across the sandy spit and onto the beach to meet him. Only with great difficulty did she manage to restrain herself. How embarrassing would that be for both of them! Instead she watched his progress.

At first he looked around him and back and then finally at her. Was he smiling? It seemed so. She hoped so. With every beat, her heart was jarring in her chest. The wind blew her skirt about her legs as she waited. He was close now. Only a few feet away.

A Quest

Sitting down to a cup of tea with Joan the following morning I asked my neighbour, 'So tell me about this quest of Angharad's.'

Joan thought for a moment. 'I don't rightly know. She wants to go back to our childhood home, Cerrigydrudion. She hasn't been back since she left to go to University, except for weekend visits to our parents. And then of course she hasn't been back since they both died. She had a miserable childhood you know. She was very overweight as a child and was always playing imaginary games that she dragged me into. Sometimes we were fairies, down by the stream near the farm. Other times we were princesses waiting for our princes to come on white horses and take us away.' Joan smiled in recollection.

'Where we lived there was a very old church,' Joan continued. 'And I think she's trying to research its history. Also on the field above our farm there were enormous great stones, or rocks. So very strange, alien really. You know, they just didn't look like they belonged to the rest of the landscape. You can't help but wonder if druids put them there or whoever built Stonehenge. At least that's what Angharad thinks. She has lots of strange ideas, my sister,' Joan added.

'But she's always interesting,' I said.

'She is that! Never a dull moment with Angharad. Here's the letter,' Joan said, fishing it out of the pocket of her dress.

'Thanks,' I said and placed it on the table between us. I felt my spirits lift a little. This was exactly what I needed: a diversion and an interesting one to boot.

'I'd love to go back, you know,' Joan said after a moment. 'I could take her back home. We could call on all the local families and see how everyone is doing. I could talk about all the wonderful things Angharad's done and she could see how everyone else has just stayed put and not achieved half of what she's done in her life. That would make her feel better I think.'

'She's that unhappy?'

'Not exactly. But when she thinks of Cerrigydrudion she thinks of that fat little girl with no friends. I'm sure she does.'

'Would it be all right if I wrote to her, do you think?'

'Of course, love.'

'I mean I used to send her the odd postcard but I think it is about time I wrote her a letter.'

'She'd like that.' Joan paused. 'Oh, she has a sharp mind, my sister. She was always asking questions as a child and she hasn't stopped.'

Joan seemed sad as she made this remark but after a moment she brightened and said, 'To be honest I think all these questions keep her alive.'

'But she's not that old,' I said, alarmed.

Joan waved her hands. 'You know what I mean.'

'Yes.'

'Well, I'm sure she would love to hear from you.'

'Thanks, Joan. I intend to really catch up on my letter writing while I'm here.'

'What do you mean while you're here, Peg?' Joan's face fell. 'I thought you were here for good.'

'I'm sorry, Joan, but I haven't decided yet. But I'm definitely here for a month or two. I thought I'd take that time to go through the house, sort Mum's things out and work out exactly what I want to do.'

'I thought you'd come here to live. But of course....' Joan blushed with embarrassment. 'Maybe I was jumping the gun. I thought from your last letter that you had decided to live here in your mother's house.'

'My last letter was a little hasty. I wasn't thinking clearly. Maybe now and staying here, I can really decide what I want to do with the rest of my life. There's Sarah to think of.'

'Of course, love.' The disappointment in Joan's voice was palpable and there were tears in her eyes. She stood up to go. I gave her a quick hug and thanked her for the letter. Alone I couldn't resist the temptation to open it. Reading about Wales was much easier than trying to work out what to do about this house, my broken marriage and the rest of my life, in fact. I thought about the two sisters pretending to be fairies and princesses and my heart went out to the overweight Angharad, whose prince had never come. No knight in shining armour that dazzled the eyes.

I walked to the window overlooking the bay. My eyes had been dazzled that day on Sandy Point with Tom, I thought bitterly. But it had just been the hot Australian sun shining down on us. Nothing more. Unwittingly I could see him now striding down the beach, his much younger self walking towards me. How could I have resisted him? Well, I should have, I told myself and studied Angharad's strange sounding address at the top of the first page.

I had just begun reading the body of the letter when there was a knock at the door. I opened it to find three of my mother's friends, staring at me with compassionate yet curious expressions. Sighing, I put the letter aside and welcomed them into my mother's home.

The Queen Mary

He walked up the beach with a determination that startled her. One moment he was on the beach and the next on the sandy spit but as he moved towards her his foot caught on a piece of driftwood. When he stepped over it and recovered he stood up right in front of her, just inches separating them.

For a moment Peggy gazed startled into his eyes and his seemed just as surprised at her nearness. But then in the next instant she experienced an unfamiliar sense of power. She was in command as long as she didn't gaze into those dark eyes for too long. She had the strength, the clear head. Their eyes were locked. Neither of them moved and all this without a word spoken between them.

Finally Peggy stepped back from him and as she did so he seemed embarrassed and unsure of himself. He turned in the direction of Salamander Bay, taking in the view.

When she didn't say anything, he moved a few paces towards the bay and then, as if drawn by an invisible thread, back to her again. All the while she knew she mustn't speak. Not yet. It would break the spell and everything would become mundane, the intense feeling of anticipation gone. Reality would intrude and reveal names and explanations, cutting off the strange possibility of now.

She wanted to do so many things. Just watch him for ages as he stood by her side. Touch the dimple in his left cheek; touch his hair that was more golden than yesterday in the shadows. She wanted to ask him a thousand questions, grab him close and kiss him, so endearing did he look in his confusion. For a second she thought that's what he was about to do. He moved closer to her and then away again, running his hands through his army haircut.

It was so exciting to be close to such a good looking young man. Betsy or Emily weren't here to steal him from her. He was hers. Today, this minute he was hers. Until he spoke anything was possible: they had been seeing each other for a while now. They got on so well. Everyone said they looked good together. Her red hair and fair skin complementing his blonde hair and olive complexion. Where did he get such colouring? Of course, being his girlfriend, she would know this. Know everything about him. But they hadn't seen each other for a few days and that's why he was nervous.

The breeze caught her skirt and whipped it up. She grabbed at it, brushing down the green and white striped material. With the breeze up and lifting whitecaps on the water and the sun beating down, Peggy waited. They stood exposed, trapped together on this sandy strip. To move away would be almost like a rejection. They had encountered each other and they could not retrace their steps. Was he sorry that he had walked up to her so quickly; making such an obvious move towards her?

She realised in the bright sunlight that he wasn't as old as she had thought yesterday or as tall. Five feet eight or so but that was a nice height against her wretched stumpiness of five foot, a bane of her life, the other her red hair and freckles. No freckles on him, just blonde hair and olive skin.

Her daydream continued. They both loved the bay and being near the water, long walks in the bush or on the beach. She still felt in control. She was in control until she looked into his eyes again. And then it was she who was confused. He was extending his hand. Was she supposed to take it?

But he mustn't speak. That was all she could think. He mustn't speak first. He had spoken first yesterday. It must be her today. For some reason it must be her. He was introducing himself. That's what he was doing. He was about to say his name. 'Perhaps you aren't supposed to talk to the locals,' she said in a rush.

His hand fell to his side. 'Maybe, but I'm getting kind of tired of regulations.'

'Me too.'

He moved a step closer to her. 'Your father?' he asked concerned.

'No, Mum. Dad died years ago, when I was a baby.'

'Gee, I'm sorry.'

'It's all right. I don't remember him.'

'But tough on your mother.'

'Yes, it has sort of made her…' Peggy searched unsuccessfully for a word to describe her mother. He was observing her with a serious expression on his face which wouldn't do. She didn't want to be serious today. That was the last thing she wanted. She flapped her arms in bewilderment.

'Overprotective,' he supplied.

'Yes.' She took a step towards him. 'How did you know?'

'A lucky guess.' Now he smiled and extended his hand. 'Howdy, Miss. I'm Tom Lockwood. I'm based at the Country Club.'

She took his hand and said, 'Peggy Ashburn.'

'Pleased to meet you. Like a walk?' He paused. 'Back along the beach?'

'Yes.' They skirted the driftwood and once when Peggy sank a little in the damp sand near the waters edge, he held her hand briefly to steady her. Peggy was in heaven. Along the main part of the beach they began to walk in step. She normally walked quite fast but carefully she slowed her pace down. She wanted him to herself for as long as possible.

'Did you come on that ship?'

'Your Queen Mary?'

'Yes that one, in the next bay.'

'It's the Westralia and no I never came on it. I've been here a few weeks working from the Country Club along with some other American officers.'

'It's nice there, at Shoal Bay not that us locals can enjoy it now.'

'No, but it was necessary to…' he hesitated. 'Acquire it.'

'I suppose so but for a while now I haven't been able to climb up Tomaree, or Stephens Peak.'

'Tomaree, the one with the guns?'

'Yes.'

'Well I'll be! You haven't climbed up that! It's a sheer cliff in some parts.' He was laughing in surprise.

'Only looks it. It's not bad to climb.'

'I'm impressed,' he said smiling and nodding at her.

It was such a relief to talk like this, to reveal that yes she had climbed Tomaree and he hadn't asked why, only commended her. He was the type of person who wouldn't misinterpret her. Unlike her mother.

Tom would be able to handle her mother, she felt sure. With his easygoing ways he could ignore her mother's unrelieved sense of doom about so many things. All she could do was respond to their conversations lightly and ignore the dire warnings. He would be able to cut through all the despair with one of his dazzling smiles.

Smiling back at Tom she said, 'You're meant to be.'

He laughed. 'Well, I am,' he said, looking at her steadily.

Flustered, she said, 'I've suddenly thought of something. I heard Mr Roche talk about the Donald Duck Inn,' Peggy was laughing. 'That's where...'

'Yes, I believe that's the Country Club's new name, Miss Peggy Ashburn.'

Now they were laughing together. When she stopped he was gazing at her.

'You have a nice laugh.'

'Thank you,' she said and blushed.

'Have you lived here all your life?'

'Yes.' Peggy hesitated. 'Well, since I was three. Before that my Dad was alive and we lived in Newcastle. In Mayfield. Have you been there? To Newcastle I mean.'

'Yeah, once already for work, organising a few things. It sure is a hike and that boneshaker of a bridge!'

'Tilligerry?' Peggy laughed.

'I won't even try to say that. Besides it's much nicer here. Sort a like Tahiti or Hawaii.' But he didn't look up in the direction of Yacaaba. Instead he was looking at her steadily as he spoke and for the first time that afternoon Peggy felt a rush of nervous tension. Those brown eyes of his were dangerous. Best not to look right into them she decided and unwittingly did just that. He didn't look away. He was staring at her unashamedly now. She held his gaze for a minute or two and then turned away, blushing again.

'You won the staring competition,' Peggy told him.

'Did I?' He seemed pleased with her reply. 'You are not like other girls, Miss Peggy Ashburn,' he told her.

'No, I'm not,' she said, despondently.

'I meant it as a compliment.' They had stopped walking and were facing each other in the middle of the deserted beach.

'Thank you, but in what way?'

He looked around him for a moment and as he did Peggy noticed he was nervous again. She had put him on the spot. 'It doesn't matter,' she told him.

'It does. Don't you think relationships between the sexes are important?'

'Yes but why does everybody make a big thing about it? Can't people just start as friends?'

'A lot a girls want to make a big thing about it.'

Peggy nodded thinking of Emily Post. 'Well, I don't.'

'I'm mighty pleased to hear that. But I knew it already.' Tom moved a step closer and took her hand. She was breathless and intensely aware of his touch and his nearness. Feeling light-headed, she closed her eyes. He didn't speak until she opened them again and she realised as she did so that he had been watching her the whole time. 'Friends?' he asked.

'Friends,' she told him.

Tom sighed and with reluctance, let go of her hand. They walked in companionable silence to Dutchmans Beach and then on up through the Christmas bush. As they neared the track along the cliff Tom experienced a sudden panic at not seeing her again. He must see her again. She was the sweetest girl he'd met in a long time.

Tomorrow was Saturday. It would be swell to ask her out on a real date but maybe too soon. He glanced at her walking by his side. She was so young. No, Saturday week would be the way to go. Some girls were coming from Newcastle he'd heard so there was no reason why she couldn't come. And maybe she could go with another girl. Well, at least arrive with another girl.

That was it. They could have a few walks next week and a

proper date the following Saturday. With it all formulated in his mind, he was at a loss for words when he turned to speak to her.

She had a way of looking at him that transformed him into a schoolboy. It hadn't happened in the valley but then they hadn't stood that close as today. At the beach when he had stumbled and then stood up right in front of her, he was firstly startled by the greenness of her eyes and then amazed at the expression in them. He had seen so much in their depths in an instant. Surprise, amusement and something else he hadn't been able to put his finger on since. That was why he had stared at her for so long just now trying to work out what it was, but that second time it was missing.

Of course the real reason he was so out of his depths today was the sight of Miss Peggy Ashburn unbuttoning her blouse to the wind. The image still burned in his brain and he knew it would haunt his nights for a hell of a long time. He kept telling himself he had caught her in a private moment. She was hot, there was no one around but that didn't help banish the sight of her with her blouse unbuttoned. God, if she would only do that for him!

Earlier on the rocks at the end of Dutchies he had stopped to look around, hoping and praying to catch sight of her. She said she would go and see the ship today. He had timed it carefully. Remembering when he had seen her in amongst the white flowered bush yesterday, he set off around the same time today and he had been scouting for a glimpse of her for half an hour. When he spotted her, he felt a simple pleasure at the sight of her up the beach from him and then she undid her blouse. The surprise of it took his breath away. And then as he began walking up the beach towards her, he knew it was going to be hard to speak to her and not reveal that he now felt differently towards her. Very differently.

Betrayal

It rained on Friday, 28th July, the day of the funeral, a fine, drizzling rain. Real English weather as Mum would have said. She would have been pleased. I cried a lot, surprising myself. I have always had so many conflicting feelings towards my mother that when grief overtook me during the service I was startled and unprepared. Finally my emotions, in regards to my mother, were wholly engaged in one direction: a tear-drenched, sobbing grief and I abandoned myself to it.

Joan was a comfort again, and the other ladies too. After the service they took over the afternoon tea at my mother's house. I sat through the rest of the day in a blur of tears, sipping I don't know how many cups of coffee, in an effort to wake myself up, revive myself somehow from the languorous melancholy that was beginning to invade my body.

That was yesterday. Today all I wanted to do was sit and vegetate, be still if that was possible without thinking of my mother's room, yet to be faced, or Tom. Tom... I mustn't think about him now. While waiting for the kettle to boil I studied the familiar slant of sunshine that falls on the porch this time of the morning during the winter months. How I would rejoice at the first sight of it! The warmth in the depths of cold.

Many insignificant memories such as this in regard to my mother's house and the landscape of my youth are still, after all these years, viable threads crisscrossing my consciousness: the appearance of the bay after a storm, the way the sun seemed to follow me home on the long walks back from Shoal Bay, how loud the Tomaree guns sounded when fired, Mrs Mann's beautiful smile and the expression on Tom's face when we met on Sandy Point. Could it really be thirty years ago this September?

Like Scarlett I would think about that tomorrow. Instead today

I would read Angharad's letter. I fetched it from my bedroom, clutching it like a drowning woman a lifebuoy. I dragged a folding chair out on the porch and placed my coffee on the brickwork in front of me. Sitting down in the low chair, the bay was no longer visible. Just an immense ice blue sky. It was chilly this morning, a real winter's day. I opened Angharad's letter,

'Ynys Affalach'
Penglais Hill
Aberystwyth
12th July 1972

Dear Sis,

Having a wonderful time planning my holiday trip and a little nervous too about seeing Cerrigydrudion again, but I feel it is time to go back. Remember the great stones heaped in groups across the plain above our farm? And the games we used to play? The stones were our fortress, our smooth, rounded battlement. We pretended we were watching out for the knights returning from battle. Our princes on horseback. I wonder sometimes how I missed mine. Was my head down in a book when he rode past? Probably. Do I mind that I didn't get married and have children? I think the answer is back home somehow although I'm not sure why. Please forgive these childish and maudlin thoughts. I am feeling my age lately and philosophy hasn't been a comfort this last month or so, even Descartes.

Unless I begin to weigh the scales of my life carefully, it seems that I will continue in this vein of self pity and regrets. Cerrigydrudion must be faced. Hopefully I will arrive and find just a small town with a beautiful church. That's what a stranger would think but I dread encountering all the old associations and discovering too that I

*have taken the wrong path in life. Regrets? Well,
that's what I think this trip is all about. To put my
life into perspective…'*

To put my life into perspective. I let the letter fall to my lap.
Wasn't that what I should be doing? Trying to put things into
perspective. Trying to work out why Tom betrayed me. But unlike
Angharad I am not ready to go back. I don't want to go back to
that afternoon. I have been running away from it for nearly two
months now but today there was no escaping the memory. It
pounced as I sat gazing at the pale blue sky.

I could feel the heat of that June day, the confusion. It all came
rushing back with a clarity that was startling. I lost everything in
a matter of minutes: firstly my dignity, next my understanding of
our relationship and what we meant to each other, and finally my
lover. Layer after layer until the threads of my life in Wyoming
were stretched tight in that awful moment when I discovered the
two of them. The threads snapped before he had a chance to
speak… Actually I didn't give him a chance to speak.

It was an unusually hot Wednesday in early June, everything
so still – even the plains. There was no wind at all and so hot in
the classroom. The plains were shimmering in the haze and the
children were listless. After math I realised that it would probably
be better just to read to them in the afternoon. They were clearly
not up to the comprehension test I had planned.

A few had nodded off as I started on a passage from
Huckleberry Finn. When Jessie Schultz fainted, I rushed to pick
him up. He was so small in my arms. I glanced around at the other
children. Marybeth looked pale and Johnny was drowning in
sweat. How easy when you teach to forget what babies they are,
most of them only seven or eight. I consulted the principal. There
were only two other combined classes and she made the decision
to close the school two hours early. Mrs Schultz was contacted,
along with the school bus driver. He was a retired gentleman and
luckily at home. He was on his way.

As the children filed slowly into the hall to retrieve their
satchels, I stepped outside and watched the plains. A breeze was
springing up. I could see its passage by the ripple in the grasses,
moving ever closer. It was cool when it reached my face, so much

cooler than the classrooms. I ordered the children to sit under the large cottonwood tree until the yellow school bus came down our road. They came alive at such a treat and sat down in the dust in a semi-circle around the cottonwood, some lifting their faces to the breeze.

I stood for what seemed like ages, studying the strange but familiar picture in front of me: the pale grassland, the glimmering leaves of the cottonwood and its fluffs of 'cotton', like snow in summer and the children sitting cross-legged at its base. It was an image I knew would stay with me for a long time. I listened to their chatter and for the sound of the bus.

Finally I was able to get away. It was a ten minute drive home along a quiet back road. My car had been steaming when I opened it and although all the windows were down, I was covered in sweat within minutes. I couldn't breathe properly and my mind was in turmoil. I had discovered something about Mrs Schultz but there was no time to think about it now. Perhaps I could talk to Tom later and see what he thought. Maybe I was just grasping at straws but it would explain so many things.

For the moment, all I could think about was getting home, flicking on the air conditioner and standing in front of it with a glass of cold water. That's what I tried to concentrate on but as I drove I became aware of a growing feeling of disquiet. Something was wrong, something other than the news about Mrs Schultz and the terrible heat.

My unease increased when I saw Tom's car. I pulled into the driveway. Whatever was he doing home at this time of the day? I pushed on the front door. It was open. The house was hot and the air very stuffy. No use opening the windows as the breeze hadn't reached here yet. I put my bag down and walked up the stairs. In the hall dividing the bedrooms off, I saw a woman's bag. It was then I heard a muffled cry from our bedroom. I grabbed this other woman's bag and ran down our short hall propelled by fury, hurt, disbelief, all welling in my chest.

When I lunged open the door, there was only a brief instant of *Yes, of course* and then I attacked. I swung the bag down on their naked bodies. They were both so shocked they didn't speak. Barbara didn't even cry out, she was so stunned by my actions.

There was a scrabbling of clothes. Tom made to say something but I put my up hand to stop him. I was out of breath and incapable of speech. What could I have said anyway? What do people say in such situations? And I definitely didn't want to hear anything he had to say. He had said it all without speaking one word.

As they dressed quietly I let Barbara's bag drop to the carpet. Large sobs began to rack my whole body. I backed away from them and somehow managed to make it back down to the kitchen. I finally had that glass of water in an effort to calm myself. And that's what I did. I calmed down and just drove away. I drove for miles and miles. I suppose I've been running ever since. Running from Tom, fearful of speaking to him but somehow I must face him and that confrontation can't be put off forever. I need to really communicate with him for the first time since it happened. I must go back to that hot June afternoon.

Betsy

Peggy was excited. Finally, after being away a month, Betsy, her best friend was home. It was lovely to see Betsy again. She had been visiting her aunt and Peggy had been counting the days until her return. The two girls met up at the park and were sitting watching some of the naval ratings from the Westralia march past. The young men were dressed in white canvas uniforms, which looked terribly uncomfortable, square necked shirts, and incongruously they had on pith helmets.

Just as Peggy was about to say something about the helmets, one of the drinkers at the Sea Breeze Hotel yelled out, 'Where are you boys off to? South Africa?' A few of the ratings looked sheepish and from the hotel shouts of laughter resounded. 'Good to see them though', the same man yelled a moment later when someone else could be heard upbraiding him.

'They do look funny, don't they?' Betsy remarked.

'What the seaman or the helmets?' Peggy was in a teasing mood.

'Peg, the helmets.'

'I wonder where they are off to.'

'Dad says they are building a whole lot of roads and pathways at Fly Point. Not sure what for though.'

'Maybe for some kind of quarters or something.'

'What do you mean?'

'For all the boys,' Peggy said pointing to the line of young men snaking along the road. They can't stay on board the Westralia for ever, can they?'

'Maybe they aren't going to stay.'

'Maybe, but then why start building?' Peggy said, a little doggedly.

Betsy sighed. 'You are always so practical, Peg.'

Peggy turned quickly to gaze at her friend. 'What a nice thing to say.' She paused. 'I think.' Both girls laughed.

'I missed the bay,' Betsy said sighing, and pushing her dark hair from her face. 'I didn't think I would but I did. I thought it would be exciting in Newcastle, but it was just crowded. And it doesn't look like I'm going to be able to work there. Auntie Sybil made some enquiries. There's plenty of jobs but most of them are for the war effort and I'd be snapped up by Manpower before I knew it. I could start out as a secretary for a legal firm and end up working in a factory. That's what Aunt Sybil said. So Mum won't risk it. She doesn't want me working in some factory. She'd rather have me helping her at home. And it looks like that's what I'll be doing. Washing and ironing. Digging in the vegie patch.'

'Well your Mum does need the help with you and your brothers to take care of.'

'And Dad. He's more work than the rest of us.' Betsy tossed a blade of grass away from her and frowned. 'But then why did I bother going to high school in Newcastle? All that studying and travelling for nothing.' Betsy clasped her knees and put her head down. 'Pity your mother wouldn't let you go on.'

'Yes.'

'And it wouldn't have been wasted on you.'

'Oh, I don't know. I still haven't worked out what I want to do.'

'Whereas I've done it all for nothing.'

'Don't say that, Betsy. All that learning will come in handy after the war,' Peggy offered.

'Yes, but when will that be?'

'I don't know. But it's kind of exciting here in the bay because of the war, don't you think,' Peggy remarked, gesturing towards the ratings in the distance.

'I didn't see a good looking one amongst them. Did you?'

'Betsy, you sounded like Emily.'

'Goodness! Did I? How dreadful.' She paused looking towards Fly Point. 'I'd rather Jimmy. How is he? I haven't had a chance to say hello yet.'

'He's fine and he's all yours.'

'What?' Betsy grabbed Peggy's arms in her excitement and

both girls jumped to their feet. 'Can I have him?'

'Of course you can but he was never mine to give.'

Betsy waved her arms in exasperation. 'Whatever that means. Let's go for a walk there now and see if we can see him.'

'Let's go after the sailors instead.'

'Peggy are you teasing?'

'Yes,' she told her friend feeling a hundred to Betsy's seventeen. Since meeting up with her friend an hour ago, Peggy had been hoping to tell Betsy all about Tom but it was proving hard to find an opening. *Oh by the way I met this gorgeous American...* There was no telling her anything until she had caught sight of Jimmy.

The two girls turned down Stockton Street and then stopped a little way from Snow Man's garage. They began to chat, Peggy with her back to the garage, Betsy straining to catch sight of him.

'It's no good. I can't see him at all.'

'We'll have to walk past then.'

'You know I don't like to do this sort of thing.'

'That's why you don't have a boyfriend, Betsy. It's not because you're not pretty. As you keep saying. You are pretty. You're just shy. Now let's walk past and see what happens. Come on, deep breath.'

Betsy glared at Peggy. 'I don't even have my blue cotton on. It's my nicest dress.'

'You look lovely in what you are wearing. Red suits you. It's new isn't it?' Peggy asked, contemplating the red checked skirt and matching top with tiny pockets just below the waist and heart shaped buttons. It really looks good with your black hair.'

I wish I had black hair, Peggy thought not for the first time. And here she was wearing yellow – a dress her mother had made and which didn't suit her in the least. Thank goodness Tom was nowhere in sight. He would change his mind about her if he saw her today. Everyone knew redheads shouldn't wear yellow. Everyone except her mother. The thought was only momentary. She was anxious to help Betsy. Her friend really needed her confidence boosted.

She moved a little closer to Betsy's side. 'Keep talking to me and if he comes over then I'll make up some excuse.' Betsy nodded, already too nervous to speak. After a moment Jimmy did come over and much to Peggy's surprise he didn't appear nervous, quite confident in fact and very pleased to see Betsy. They began to speak. Peggy mentioned seeing a friend and began to walk home. As she passed the garage the owner's beautiful wife Mrs Man, who was working on one of the pumps, smiled at Peggy.

Just around the corner of Stockton and Donald, Peggy sat down for a moment in the dirt. Never mind the wretched yellow dress, she decided, feeling hurt and bewildered. She was not bewildered that Jimmy should like Betsy. All the boys in the bay did. But instead she was shocked by his transformation: from one thing with her, to something entirely different with Betsy.

Had she done that to him, made him awkward and nervous? Had he actually been dreading speaking to her? Had she caused him weeks of worrying by walking nearby, hoping that he would come out and say hello? The whole of August she had tried to gain his attention. Walking past the garage when she knew he would be there. Looking out for him near his house when she thought he might be walking home. How stupid it all seemed now after meeting Tom. With Tom it had been the opposite. Suddenly he was just there. Jimmy had been here for weeks. Here, working in Stockton Street, but not here for her.

They had known each other since kindergarten. Played chasings. They had even climbed Tomaree together. And then Jimmy went away for two years to train as a mechanic in Newcastle. He came back just five weeks ago and Peggy had been immediately drawn to him. He looked so much older. His voice was deeper and had his shoulders ever been that wide? His strange new maleness was all she could think about for weeks. It had fooled her into thinking he was somebody else. But he was still the same old Jimmy from way back.

To think how she had almost thrown herself at him! It was embarrassing and his keenness to speak to Betsy only made it worse. Peggy kicked her feet in the dirt. She was an idiot. And then she remembered Tom. Was that what she was doing with Tom? Throwing herself at him too? Was he even now wondering how to extricate himself out of a very embarrassing situation?

Considering what to do about a silly seventeen year old who was chasing after him.

But wait a minute. Had she chased him? Peggy racked her brains over their three encounters. No. The first had been sheer, heavenly luck and the second he had obviously sought her out. Hoping to find her walking towards Salamander Bay and he had. And the third time he had been waiting outside Ocean View. He only had a minute he explained and that's when he invited her to the dance and gave her a pair of stockings. So she hadn't been chasing him. He had been chasing her. What a lovely thought!

She had to speak to Betsy. She had completely forgotten about the dance tomorrow night. Well, only this last half hour. Tom said he would meet her there and that she should bring a friend. A sort of double date.

She recalled how sweetly he had asked her, assuring her twice that they could just meet up at the hall. So it wasn't an official date, thank goodness. She wasn't ready for a real date yet. The whole thing with Tom was happening so fast she needed time to think and it would be nice for Betsy to meet him. And then in a week or so they could go on a real date. Maybe to the pictures. Blissfully her mind ran on with the image of the two of them sitting close in the back row of the Arcadia when Peggy was startled by Betsy's voice.

'Whatever are you doing sitting in the dirt?' Betsy was laughing happily.

'Thinking. Tell me what happened.'

'He's asked me out.' Betsy was jubilant.

'When?'

'To the pictures tomorrow night,' Betsy paused. 'What's the matter? You don't look pleased.'

The girls began walking again. 'I am. It's just that I was hoping you'd be free Saturday night.'

'Why?'

'I've been invited to the dance at the Church Hall and was hoping you could come, as a sort of a double date.'

They were nearing Peggy's home so she grabbed Betsy and steered her on past her house and towards the track that zigzagged down the slope near the beach. 'Let's go and sit on the beach and

I'll tell you.' Peggy ran on ahead, down through the bush. Betsy followed, puzzled, taking her time and watching her footing. Finally Betsy caught up and both girls sat down on the sand, Betsy carefully tucking her skirts under her. In the bay a flat sort of barge like boat was roaring past on its way to Shoal Bay. Peggy squinted in the sun and could just make out a number of American sailors on board.

Still fussing with her skirt, Betsy asked, 'So what's happening. Tell me! Who is he?'

Peggy couldn't keep from smiling as she began to tell Betsy about Tom. 'His name is Tom Lockwood and he's with that overseas school at the Country Club. He's only been here for a few weeks. I met him a week ago on the Thursday near Dutchies.' Peggy turned towards her friend and gazed into her eyes.

'You should see him, Betsy! He's not that tall but he has the nicest face, blonde hair and the darkest brown eyes you've ever seen!'

Betsy inched away from Peggy. 'Why is he at the Country Club? He's not American is he?'

Peggy's eyes widened in disbelief. 'What do you mean by, he's not American is he? Yes he is American and he's very nice and he's over here helping us. What are you really saying, Betsy?' Peggy drew her words out.

Under Peggy's scrutiny Betsy stood up and moved away. Without turning around she said, 'I've been hearing all about the Americans from Auntie Sybil. Eddie was in Sydney when they arrived last April and evidently they took over the place. He couldn't get a room anywhere. They had taken them all and he couldn't get a drink either. The barmaids were serving all the Yanks first and only bothering with the Australians when there were no Yanks. They take over everything.'

'Is this what your Aunt Sybil thinks too?'

'Well, I'm not sure if she's met any herself but what Eddie says is good enough for her.'

'And good enough for you?'

'Oh, Peggy I don't know but don't you think it's kind of disloyal to go out with an American instead of one of our boys.'

'I haven't met one of our boys!'

'There's the DIB at Gan Gan.'

'I don't know any of the DIB. But now there's a dance to go to and we're invited.'

Facing Peggy squarely this time Betsy said, 'I'm sorry, Peggy. I have a date and he's joining the AIF soon. Why don't you ask Emily?'

'It looks like I'll have to.'

'Don't make me feel guilty. I just don't think its right. We should put our boys first,' Betsy paused, looking back towards Magnus Street. 'I'd better get home. Baby Charlie will be driving Mum mad right about now.'

Peggy didn't return Betsy's wave. With the sun low over the bay she stood and watched her friend walk back home. She could tell by the set of Betsy's shoulder that she was upset, but that was just too bad. How could she be so narrow-minded? Hadn't they joked many a time about her whiny cousin Eddie. Always complaining about anything and everything. Now here she was taking his every word as gospel and agreeing with Aunt Sybil. And both of them never having met an American!

This was something she hadn't foreseen. She hadn't even guessed that her friend would feel like that. How self-righteous Betsy had become in the space of an hour. Suddenly she had an Australian boyfriend and was high enough up to look down on her life-long friend. A friend who in her opinion was crazy enough to go out with a god damn Yank, as no doubt Eddie would call them. Well she was going out with him. And she would have a good time, despite having to ask Emily instead. Though truth be told, knowing Emily, she probably wouldn't see much of her. She would be too busy fraternising.

With one last glance out to the bay, the sun dipping down making the water sparkle, Peggy crossed the road and followed the track up the slope to Magnus Street.

Snapshots

The door to my mother's bedroom has been like a reprimand this last week. How useless it makes me feel. *Here we are. You can open it now.* But of course I can't. For most of my life that door has been closed. It was my mother's bedroom and what right did I have to go in there? There was nothing of mine in there. I remember she told me that once. *There's nothing of yours in there.* It was my mother's private room and little girls had no right poking about in there. That's how it had been all my childhood.

At about twelve years of age I started to wonder why I couldn't go in. Betsy was allowed in to her mother's bedroom but only when her mother was in there, which was fair enough. Her mother would be sitting at her dressing table brushing her hair or putting her makeup on, grabbing a few moments away from her children. Once or twice I had been with her in the bedroom and it had been disconcerting.

Mrs Wallis was in her housecoat and studying her reflection in the mirror. She turned and checked to see if Betsy's hair was tidy before letting the two of us go down to Blanch's store. I recall glancing back twice at that half open door.

'Can you just go in?' I asked.

'I've got to knock first.'

'Oh, I know that. But if you knock can you go in?'

'Yes, of course, silly.'

How strange. My mother was such an early riser that I never encountered her in a housecoat, let alone sitting at her dressing table brushing her hair. In the next week or so I tried waking up early to catch my mother in her bedroom but each time she was up and dressed, having a cup of tea at the kitchen table. Eventually the early mornings caught up with me and I gave it away. Once, thinking my mother was out shopping, I had reached out to open the door when she spoke.

'How dare you go into my room, Peggy Ashburn. What do you think is in there that you might be interested in? Tell me. Tell me!'

I had never seen my mother so angry and I had never felt so ashamed. 'I'm sorry, Mummy. I'm sorry,' I sobbed over and over. As I ran to the beach below Magnus Street I couldn't remember why I had ever wanted to go in there in the first place.

And then gradually I became used to the idea. It was almost an extension of her personality, that closed door. Just as I couldn't open the door, so I couldn't ask my mother certain questions. Such as: *What was my father like?* She would answer a few things about him and then the matter was closed. Just like the door.

So all I knew was that he had been a good man. Hard working and from one or two remarks I guessed that my father had possessed a wonderful sense of humour. Not that my mother had said so, but little things that she let slip suggested that he had been funny and quick witted. I knew that he had worked at BHP while they were living at Mayfield and that he had died in an accident at work. No details of the accident. Just that he had died and soon after we moved to Nelson Bay.

I walked towards the teak buffet inside which Mum kept her best linen. On top was Dad's photo, the only one I had ever seen. It was a head and shoulders shot and looked to have been taken in a Newcastle studio. The man staring back at me had a pleasant rather plump and almost jovial face. Not the sort of man I could imagine Mum marrying but then I couldn't imagine Mum at twenty. What had she been like? Had she been happy? God, I was heartily sick of questions that I couldn't answer. In frustration I marched over to my mother's door and flung it open.

The first thing I saw was the rose curtains, light sheer curtains with a heavy backing, so the room was fairly dark and the pink roses weren't visible from outside. I pulled the curtains open and looked at Magnus Street and the bay beyond. The whole sweep was before me.

Across the bay and to the left was Pindimar, a shoreline of grey green trees coming down to the water's edge. Next the land mass of Corrie Island which I could just make out. Directly in front of me was Tea Gardens. Nearby I knew, but couldn't see, the mouth of the Myall River spilled into the bay. To the right of this was Hawks Nest. There seemed to be a few new houses on the shoreline since my last visit which was to be expected, considering the beauty of the spot. Mum and I went there only twice when I was a child but I still remember it well enough. On my further right and stretching away to Yacaaba Head, was the sandy strip of land called Windi Woppa.

Sighing, I turned from the window. The room was quite spacious with only the single bed. This had a pink and white flowered cover on it and a large oak wardrobe with intricate carvings on the doors. Near the window was a comfy looking armchair with a strange design on it, a sort of curlicues and stems and funny stylised flowers. The pattern was vaguely familiar and so was the chair. Perhaps at one stage, when I was very young, it had been in the lounge room. I sat down in it and leant back. Already I felt inexplicably tired.

After a moment I opened my eyes to stare at the dressing table on the other side of the room. It was a rather nice dressing table, very feminine with curved lines and a bevelled mirror. Its surface was bare, only a brush and comb set, a small bag, possibly for makeup and one bottle of perfume. Just her lavender water I guessed, from this distance.

I closed my eyes and remembered that long ago summer's day. It must have been summer as both Betsy and I had on little cotton shifts. I was wearing another green and white striped outfit. Mum obviously liked stripes or maybe they made for easier sewing. I recall trying to work out exactly what all the stuff was on Mrs Wallis's dressing table. Countless lipsticks, hair ties, brooches, scattered about. A lot of things she must have accumulated when the family lived in Newcastle, but there were also lovely bottles, sort of Aladdin's lampish with dark brown liquid inside. And I particularly remember an exquisitely blue bottle with something about Paris on it.

I wondered even then where they all came from. Now I find it fascinating to think how much Mr Wallis must have speculated on the same thing. Surely more than: *Something my sister Enid sent me.* Of course the whole of Nelson Bay found out late in 1946 when Mr Wallis, making a rare and sudden visit to Newcastle, caught sight of his wife with a strange man in the Great Northern Hotel. Mother's letters to me were extremely lengthy with all the details for several months. How I worried for Betsy then, no wonder she put her marriage forward. To escape just like I did; to escape without looking back.

But sometimes you have to look back to work out where you are going. To check that the road you are following is going the right way. Only by turning back and considering, really taking into account the past, can you see whether you are veering off at right angles or marching straight ahead to what you really want. Had I done that when I married Tom? No, of course not and I'm sure neither did Betsy. Was she regretting the haste just as I had begun to? Was she even still married?

I closed my eyes again and cursed myself. I couldn't even remember where she lived. Vaguely I recollected somewhere in the south of England. A very English sort of name. Sevenoaks. Yes Sevenoaks. Mother had devoted a whole letter on Betsy's move and her new home. Betsy wrote to her for a while but then the letters must have stopped. How that must have hurt her!

In my letters I wrote: 'Any news from Betsy?' Mother never answered that question. The truth was Betsy probably just got so busy with all those babies – five I think it was – that she didn't have time to write and then how awkward to resume again when you realise a year has passed. Well now was the time to write, no excuses but first I would have to find her address amongst mother's things. It was probably somewhere in the buffet drawer or in the phone table. I must look for it today. But not now. I doubted it was in this room.

I stood up. That was enough thinking of Betsy or Mrs Wallis for the time being. I wouldn't find either of them here, but I might find my mother. I walked over towards the almost bare dressing table when I noticed the dressing table wasn't bare at all. It was covered almost completely by the past. A past I had never seen.

The cream painted surface of the dressing table was topped by a sheet of glass cut to the same size and underneath the glass were at least fifteen photos of my mother and father. In a sudden, frantic urge, I cleared the dressing table of its few things and threw them on the bed. I then lifted the glass and placed it carefully on the bedcover.

Breathless, I picked up photo after photo. In the first one that seemed to scream at me for attention, my parents were looking so happy and all dressed up, standing in front of a dance hall it looked like, somewhere in Newcastle or Mayfield. My mother was wearing a very pretty dress. It seemed to glitter against the dull background of the photo. It was hard to tell the exact colour but my guess was a dark silvery grey. It was long waisted with pleats, my mother's hair was bobbed short and around her neck she wore a very long dark necklace. Jet perhaps? I was stunned by the outfit. She looked so glamorous and so young. Was this really my mother?

Reluctantly I put the photo down and turned my attention to the others. Three were taken in the backyard of what must have been the elder Mr and Mrs Ashburn's Mayfield house with about half a dozen rose bushes in full bloom and behind them what appeared to be a very well tended vegie patch. There were my grandparents, I guessed, a rather grim looking couple trying to smile for the camera and between them stood my parents.

In one of the three photos there was a white blanket on the grass but nothing on it. Where was I and who took these photos? The rest of the photographs were holiday snaps at a beach somewhere or a lake maybe. There wasn't one photo of me or of the small timber house my mother told me they lived in for a year when I was a baby.

In one holiday shot my mother and father were leaning against each other awkwardly as if they had just shared a joke and had fallen together giggling. The camera had caught them moments after and the laughter was still in their eyes. Behind them stretched a shore speckled with a few houses. Too close to be Tea Gardens, so I had no idea where it was. I was too amazed to consider where it could possibly be.

I studied each of the holiday snaps to try and work out if it was just the one year or maybe repeated visits. In all of them Mum wore a dark, ribbed swimming costume just above the knee with a v neckline. Dad wore a similar outfit in some but in others he was wearing a white shirt and pale coloured shorts. In all of them they looked so happy.

After leaning on the dressing table for some time gazing at their smiling faces, I began to feel dizzy. With the bed covered by my mother's things I walked over to the patterned armchair and slumped into it. Was it them? Was it really them? And if, so where was I? Some part of me was unable to acknowledge the fact that yes, it was them and they were happy. It wasn't that I was jealous. Just puzzled.

The obvious answer was that the photos were taken years before I was born, therefore before the summer of 1924/25 and judging by the clothes, which looked about right, but something was amiss. I didn't know what but something was wrong. In several of the photos my mother looked maternal. Was that possible, considering there was no child in the photos? But she did.

She looked like a happy young woman but with more experience in her face than a honeymooner. She had the look of a young mother having a holiday knowing her beautiful baby would be there when she got back. What a leap of the imagination but I felt sure there was a grain of truth in it. I could almost feel her expectation, but where was I in these photos of her life?

Somewhere there must be photos of me in the backyard of Mayfield sitting on the lap of doting grandparents. *Mummy will be back soon*. But did she ever really come back from those holidays? Not looking like that she didn't. There were pictures of a stranger that looked like my mother on the dressing table. The mother I knew had never been skylarking on the beach. Had never been to dances. Had never in her life been so happy. Did I ever really know her? Or was the answer that I lost her many years ago?

A wave of nausea passed over me. I had to get out of the room. The wardrobe loomed large as I passed it as if to say: *I know. I know everything*. I glanced at it once before leaving the room and closing the door. I escaped to Joan's and luckily she was home. She opened the door, took one look at me and said, 'You look like you've seen a ghost.'

I nodded. 'I have.'

'Cup of tea is it? You can tell me all about it.'

The Dance

Peggy and Emily stood a few yards down the road from the hall, watching a group of young women arrive.

'They look...' Peggy struggled for a word, wondering if it was just her but the girls appeared rather colourful to say the least. 'Forthright', she told Emily at last and the other girl burst out laughing. 'You're a turn, Peggy. You really are. Thanks for inviting me. Let's show these Newcastle girls what for.'

'I'm glad one of us is feeling confident.' Peggy looked down at her white voile dress. She felt fourteen in it despite the rather low neckline. Emily looked sophisticated in a pretty emerald green which showed off her blonde hair. In an exuberant mood she grabbed Peggy's hand and together they walked up to the church hall. A young naval rating motioned them inside. No need for tickets just as Tom said.

It all happened so swiftly. One minute standing by the school, the next blinking in amazement at the sight of so many people. She was inside and couldn't escape without making a complete fool of herself. For a few minutes, too nervous to look around, she stood near the entrance trying to formulate a reasonable excuse to leave. Her mother had suddenly taken ill. She had suddenly taken ill. She closed her eyes. Where was her customary devil-may-care attitude? It had completely deserted her. Why was she feeling so timid? It was the dress. That was the reason. It was the wretched dress.

And then in the instant she opened her eyes, he was in front of her.

He looked wonderful in his uniform and different too. It must be his dress uniform. Tom was wearing a very dark green jacket, a different cap and light grey trousers. He looked so impressive yet still very approachable, she decided, as she looked at his smiling face. He had removed his fancy cap with the badge on the front and was bowing. She felt drawn into his arms, a magnet pulling her to him. Emily nudged her. She introduced them and in the next breath they were away on the strains of a waltz, moving across the floor, the hall a blur.

They seemed to be dancing quite fast and she couldn't recall the tune. As they danced she caught sight of the chairs around the hall. Some empty, some filled. On the next spin she thought she saw Jimmy's sister June. Whatever was she doing here? She was only fourteen. Snuck in obviously. She bit her lip worrying about her and then lost sight of the girl.

Peggy was surrounded by colours: the softer hues of the girls and women's dresses, the khaki, dark green and dark blue of the officers' and servicemen's uniforms. How beautiful it all was. Just like a fairytale. But she was no Cinderella. She was dancing like an elephant, Peggy told herself. He danced expertly while she felt clumsy. She was so rusty. When was the last time? Stupidly she searched her memory. With Emily's brother last year. Her neck had hurt straining to look up into his eyes.

She glanced up at Tom's. How brown they were. So intense. She looked away. They were moving together more easily now, almost fluidly. She was incredibly aware of her own body, her sense of touch amplified tenfold by his touch: the feel of her skirt against her legs, the lace on her neckline, the fabric of his uniform under her left hand, his breath on her forehead. Her thoughts spun in a crazy web wrapping them together. She felt herself go limp and in the same instant Tom tightened his grip on her waist.

Peggy could feel the weight his hand brought to her body, the touch of his fingers against her dress. Was he aware of her shaking underneath his touch? She tried to concentrate on his neck and chin. They were directly in front of her line of sight. But again her eyes were dragged to his. He smiled and the smile stilled for a moment her reaction to his nearness.

The song was coming to an end and she was able to catch her breath. Tom brought them to a stop near the doors that closed off part of the church used for services. He moved his hand from her waist and then as she turned to him, took hold of her right hand. Her waist felt cold without the touch of his hand. She clasped his hand tighter.

They stood for a few minutes in companionable silence. Peggy glanced about and spotted her friend with a gentleman in a beautiful double-breasted jacket. It was very dark blue, almost black trimmed with gold buttons and braid.

'That your friend over there?' Tom asked.

'Yes.'

'Well she's done well for herself. That's the Captain of the Westralia.'

'Trust Emily.' She found herself laughing with relief and amusement.

'You don't need to worry about her now. She's right for the evening,' Tom remarked.

She certainly didn't. But she was worried about June Hartley.

'Is everything all right?' Tom asked after a moment.

'While I was dancing I caught sight of June Hartley. She's very young. Fourteen actually. She was wearing a pink dress, sitting over there I think.' Peggy pointed to her right. 'I thought if she was still here something should be done.' She glanced at Tom who was scanning the crowd carefully.

'I can't see no-one like that. I guess she left. Like me to ask some questions?'

'Yes please.'

'Here sit down.' Tom led her to a nearby chair. 'I'll go and see what I can find out and bring you back a drink. What would you like?'

'Just a lemonade, thank you.' Peggy stared after him. Where would he get a drink now, she wondered. It was past six o'clock. As if reading her thoughts Tom paused and turned around. 'Where from?' she asked raising her eyebrows at his quizzical expression.

He broke into a broad grin. 'Don't ask. Here's hoping I can find the spot again.' Peggy laughed.

She watched Tom cross the hall. He really was gorgeous and she noticed two or three women's heads turn as he passed. Well they couldn't have him. He was hers. All hers. Thinking about June made her consider her own age. Had Tom guessed she was only seventeen? She would have to tell him. The sooner the better.

And later, if they were still going out, Mother would have to meet him. Whatever would she say? Peggy didn't like to speculate. At least she hadn't banned her from going to the dance. In fact she seemed to have eased up lately. Her mother had started helping at the ladies auxiliary and she was often rushing off at odd hours. But she seemed happier, that was obvious. And Peggy had long ago noticed that if her mother was busy she was generally easier to get along with. The same could be said for most of us, Peggy decided, particularly now with the war on.

At that moment Emily waved at Peggy over the back of yet another officer. When they exchanged glances Emily jerked her head towards the entrance of the hall where Tom had just disappeared from sight. 'Wacko' she mouthed in an exaggerated fashion. Peggy nodded and smiled at her friend, inwardly relieved that at five foot eight or so Tom was too short for Emily. So Emily fancied him too. *And* a lot of women in the hall. When the slow number finished Emily walked purposefully over to Peggy.

'You never told me he was *sooo* good looking. And a First Lieutenant too.'

'He's too short for you,' Peggy said quickly without thinking.

'Well, you do fancy him, don't you?' Emily's eyes were boring into hers. 'You've got competition. You'll have to stay on your toes. And where has he gone by the way?'

Immediately Peggy was reminded why she really didn't like Emily. She could be a cat sometimes, so jealous of what other people had. And that insinuating tone of hers! Where did it come from? And why, when things were going well for someone else did she have to throw a spanner in the works? There was just no need. Emily was so pretty. Grudgingly Peggy said, 'He's gone to see if June Hartley got home all right. She was here earlier.'

'She wasn't!'

'Didn't you see her?'

'No, too busy,' Emily said laughing. 'Oh, there's the Anniversary Waltz. John wanted this one,' and she was off to the other side of the room.

Peggy sat down and listened to the slow bars of the song. Mercifully Tom wasn't back yet. She wasn't sure she was up to the closer dancing of such a song. Her head had been spinning with just his left hand in hers and his right on her waist. How would she feel if he moved any closer? Maybe she would find out. He was moving towards her now with a serious expression on his face. Peggy stood up. He walked right up to her to whisper in her ear, 'Her father came and got her.'

'Thank God. She must have gone quietly.'

'She did. I think she realised the game was up when no one danced with her. All the guys here are...'

'Gentleman,' Peggy supplied.

'Yeah, that's one way of putting it and I think most had a fair idea of her age. That's why they never asked her to dance. And, speaking of ages...'

Peggy tried to hold his gaze and speak confidently. 'Eighteen this December.'

Tom was visibly relieved. 'Did you think I was younger?' Peggy asked feeling quite annoyed.

'Sorry I just had no idea. On the beach last week you acted so much older. Say, twenty two.'

'Twenty two!'

Tom was laughing at the indignation in her voice. He took her hands and said slowly, in that measured drawl of his she was becoming fond of, 'I meant it in a nice way. You're sort a grown up in some respects. In the way you think, the way you look at things. But your face is young. So tonight I was thinking maybe Miss Peggy Ashburn is only sixteen.'

'It's the hair, isn't it?'

Tom was really laughing now and squeezing her hands. 'I love your red hair. Hey, it's more auburn anyway.'

Peggy was so grateful for that remark that when the next slow dance started she willingly moved into Tom's arms. But within a few bars the intense feeling returned. There was no way to fight it. She wanted him to hold her tight and as she moved nearer she felt the brush of his lips on her forehead. His grip on her right hand tightened. She gave him a squeeze in return.

When their eyes met, the expression in Tom's seemed far off, almost sleepy. She desperately wanted to touch his forehead, the dimple in his left cheek. Peggy felt again, like she did in the valley the other day, that she was surrounded by the sea and the sky intermingled. She was being tugged slowly down. Sometimes when this happened she panicked and shook herself free of the illusion. Other times like now and in the valley, she let go. At one point she would level out. She always did if she could bear to go with it. She would stop falling, stop sinking and begin to float. And then the feeling of being buoyed up would take over. The awareness of a light above her, but this time Tom was the sea, a dark green sea tangling around her like seaweed, around her shoulders and against her cheek. It was then she realised that her cheek was resting against his shoulder. The material of his jacket was woollen and all she could see – dark green everywhere. She closed her eyes and felt Tom stroke her hair and her cheek and kiss her forehead again. The music stopped and he whispered in her ear.

An hour later after escorting Peggy home he was back on the beach. Back where it had all happened. God what was he thinking! What had he done? It was ruined between them, completely ruined. She hadn't wanted him to meet her mother. Instead she had just stood below her house and watched him walk away. Twice he looked back. She was still watching him, her white dress almost luminous in the dark night. That would probably be the last time he would see her. There was no other possible outcome. None.

Tom sat on the small beach below her house with his head in his hands, trying to go over the whole thing in his mind. When they were dancing, he should have known then, she would be different. He should have taken better care of her. Instead what had he done but led her away from the safety of the hall? The excuse: a walk on the beach. She had seemed to sink into his arms on the dance floor, really to merge with him and he wanted that sensation over and over. On the beach when she began to sink into the soft sand and with the moonlight on her face, he pulled her to him again. This time he kissed her deeply. He felt her arms tight around his neck, her body pushed very hard against him. Was she deliberately torturing him?

He couldn't stop kissing her and she didn't stop him. He

waited for a warning from her. There was no murmur of protest, no pulling away. What did she do instead but keep responding to him! There was no teasing in it; no carefully leading him on only to pull the rug from under him at a certain moment for the greatest impact. No. It hadn't been like that at all. She was completely with him in this. He could sense it. Know it. Know she was experiencing the same strong pull towards him that he was feeling towards her. His hands were on her breast and still she didn't stop him.

That was when he started to understand the difference, realise the intensity of her responses to him. She must be able to feel his body hard against her. At that moment when he pulled her to him, her hip tight against his groin, he waited for her to recoil in disgust as one girl back home had done, but she didn't. If anything she moved closer. Now as he touched her breast he fought the desire to unbutton her dress. She was too young. It was too soon. He told himself this over and over but the words only became an undercurrent to the touch of her lips and her hands on his neck.

Gradually he was able to slow his responses a little. By God, he had been rushing things! He reined himself in and began to enjoy her kisses even more. As he kissed her more tenderly, her hand slipped from a grip at the back of his neck to a gentle stroking through his hair. Still they hadn't said a word, he thought. Not a word, just thousands. She was saying so much to him now in the silence. It sounded like: *I need you. You see I want you as much as you want me. I am not playing games. I don't know how.* That's what she was telling him.

How unlike Mary she was, who gave nothing of herself without expecting something in return and that reward not affection or love but something tangible like a new bracelet, a locket, something she could touch, fondle rather than him. *See what he gave me.* She actually said the words one time. He only worked it all out much later but that's how it had been. *I let him touch me down there and now I have this wonderful locket. We spend the night together and soon we'll be engaged.* Always a withholding until she was sure of the outcome.

Now, here in his arms, was Peggy not withholding at all. Only giving and giving. Still he touched her breast and still she kissed him. He caressed her once more and heard her moan. It tore through him. He held her tight and rocked her in his arms, calling her name over and over. This was too much. It was all too much and too soon. With a sharp intake of breath he pulled away from her.

She looked at him surprised and then smiling, stroked his face. It was the undoing of him. He grabbed her again and almost crushed her against him as the sobs tore through his body. He couldn't bear it. He just couldn't. His feelings for her were overwhelming. Of all the girls he had been close to, all the women he had made love with these last few years, and it wasn't many, why was he experiencing this now when his commitment to this small fishing town was so uncertain. He could be posted anywhere in a matter of months. Why had he met her now, at the worst possible time? And how had she done this to him so quickly?

But no, that wasn't right because he could see the same thoughts, the bewilderment mixed with affection, in Peggy's face. He let her look at him with the tears in his eyes. Again he was mistaken he wasn't letting her. She was forcing him to hold her gaze. Her hand was on his chin. He had no alternative but to meet her gaze. And then her expression darkened.

'I'm sorry. Please forgive me,' he whispered.

'There's nothing to forgive. I should have stopped you. Isn't that my job as a *nice* girl.' She said the word bitterly and broke away from him.

He ran after her. 'But that's what you are. Don't you understand?'

'No Tom, I don't understand.' She stopped then and looked around her as if realising where she was for the first time. Slowly she turned to him. 'You'd better take me home.'

With a sudden stab of pain he noticed she was brushing tears from her own eyes. As the moon disappeared behind clouds they began to walk up the steep incline towards Magnus Street. After a moment Peggy stopped abruptly.

'No, first I have to tell Emily I'm leaving.'

He took her to the hall and spoke to a number of his friends while Peggy spoke to Emily. They both made excuses and left. He would make sure tomorrow that the other guys at the Country Club understood that Peggy hadn't been well and that's why they had left early. Also that she was his girl. She *was* his girl, even if Peggy didn't understand that right now. He couldn't think about anything at that moment except winning her back but as they walked along Magnus Street, an impenetrable silence fell upon them. When he left her below her house he told her, 'Peggy I want to see you again.' He went to reach for her hand but she seemed miles away.

'I don't know, Tom. I just don't know.' They were the last words she spoke to him.

By God, he had ruined everything, he thought, tossing a handful of sand towards the water.

Working from the Known

Of course at first I wanted to rush our cup of tea and race back to my place to show the photos to Joan but she persuaded me that it was best to sit quietly for a while. She listened to all my wild speculations and theories that had seemingly sprung from nowhere: that I was adopted, which explained why there were hardly any baby photos of me, a fact that came to light when my daughter Sarah was born. Or I had been a terrible baby and that's why my mother looked so happy in those snaps at the beach – she was free of me for a while. That maybe it wasn't my mother in the photos but an aunt I had never known existed. On and on I went until I came to a shuddering halt. 'What's the matter with me, Joan? Why can't I accept the photos for what they are?'

'And what are they?' Joan asked gently.

'They are photos of a young woman having fun at the beach.' I sat back in Joan's comfy chair. 'But I suppose I never thought of mum as having fun. Though why shouldn't she? It's just that she never seemed to. When I was young she was mostly alone. I remember vaguely a few people visiting when I was little but either she didn't make them welcome or they just didn't want to come back.'

'She didn't have any family out here did she?'

'No, she didn't. She never talked about England or her family. There used to be letters I think but then they stopped. I can't remember when though. I think she had a brother but he died in the Great War.'

'It must have been hard for her coming out here, leaving her family behind. But then you know all about that, Peg.' Joan was studying me with a sympathetic gaze.

'Yes, it was hard.' I ran my fingers through my hair. I felt tired merely remembering. I looked down at the carpet, aware that Joan was waiting for my answer. 'But you don't really think about it at the time. When you make your decision I mean. I suppose Mum didn't either and then she fell out with Dad's family after he died. I think that Mrs Ashburn was very difficult.' I frowned. 'I'm not sure why, just a feeling I had as a child. I would have liked a grandmother. One Christmas that's actually what I asked for: a grandmother. How it must have hurt Mum. It was a pity she couldn't continue seeing the Ashburns.'

'I gathered too, love, that there were problems. I remember thinking when she first arrived that she seemed relieved to be here, rather than pleased. It was like she had been travelling for months and liked the fact that Nelson Bay was hard to get to.'

'You know,' she said, putting down her teacup. 'A red notebook, I have, that Angharad sent to me. To put things in, see and she started me off with a quote. A very useful quote.'

'Mind,' Joan continued, 'I laughed at first when I opened it, many Christmases ago. Me, writing my thoughts down. That's what she had suggested. Well, I don't worry about that. Too hard to get my thoughts straight at the best of times; let alone organising them on paper. But I write other people's down. One of my favourites is that saying of Proust's.' Joan was completely still for a moment. '"The real voyage of discovery consists not in seeking new landscapes but in having new eyes." Some people put things so beautifully don't they?'

I smiled as Joan spoke the word. She said it as 'bootifully'. What a wonderful sing song accent the Welsh is, I thought.

'I've got lots of Angharad's dead Greeks' sayings and others,' Joan went on. 'Bits of things I read in the newspapers. Once she mentioned in her letter something an author had written, an historian I think it was, and I wrote it down. I think it is in the red notebook.'

Before I could answer, Joan had bustled off into her bedroom, the door open to reveal a crocheted rug on her bedspread that Mum had made for her a few birthdays ago. I took another sip of tea to calm me and waited. I could hear rustling sounds and the odd oath or two, which made me smile. But I was dreading to think what platitude Joan would come up with and how it could possibly help me now. I was itching to go back home and have

Joan look at the photos but she obviously had other plans.

She finally returned with the notebook, a large one as it turned out and settled herself back in her favourite armchair. 'It's about what you're doing in a funny sort of way and the pitfalls which you probably have already fallen into.'

I had no idea what she was talking about and was looking towards the door hopefully when she said, '"Working back from the known to the unknown, that easy but perilous method", Arthur Wade-Evans quoting someone else I believe.'

'So what are you saying Joan?'

'That you can't hope to understand your mother in the 1920s when you really didn't know her in the 1940s.'

I flinched. How right she was. I really didn't know her. Had never known her. How could I possibly start now? 'And now it's too late,' I said. 'Is that what you are saying?' I was angry now.

'Not completely, like. A difficult woman she was. I know that. You know that. I worked around her and I decided early on to accept her the way she was.'

'And in a nice way you're saying that's what I should have done. Accepted her and not left her to be alone all these years.' I was fighting back tears.

'There's the rub isn't it? That's what really hurts. You can't blame yourself for falling in love, now can you?' Joan stopped to look at my tear-stained face. 'But it seems you have all these years. That's obvious. You've blamed yourself. Well Peggy, I think you should know something.'

I turned to face Joan, startled by her tone of voice and feeling seventeen again. 'Made you go, she would have. If you had hesitated she would have insisted. I'm sure of it. But unfortunately, in a way, you never hesitated. You never got the chance to see that she thought you should go. You just up and went when your papers came through. But she thought you should go just the same.'

'How can you possibly know that,' I asked, annoyed at the self righteous tone in Joan's voice.

'The way she talked about you and Tom and your life out there. She knew you wouldn't have been happy if you had stayed.'

'But how can you be so sure she felt we should be together? Did she actually say that?'

'More or less,' Joan threw off as she got up to walk into her dark green kitchen. 'I'll just make another pot.'

Another cup of tea! I thought. We'd never get back to the photos but I was aware that Joan didn't want me to get back to the photos for a while. I wasn't sure why but there was some philosophic thinking in there, I felt certain. But perhaps she was right. If I looked at them in this agitated state I would draw the wrong conclusions. Already my memory or at least my perception of the sort of person I thought my mother had been was clouded by this piece of news from Joan: that my mother had believed in what Tom and I felt for each other. Wasn't that what Joan had just said? I sat hunched forward, rubbing my forehead. I was confused, my mind muddled.

Frustrated, I followed Joan into her kitchen. Studying the row of Toby jugs on a shelf near the stove, I asked, 'So what you are saying is that Mum believed Tom and I loved each other?'

Joan plonked the teapot on a tray along with a plate of shortbread biscuits. 'Another one is it,' she asked reaching for my cup. Sighing in exasperation, I handed it over.

Joan glanced at the clock as she left the kitchen. 'Well there we are, it's time for afternoon tea anyway.'

Defeated, I took my cup, sat down again and tried to open my mind out to these new thoughts of my mother.

'What was I saying, Peg?' Joan asked with a mouthful of shortbread.

'That Mum believed Tom and I loved each other.'

'Well of course I moved next door to your mother five years after you left, you know. So I missed your first visit back with baby Sarah in 1950 wasn't it? Just missed it I think by only a few months. She talked of Sarah a lot you know. And you and Tom.'

'And?' I asked leaning forward in my seat.

'Just before your next visit it must have been. When was that love?'

'My last visit was 1967.'

'That's right. You've only been back twice, not counting this time haven't you? And Tom didn't come on either of the times did he now?'

'No,' I answered sitting back in my seat, resigned. This was going to take all afternoon.

'Well about a month or so before you were due to visit see, she started talking about you and Tom. Just little things. Her memory of the two of you together, all the details of your marriage. How in love you were. How terrible it had been for you waiting for him during the last year or so of the war.'

I almost dropped my tea cup, putting it back on Joan's small coffee table.

'Joan, you must be mistaken. She didn't want me to wait for Tom, even though we were married. It was as if she thought I should pretend he just didn't exist. As if he would never come back.'

I was crying now. 'I remember clearly her saying to me once when we argued. 'There's no point in waiting. I should just get on with my life as best as I could.' That's what she said. As if Tom didn't exist. I was married to him but he never existed. She just wanted me to pretend I had never met him.'

'She wouldn't have said that, love. Pretend you'd never met him. You were married to him. She would never have said that. That's not your mother at all. Now, get on with your life as best as you can, that's your mother. It probably just felt like that. Felt like she didn't care, mind. But she did. Maybe she worried that he wouldn't come back for you and wanted to prepare you in some way.'

Without getting up Joan produced a handkerchief like a conjurer.

'Where did that come from,' I sniffed.

'Oh, I had it here in one of me pockets.' Joan rummaged through her apron and produced a pencil and a piece of string, a peg from another pocket.

I laughed despite myself. 'Now I'm totally confused, Joan. Maybe I'm not remembering her right. Does that make sense?'

'Oh aye. A strange thing is memory. It can get twisted, transformed really by a lot of things. Fair play, it was a terrible time you were going through. Worrying about Tom, arguing and misunderstanding each other. And you convincing yourself she was thinking and feeling certain things that probably never entered her head. And that's how you remember it now. After all this time you thought your mother said, "Just pretend you never met him."'

'But in reality she never said it?' I asked.

Joan nodded. 'I can't imagine the Helen I knew saying that.'

'I just thought she did. Or maybe I only thought she felt that way.'

'Ah, now, that's an entirely different thing isn't it? They're your thoughts. Both of them are your thoughts. You probably thought too that she was hoping he wouldn't come back.'

I felt a tightening in my chest. 'Yes, I did, Joan.'

'But she may not have been thinking that at all. In fact knowing your mother, as I believe I did, I'm fairly sure she wouldn't have wished that either.'

'Now I'm totally confused.'

'Made it worse, have I?'

'Oh, Joan, the photos, now you saying that Mum believed Tom and I were in love.' I paused for a moment. 'Was it how she talked about us before that last visit?'

'Yes, Peggy. When she thought Tom was coming, remember.'

'Yes, and the last minute he couldn't make it.'

'Well, she was talking a lot about the two of you as if to sort of get reacquainted in her mind like. But it was more the way she talked about the two of you, not what she actually said that made me think you really were in love.'

'So Mum really did believe we were in love?'

'Not believe. That's not the right word, Peg, more like knew.'

As Joan said the word 'knew' I felt a strange pause. The world had stopped for a moment and I didn't want it to start again till I had grabbed what seemed to be hovering at the edge of my consciousness. What was it? I couldn't make it out.

I sat still for a moment, completely still and gazed about Joan's simple house. All her knick-knacks, her wallpaper, the rugs everywhere were so different from my mother's house but nice, welcoming. If you looked out at the world from this house was your view of the world different? Did the cheerful rooms somehow colour Joan's view?

Had Mum's more austere furnishings, the white walls and the rather bare rooms, stripped back somehow her perception of life? Removed the soft touches that make life bearable? I didn't know. Was there any way of knowing such a thing? But maybe what we gather about us *is* a manifestation of ourselves and an indication of the way we look at the world. Or maybe the way we want the world to be. I put my head in my hands. I couldn't get a single thought straight. It was all a terrible mess.

'Oh dear, I really have muddied the waters, haven't I? You look like you need an early night. What about I make you a bit of Welsh rarebit for tea? Then you can go home, have a bath and go to bed. But I want you to promise me one thing.'

I looked up. 'What's that?'

'Well two actually,' Joan said, looking at me rather sheepishly.

'Yes, I promise.'

'That you won't look at the photos again tonight or worry about them.'

'I promise.'

'And that you won't look at a note I'm going to give you, until tomorrow.'

'Yes Joan. But what sort of note?'

'A list,' Joan said, disappearing into the kitchen again.

Stained Glass

Peggy stood for what seemed like ages after Tom left her. She didn't turn around until she was sure he would be gone from sight. When she did swerve around and he wasn't there, a terrible desolation washed over her. She had said all the wrong things. It wasn't his fault. Was it hers? She couldn't think straight. She sighed. *What had really happened?*

She faced the moon, free of the clouds now and watched its clear brightness. Her dress seemed to be absorbing some of that brightness. She felt like she was glowing, shining somehow. She remembered how Tom had cried in her arms. Why had he cried? Wasn't that the real question that was bothering her? Wasn't that the one that needed answering?

Peggy gazed down at her luminous dress and then back up at the lounge room windows. It was hard to tell if a light was inside or not. Peggy was sure her mother had the tightest fitting blackout curtains in the bay. Had her mother carefully parted the curtain and seen her standing below?

Inside was another world. There was no way she could go in just yet. Her heart was beating fast; her dress was shining, her lips still throbbing from Tom's kisses. For a minute more she stood and stared at the moon. She was transfixed until a breeze sprang up and ruffled the lace against her breasts.

How quiet the street was and dark! Peggy took off her high heels and with one last glance at the weatherboard house with the brick porch, walked past and on towards Mrs Linden's. An inside light was on. She could see it winking through a crack in Sarah's blackout blind and almost immediately she felt better. With quick steps she walked up to stand on Sarah's rather large verandah.

Peggy glanced to her right, towards the window, forgetting for a moment she wouldn't be able to see anything; that for ages now because of the blackout she couldn't look in through the stained glass and see Mrs Linden reading or writing a letter. How often had she done that since she was ten? Looked in through the stained glass to see Sarah Linden seated in that rather old fashioned chair of hers; marvelled at how she changed colours depending on which part of the window Peggy was looking through. Pink if she looked through the stylised rose part of the stained glass; yellow if she looked through the background part of the design.

Leaning close, Peggy ran her fingertips over the uneven surface of the glass. In the darkness and with the blackout blind behind, it was impossible to tell which part she was feeling.

Softly Peggy tapped on the window. After a moment Mrs Linden pulled the blackout curtain aside, gazed at Peggy and then nodded. What a wonderful sound it was to hear Sarah's door opening!

'Sit down over here.' Mrs Linden pointed to a smaller armchair opposite her own.

'I shouldn't stay. It's probably too late even to be here.'

'It's not that late and as you know I stay up until all hours.' Mrs Linden studied Peggy's face. 'I think you need a drink. I won't be a moment.'

Peggy watched as Mrs Linden moved from the lounge room and into the dining room behind her. She didn't turn around to see what the older woman was doing but heard the clink of glass. In a moment a crystal tumbler was in front of her, half filled with a beautiful dark golden brown liquid.

'It's brandy. You need it. But don't tell your mother I gave it to you. Slowly,' Mrs Linden added as Peggy brought the glass to her lips.

The liquid burned her throat and for a moment she was incapable of speech. Just as the glow had gone from her dress, now she seemed to be glowing from inside. She leant her head back against the top of the armchair. Closing her eyes, she heard the sound of Mrs Linden's book closing. Peggy opened her eyes to see Mrs Linden's beautiful hands place the rather large red book on the small table beside her.

'What are you reading?'

'*Gone with the Wind.* I've been meaning to read it for years and I have now finally got around to it.'

'Is it good?'

'Yes, it is. I think you'd enjoy it Peggy. I'll lend it to you when I've finished. But in the meantime it seems that something is very wrong. Would you like to tell me about it?'

In the soft glow of the lamp, Peggy studied Mrs Linden. The older woman had never looked more beautiful. Her chestnut hair, usually worn in a large bun, was falling free now, in waves about her shoulders. She wore an apple green negligee, with a matching short jacket tied loosely across her shoulders and her bare skin, especially around her neck and throat, was an almost pearl white. Many men, Peggy thought in that moment, would find her irresistible.

'I don't know where to start.'

'You went to the dance?'

'Yes. Tom met me there.'

Mrs Linden raised an eyebrow and smiled. 'Tom?'

'I haven't been to tell you about him, but I've wanted to. It's just that it's all happened so fast. We met on Thursday last, near the Christmas bush. He's American.'

'What a beautiful place to meet.'

'Yes, and then on the beach again on Friday. Yesterday week that is. And then the other day he asked me to come to the dance. Not as his date exactly. But he told me he would meet me there.'

'And he did?'

'Yes.'

'And?'

Peggy didn't know how to explain. She fidgeted with her hands and then suddenly got up as if to pace about the room but feeling woozy, she sat down again.

'Does he know your age?'

'Yes. He asked me and he's twenty three.'

'And based at the Country Club?'

'Yes. He is so nice, Mrs Linden. He's wonderful. He has blonde hair and the darkest brown eyes you've ever seen. And he's so friendly and polite. And he danced divinely. I was terrible tonight, so out of practice but he didn't say anything. Then it was a slow dance and something came over me.'

Mrs Linden smiled in encouragement.

'I felt like I was drowning but in a nice sort of way. I just wanted to be close to him. It felt like it was the only place to be.'

'And it is the only place to be. With someone you like very much. But you both got carried away, I take it.'

'Yes.'

Mrs Linden had lit a cigarette and the smoke drifted up lazily. 'Did he take advantage of you?'

Peggy hesitated and Mrs Linden paused, gazing towards the window as she smoked. Her expression was serious and far away. Peggy waited, unwilling to interrupt the older woman's reverie. 'Did he do anything you didn't want him to?' she said finally.

'No.' Peggy caught her breath and frowned. 'How did you guess?' she stammered and blushed. 'I mean he kissed me for a long time and he touched my breast. And I wanted him to. That's the thing. I wanted him to.'

'That's perfectly normal, Peg but of course you can't let him go much further.'

'I know that but I feel awful for letting him do that and now I think he...'

'Don't tell me. You're worried he might think you cheap.'

'Yes,' Peggy said, moving uncomfortably on the chair.

'Have some more of the brandy. Finish it off,' Mrs Linden added after a pause. She had stood up and was now pacing about the room.

'But there's something else,' Peggy said.

'He did something else?' She turned sharply towards Peggy.

'No, not exactly. It's just that he cried in my arms and I don't really understand why. Then we sort of had a misunderstanding. The whole thing became about him touching me. But instead I really wanted to know why he cried. I still want to know.'

'How fascinating. I'd like to know why too,' Mrs Linden said. At the window she continued, 'If I could say the same,' Mrs Linden paused. 'That a man had cried in my arms. My life might be very different now.' Peggy didn't answer. It seemed Mrs Linden was speaking to the night and the moon. After a few moments she came back and stopped in front of Peggy's chair. Kneeling down, she took the girl's hands. 'Why don't you start from the beginning and we'll see if we can work this all out.'

He first caught sight of her on the sandy track near the beach. She was walking towards the Country Club. He and another officer had come outside when they heard wolf whistles from nearby. Tom leant against the wall near the front entrance as she drew closer. It was Peggy's mother.

It must be, he decided, taking in the chestnut hair and the tilt of her head. But in another instant he realised it wasn't. This wasn't Peggy's mother any more than he was her brother. She wore a white linen suit and was immaculate, confident too. No wonder the boys had whistled. She was beautiful in fact but he felt wary. Something wasn't right. Immediately he was on the alert.

She was about five feet away and looking at the two of them, Bob Morecroft, an RAAF officer that he billeted with and himself.

'I'm looking for Lieutenant Tom Lockwood.'

'You've found him.' Tom stepped forward in the same instant Bob moved away. He extended his hand. 'First Lieutenant Tom Lockwood at your service.'

Her grip was firm as she shook his hand but the look she gave him was deprecating. He felt put in his place. His rank meant nothing to her and she made him feel that he had spoken glibly instead of politely. These Australian women sure were challenging, he thought.

'Sarah Linden. Is there somewhere we can talk?'

'Shall we go for a walk on the beach?'

'Oh, dear.' Sarah paused. 'After last night is that advisable?'

He heard Bob snicker from the doorway. Damn her, but he deserved that.

'There's really nowhere else,' he remarked, looking around.

She shrugged her shoulders and taking this as an assent, Tom led the way across the road to the beach.

He was blushing and he could feel the colour staining his cheeks. Trying to gain some ground he asked, 'How did you get past the guard?'

'Told him I was on special business and winked at him.'

Tom studied the older woman. The audacity, but she didn't seem to care.

'Look, Tom, I don't care what this town thinks of me. They have already made up their minds about me. They envy me my money and my freedom and secretly wonder why I live here.'

'And why do you?'

'Because it's one of the most beautiful places in the world and I appreciate beauty. Need it actually but that's none of your business.' She paused to look for a cigarette in her handbag. Tom retrieved one from his pocket and lit it.

'Thank you. I'm rather short at the moment. As are most of us.'

'Except us Yanks, right?'

She didn't answer, simply smiled.

'I'll get you some.'

'I would appreciate it,' she told him looking away. They both smoked in silence for a few minutes, still standing. Tom surveyed the blue water all around him, waiting for her to speak.

'I'm here about Peggy.'

'I guessed as much. How is she?'

'She's all right. She told me everything.'

'Everything?'

'Yes, including the fact that you cried in her arms. I'm hoping that was a genuine expression of your feelings, not a lead up to the usual, '"I don't know how long I'll be here. I don't know how long I've got routine."'

She really did mean business. He took a deep breath. 'It looks like I'm going to be here for a while but please don't repeat that to anyone but Peggy.'

'Of course.' She blew smoke near his face. 'Well then if you are, I'd like you to do something for me.'

'Leave Peggy alone. Is that what you want?' Tom spoke quickly.

'Only if you don't care about her.'

'I do. Very much. In fact I think I'm in love with her.'

'Hence the tears.' Sarah Linden spoke softly, looking towards the bay again. After a moment she turned back and he faced her squarely.

'Yeah, and a few other things.' As he answered, he saw her shoulders sag but she rallied quickly and raised her eyebrows in answer.

'Two years worth bottling up my emotions. Meeting a girl like Peggy *now*. The war, the impossibility of it all...' Tom paused.

'Etc., etc...' Sarah cut in, not unsympathetically. 'But you do care about her?'

'Yeah, I do.'

'Well that's all that matters, isn't it?'

He nodded.

'Then you owe her a letter and a bit more self control don't you think?'

She was looking about her now. Under the beautiful veneer he sensed another Sarah Linden. Obviously one who cared a great deal about Peggy.

As if reading his thoughts she added, 'She's like a daughter to me.'

Tom nodded again. 'I had already decided on a letter but have been trying to figure out how to get it to her.'

'I love intrigue.' Sarah stamped out the last of her cigarette. 'I have a large blue Chinese pot around the back of my house. There's jade growing in it but there's room to pop a letter in and some cigarettes. Drop it in tonight and I'll see she gets it tomorrow. I'll explain that I've seen you and why.'

'Your reason for doing this?'

'I thought I'd already told you. And I think if you haven't already got some... What do you Americans call them? Prophylactics? Then you had better see to it. Just in case,' she added.

'I'm not eighteen and I'm not totally irresponsible.'

'I hope not,' she said and walked away.

The Letter

When I got back from Joan's I did as I had promised. I didn't look at the photos but I did one thing before closing the door to my mother's room: I dragged the paisley print armchair out into the tiny sunroom next to the porch and positioned it near the window so that I could sit and look at the view. (The word paisley print had suddenly popped into my mind when I surveyed the chair for a second time.) I sat in it for quite a while before going to bed. Just sat there, dazed and exhausted, staring into the dark night.

This morning it was chilly with an unpleasant breeze blowing so I decided on the armchair by the window rather than the folding chair on the porch, to have my coffee. I sat down with my coffee and Joan's note. It was on rather nice writing paper with a small Welsh dragon in the right hand corner. Most of the note was set out in point form. It read:

> Dear Peggy,
>
> Below is what I _believe_ your mother _thought:_
> · that you and Tom were in love
> · that you and Tom should go where Tom's work was
> · that you were a wonderful mother and daughter
> Hope this helps.
>
> Love Joan
>
> P.S. That useful quote was: 'None but a fool worries about things he cannot influence' Samuel Johnson (1709-1784) English essayist.

Yes, Joan was right. It was a useful quote but very hard to put into practice. Point three was a wonderful touch. A magnanimous gesture on Joan's part or the actual truth? Surely Joan was too pragmatic to repeat anything other than what she believed to be true, i.e. that my mother thought I was a wonderful mother and daughter. I gazed at the bay. Of course it was the sort of thing Mum would never have told me; therefore it was very possibly true. I felt a lump in my throat and a sudden desire to be out walking.

Before I knew it I was on the zigzag path down to the small beach. The weather had obviously deteriorated in the last half hour. The wind was whipping up small whitecaps over the sandbanks in the bay and away on the other side Windi Woppa was just a blur. Not a day to be out fishing. The fisherman in their small boats after flathead, or maybe even snapper out to the islands, would surely be stranded on the other side of the bay. Just like they had been all those years ago. I closed my eyes to shut out the heaving bay.

It was on a day such as this, I realised, trying to brush the memory away, yet it persisted. A day like this. The wind had been up. In the shelter of the bay, not too bad but in the open water, almost a gale. The sky overcast to the point visibility must have been affected. On that day the waves in the middle of the bay were enormous, monstrous brothers and sisters of the waves that were springing up now. How quickly it all happened. How quickly it was over. I felt tugged down with them every time I thought about what lay underneath the sea, on the other side of the bay. What had lain there for nearly thirty years.

I shook myself and walked further up the beach towards Fly Point and then on up to the road. What a mess my life is at the moment! I am torn between two worlds in more ways than one. I haven't decided where I am going to live or what I am going to do. Teaching again? Or an office job. Married? Or with a divorce imminent?

At this moment my life seems to be filled with things I mustn't think of, for various reasons. I mustn't think about Tom right now. Something told me Mum must be attended to first. Therefore I mustn't think about Windi Woppa or the day little Jessie Schultz fainted. Yet how could I possibly reacquaint myself with my mother? How could I begin to know her as she was in the 1940s?

There was always the wardrobe but Joan's simple list drew me. Particularly the first point. 'I believe your mother thought that you and Tom were in love'. That's what it reiterated. But was that what Joan had told me last night? I racked my brain over the conversation. No, not quite. What had she said? It wasn't *thought*, I was suddenly sure. Not *thought*. My mind was blank but gradually as I stood there I became aware of how hard the wind was blowing and how cold it had become. The paisley print chair was beckoning.

I looked about me. The bay was grey; the clouds grey too, the whole expanse before me drained of colour while my mind seemed to be on fire. So many things jostling for attention that I couldn't think. I gazed at the bay again for one last look before turning back. Despite the wind, I felt like taking the long walk home past the shops instead of up the zigzag incline to Magnus Street.

Nelson Bay hadn't changed much since my last visit thank goodness. What a shock it had been back in 1967. On that occasion the small fishing village I had left behind on my 1950 visit, essentially the Nelson Bay of my youth, was unrecognisable. I had been so dismayed and inexplicably sad. Yes, it was convenient to now have a women's hairdresser, a cake shop, chemist, electrical store and newsagent but all the old houses that had gone in my own street to be replaced by shops! The old post office closed down and made into a residence and a new one on the corner of Magnus Street.

Of course over the years to 1967 Mum had written of all the changes but none of the news had any real meaning until I saw it for myself and faced the reality of shopfronts and footpaths, more cars and more people. Luckily this time Nelson Bay was pretty much as I had left it. The Catholic Church Hall was still there, mercifully too the Methodist Church on the hill and the Blanch name still visible in Stockton Street. There were maybe a few more shops but I wasn't sure which ones. The garden centre in Donald Street was new I decided and then walking up Magnus Street I thought maybe the restaurant was new too but wasn't completely sure.

It was to be expected, I suppose, with such a beautiful spot, that other people would eventually discover it. More people coming and buying up houses and more shops for the new residents and tourists with development close behind. I had seen it all in the States. Last Saturday I watched The Tamboi Queen cruise up and down the bay, filled with holidaymakers. Soon there would be more tourists and more cruise boats.

I had heard from Joan last Monday when we took the hire car back, about the horror of the Radburn estate. Acres of bush cleared, the land ravaged at Little Beach and then no further development for years. It seemed building was finally beginning but what an eyesore it still was. I dreaded to see it and had been so upset by Joan's description that I still hadn't walked there. And that meant, of course, I hadn't visited Shoal Bay. I couldn't put it off forever. I would have to face the estate and visit Shoal Bay soon, see the Country Club and lay some ghosts to rest.

Up the twist of Magnus Street and then the land levelled off. The wind had eased and I paused outside my mother's house. Mine now of course, but I still couldn't claim it as such. I kept walking. Right on past as I had done that night so long ago and found Sarah up late, reading *Gone with the Wind*. I sighed, staring at the Linden house.

And it all had gone with the wind: that night, Nelson Bay as it was in 1942, Tom and I but more than anything, Sarah. Taking a deep breath I walked up to her house, boarded up now and badly needing a coat of paint. As I stepped onto the verandah to get out of the wind I noticed that several of the leadlights were broken. I had expected it sold by now, with the new owners moved in.

I peered inside. Empty, of course, of all her lovely furniture: the large armchairs, the standard lamp, her beautiful sideboard. The ornate mouldings on the ceilings were still intact, a climbing rose twining through a trellis, working its way around the ceiling. How it had wrapped around Sarah and I when we talked. Surely the beautiful proportions of the room would be obvious to many, so why hadn't it sold? I straightened up at the sound of footsteps behind me.

Mrs Marley, an acquaintance of my mother's came up the steps to the verandah. 'It's awful to see it like this but it won't be long now. I'm so sorry about your loss. She was a fine woman, your mother.' Mrs Marley's long face appeared to lengthen further in commiseration.

'Thank you. And thank you for coming to the funeral.' We both looked blankly at each other. 'I was sorry to miss Sarah's,' I added, struggling for something to say.

At that instant, Mrs Marley's face lit up. 'Do you know I think she left you something? I remember your mother mentioning a letter from the Solicitor requesting she call by. She told me she didn't want to and called in to let Mr Caldwell know you would be visiting next year and could it wait until then.' Mrs Marley paused. 'You were planning to visit next year weren't you?'

'Yes.'

'Well, anyway I remember your mother saying that Mr Caldwell said the matter could wait. Funny how they often use that word isn't it? The matter this, the matter that.'

Mrs Marley was quite happy to chirp on for half an hour, despite the weather, but I couldn't wait another moment. I cut her short saying, 'I might go now and see if he can see me.'

Mrs Marley put out her hand to stop me. It stilled my sudden impulse to run down Magnus Street but it didn't stop my mind racing ahead.

'He's away dear, gone for a month to visit family in Tasmania.'

'Of course he has,' I said exasperated.

The elderly woman looked quite sympathetic. 'Awfully inconvenient I know but I don't think it was anything much she left you. Something small your mother said.'

'Thanks for that, Mrs Marley,' I said, gazing at the elderly woman in her dusty pink twin set as if seeing her for the first time. 'Did you say something about the house not being vacant for too much longer?'

'Yes I did,' she replied, gripping my arm again and becoming quite excited. 'You'll never guess who she left the house to?'

'She had no family, so I have no idea'

'Mrs Wallis.'

'Mrs Wallis? Betsy's mother?'

'One and the same. She's been nursing that brother of hers for a while now. He died a few weeks ago and she's just putting everything in order. And from what's been said around the bay, it looks like she's coming back here to live. Taking over the house and doing it up.'

My head was full again. Would I ever sort it all out? Not here standing talking to Mrs Marley, that was for sure. Not wanting to hear anything more of 'what's been said around here', I said goodbye to her as quickly as I could and escaped finally to the paisley print chair.

Sitting in it now, the afternoon was closing in and the clouds had settled into a threatening purple coloured mass to the northwest. I gazed at the heavy depths of the clouds and thought through the conversation with Mrs Marley. A letter from the Solicitor. Something from Sarah. A letter from Sarah? Sarah and a letter? That first letter. Tom's first letter!

I sat up in the chair. I had received that first letter from Tom enclosed in a note from Sarah explaining that she was helping us by allowing Tom to drop his letters into her and she would pass them on to me. Also that he wanted to see me down at Sandy Point at two o'clock that afternoon.

I cast my mind back. Sarah had found me coming out of the Methodist church on the hill that Sunday morning and pulled me aside. Mother had probably been suspicious from that moment on, but I didn't realise it at the time. Would I drop in to her place in a few minutes? I said yes but before I could speak to her further she moved away and began chatting to the minister. As I walked home with mother I tried to formulate a reason for visiting Mrs Linden. 'She has a book she thought I might like to read.'

Mother was quiet for a moment then said, 'You should do more reading, Peg.'

'Yes.'

'Well hopefully it's a suitable one.'

'Yes, Mother.'

We both pulled our cardigans about us and I walked on to wait for Mrs Linden.

'What was your excuse?' she asked me as she opened her front door five minutes later.

'That you are lending me a book. But it has to be something suitable.'

'Oh dear, that restricts us, doesn't it?' Sarah was smiling as she scanned her bookshelf. She pulled a book from a shelf to her right, *Gone to Earth* and in a slow movement that I recognised even then, would hang suspended down the years, gently placed the book and two folded notes, one wrapped around the other, into my hands. 'Go out the back near the herb garden and read the letter if you like. Or would you rather go home and read it?'

'I might not get a chance until after I go to bed. I don't think I can wait that long.'

'I wouldn't be able to either. There's a patch of sun out there where it is quite warm right now. Don't worry about my note too much. I only wrote it in case I didn't get to speak to you.'

I can almost feel the paper in my hands now. See the mark of the Shoal Bay Country Club on the top of the letter and smell parsley and thyme as I read it. If only I could read it again! How the lunch with mother had dragged interminably. And later how fast I raced down the beach that afternoon. But what happened to the letter? I read it that night I'm sure I did but then nothing. I can't remember a thing after that.

To clear my head I got up and made myself a cup of coffee. As the kettle boiled I heard thunder, lightning and then the steady beat of rain. With rain came a sudden fear and immediately a vivid flash of what happened to the letter.

I was out on the porch, scrabbling along the brickwork, feeling the cement rendering with my fingertips, feeling for a familiar rough patch and a loose brick. My memory failed me. I couldn't find it in the dark I moved quickly back into the house and turned on the porch light. It was still hard to see but then I located the loose brick. Something was sticking out. It was the letter. Tom's beautiful letter.

It was all coming back. Everything was coming back. A week or so after I received the letter I was reading it on the porch, thinking mother was at the shops but she wasn't. She was out the back, working in the vegetable patch. She came inside. I was startled and not thinking quickly enough, I shoved the letter behind the loose brick, an old hiding place of mine since I was a child. The brick was only three quarters of its proper width – so little trinkets could fit in, my peg dolly, lollies, and a small toy car of Jimmy's.

I didn't get a chance to retrieve it until the next day and when I moved the brick the letter was gone. I was devastated and soon after admitted to Tom that it was lost but didn't explain the circumstances. I was ashamed to think my mother had stolen it. For years I mourned the loss of that letter and even looked for it on my first visit back in 1950. Never mentioning its existence to my mother of course. After that time I don't think I've wondered about it since.

I was still standing in the porch and the rain was coming in. Shaking drops off my hair, I closed the front door and turned off the porch light. Sitting in the armchair, I opened Tom's letter. The paper still felt new. Crisp. Where had the letter been all this time? Obviously not in the brickwork. And when had Mum put it back? That particular question alarmed me and I shook my head to dispel it. The mystery of it flashed black and white like a butcher bird and flew away. It would come back later I knew to rest on the brickwork, waiting for my outstretched hand.

The paper fluttered in my trembling fingers.

My Darling Peggy,

I don't know where to start but firstly must say I'm sorry for alarming you by crying. That was the point the whole evening turned on, wasn't it? I cried, you looked at me and then blamed yourself for allowing so much to happen. I tried to tell you it was up to me and that you mustn't blame yourself. But then you were down the road, lost to me.

I want to explain in person what really happened but I will try first in this letter. You see, it's me who's been lost. Lost really since I left school and that was five years ago. Leaving home after high school and working in the telephone exchange in Newcastle, Wyoming. Then two years studying in South Dakota, basic training in Washington State and the sea voyage over here.

By degrees I've lost bits of myself. The kind of life

I knew, my home state and now my country of birth. I guess in that moment with you it all got on top of me. Everything I've shut out and then the fact that I was falling for a girl that lives so far away from my home town.

I'm starting to think that you of all people will understand how I feel because you love this bay so much. You see my whole landscape has changed. The grasslands I grew up in have gone, the way of life and everything familiar. I'm here, surrounded by the sea and it really is a foreign land, Peggy. It's completely different from anything I've ever known. The people are different, the food, the way everyone talks. Everything is different. I've never told this to anyone. A few words have been mentioned between us Yanks at the Country Club but we don't go into it too deeply. And then you come along and suddenly everything makes sense. You sort of pull me into it all and make me feel I'm part of this place, that I'm not lost any more. It's like I belong to you and the feeling is so strong that I can't stop myself from wanting to be part of you. Emotionally and physically.

Forgive me for saying that, but that's what made me cry. You made me cry with the beauty of who you are. I was feeling all this when you touched my face and I couldn't hold it in any longer. Don't be frightened by what happened between us and please don't blame yourself for the fact that I never stopped myself from touching you. From this moment on, if you still wish to see me, I will be responsible for the two of us. Please just keep being yourself, my dear sweet Peggy Ashburn.

Yours forever,

Tom

Yellow

In the distance, from his vantage point on the sandy spit, Tom could see two of the boats ferrying the ratings ashore from Salamander. The poor old boat crews had it tough. Busier than anyone else, he reckoned. Luckily he had a fair amount of spare time and that situation wouldn't change for a while. There could be no training of beach landings without a fleet. At least not until the seconded pleasure cruisers arrived, maybe not even then, if the boats proved unsuitable. Most of them were coming from the Hawkesbury and Sydney Harbour. It would be interesting to see what sort of training could be organised with such a fleet.

When you started to examine it all, the whole thing was a bit of a mess: holed up in the club, working with the other JOOTS staff to formulate some sort of training program. Communications was still slow. Not all the lines had been put in and he'd lost count of the number of meetings he'd had with the Naval Signals Officer at Mrs Kelly's. And to top it off the Australian Army were still using heliographs!

But the new base at Fly Point was coming along and in a perfect location – not too exposed with a good lookout to the heads. A visit to Tomaree was on the agenda for next week and he'd get to meet the radio operators and take a look at the guns, and the view. He couldn't wait to see the view from that headland. It was like a child's drawing of a mountain and from up there it would be like touching the sky. He had a sudden desire to climb the Devil's Tower back home. And he would if it was humanly possible. *And* if he made it back home. But for the moment Tomaree would do.

He would stand there in the gun emplacements with the view all around him and think my girl has climbed up here. She has claimed this headland and now me. At that he caught sight of her running down the beach. She was dressed in yellow, her red hair flying, her legs moving swiftly. She was like a shaft of sunlight breaking through clouds, racing towards him. He took a deep breath as she hurled herself into his arms, lifting herself off the sand and wrapping her legs around his waist. She was giggling, he started laughing and the two of them fell as one onto the beach.

When they both sat up and brushed the sand off their clothes, he said still laughing, 'The letter was okay?'

'What is this okay? What does it mean exactly?'

He shook his head and smiled. 'It means all right. The letter was all right, wasn't it?'

'No,' she said, with a serious expression on her face. 'It wasn't all right.'

They had fallen apart and were sitting opposite each other. Staring down at the sand trickling through his fingers, he frowned trying to think. Had he made a mess of it? It was then he felt a kiss on his forehead and he looked up to see her kneeling above him with an enormous smile on her face.

'It was wonderful. It explained everything,' she paused. 'Well, almost everything.'

'How do you mean almost?'

'Well as much as you could explain. I don't think everything can be explained do you?'

He studied her serious expression and knew without a shred of doubt that he was looking into the eyes of a young woman who lived half a world away from his home town, but who thought and felt like himself. 'You're right. I don't think everything can be explained or that we can completely know another person.'

'We might think we do,' she added.

'That's for sure. But we can't.'

'No, we can't,' she added more softly and sat back on her heels. 'But is that a bad thing or a good thing? I haven't worked that out yet. What do you think?'

'I'm still working it out too but I don't think a couple should keep things from each other because in the end that will drive them apart. All the unspoken things.'

She had taken his hand and he felt its softness in his and the sun shining down on them. In that instant he was truly happy. He reached out and stroked her face like she had done his, the other night. She held his gaze.

'It was a beautiful letter,' she told him.

'I don't know about that. I was never good at literature at high school but I believe it was honest.'

'It was. I understood what you were trying to say.'

'That's good.' He felt his throat working. No words would come. He wanted to reach for her but was still afraid of his lack of self-control. There was no cover of night but surely he could trust himself to hold her. He hesitated. Sunlight was in his eyes when she said, 'Can I hold you?'

'Hold me?'

'Yes, hold you.'

He could only nod in reply and closed his eyes as Peggy put her arms around him. Letting go, leaning against her body, he felt her heart beating under his ear.

Tears

I think I cried for nearly ten minutes and didn't regain some measure of control until I noticed that I had smudged Tom's letter in two places God! Couldn't I do anything right? My mother had kept it beautifully in some mysterious, hidden part of her bedroom, her soul. I had it for a few minutes and now it was crumpled with parts of the letter smudged. *I've lost bits of myself* was almost indecipherable and the words *surrounded by the sea* had trickled down into a sort of pool that dragged off to the right. I lay the letter out flat on the coffee table to dry and sat back down. Ink was on my fingertips. Uncaring, I rubbed them on my brown skirt.

Had I ever written him a letter like that? Of course I hadn't and never conveyed my feelings so well either. I couldn't recall one occasion in twenty six years of marriage that mirrored the same intensity of Tom's words. But this wasn't a new thought. Over the years the awareness of my inability to express my feelings for my husband sometimes came to me in the moments of greatest intimacy with him. Yes, I said the words, but did I really manage to bring the weight of meaning to them? Had they often sounded empty to Tom's ears? Just reverberations of his more passionate and devoted feelings towards me?

If I was brutally honest with myself and I must be or I would never understand what happened between us, I had to face the awful truth that perhaps I had never succeeded in telling or showing him exactly, how much I loved him.

I often reassured myself at odd times: *Of course he knows how I feel.* He knows I love him and love being with him. As the sound of the rain increased, I remembered a dinner party with the Weinsteins when Bill Weinstein had joked that his wife Gloria (a particularly clinging doll of a woman) needed constant reassurance. 'Sometimes I'm sure I say it in my sleep. "Yes sweetheart, I love you."' Gloria shoved her husband in fun and said, 'Oh, Honey really!' But in that moment when I looked at Tom, I saw something so heartbreakingly sad in my husband's eyes that I felt guilty for weeks.

The clarity of that particular memory made me catch my breath. I got up and padded barefoot around my mother's house, listening to the rain and trying to place that dinner party. It was soon after Sarah's graduation from college, I was fairly certain. That made it just over a year ago. That night had I held him in my arms and told him I loved him? More than likely he made a move for me and I withdrew into myself. How long had I been doing that? For too long. For far too long. Now with his beautiful letter returned to me I had regained another Tom: a young and ardent Tom, different in many subtle ways to the Tom I had so recently run from.

Could my fifty three year old Tom write such a letter now? No. Just as I had changed, so Tom, in the words of his own letter, had lost bits of himself over the years. Had I lost more than him? Had the years as a young wife in a new country changed me so much that there was hardly anything left of that young Peggy who had run down the beach to meet him? Did he ever realise how hard it was for me at first? Maybe he didn't, but then I never told him. I never told him a lot of things.

I never told him how much I missed Australia and my mother. I never explained the extent of my guilt in leaving my mother alone. Yes, I wrote to her regularly and phoned once a month. And Tom very generously paid for two trips out here but never came himself. I wanted him to come both times. Did I explain to him how much I wanted him to come? Just as my mother never complained about the cards life dealt her, so I tried to live my life like that too.

Everything was so strange at first. The voyage out with over five hundred other women who had fallen in love with an American just like I had. And the babies! I don't know how many babies were on board but as I was childless I was often minding quite a few to give their mothers a rest. Margery from Newcastle's Charlie and young Doreen from Sydney and her baby Orville, after his father. They are the two that I remember the most.

I wrote to them both for a couple of years. I met other women at the odd War Brides get-together in Wyoming but gradually found myself letting go and losing contact. It seems to be a weakness of mine – a lack of communication skills. Funny for a woman whose husband was a signals officer during the war and more than once risked his life to keep communication lines open. It really has been one of his strengths, insisting we talk when things got tough. Always asking me how I feel but gradually I must have worn him down, especially this last year or so. And inevitably he allowed me to grow quieter, confide in him less and move that much further away from him.

But if I'm honest with myself, it wasn't just this last year or so, I think it started, *really started* that February day in 1946, standing at the railing of the Monterey. As the boat began to pull away and the streamers tore apart, a crowd of young women pushed in front of me and I lost sight of my mother and Mrs Marley standing on the wharf. When I finally made it back to the railing I saw them walking away.

Upset as I was, I still had enough common sense to realise that they must have thought I'd gone below. Squinting to see, I felt the breath catch in my throat. That couldn't be my mother! But it must be. I could just make out Mrs Marley's arms around the woman who appeared to be my mother. The woman was racked with sobs and every now and then stopped walking as if to catch her breath, all the while being steadied by Mrs Marley. My mother's head was bent forward and she stumbled as they moved away from the crowds. I was desolate and finally felt the full force of what I had done. I cried then, great rasping sobs and hurried to my cabin.

Of course I never told Tom what I saw that day. How my mother in her grief was almost unrecognisable to me. I just told him it went fine. That Mum seemed quiet but that Mrs Marley had been a help. What else could I have said? I couldn't have told him. It was best not to mention such a thing. But I should have of course, because I'm sure that that one confidence might have ensured the existence of a lot of others.

On the Monterey I kept myself as busy as I possibly could,

met lots of girls, wrote a letter to Tom and to Mum nearly every day and, of course, minded lots of babies. Although the trip itself was both exciting and tedious, it was also a time of excruciating worry. I hadn't seen Tom for nearly two and a half years: the last time, one special week we managed to snatch from the jaws of the war machine that had Tom in its teeth.

I still, even now, try not to think about the first week of October 1943 when Tom left the bay to join the rest of the 41st stationed in Rockhampton. It was an awful, desperate time in my life. A time when I often convinced myself that I would never see him again.

But miracles do sometimes occur and we had two. The second one was that he made it through the war and the first: five days together in the Great Northern Hotel before Tom shipped out to New Guinea. Blissful days, but then of course I had to say goodbye to him all over again.

Nearly two and a half years apart. Would he still look the same? Would he still be my Tom? And what would he think of me? Would he catch sight of me on the rails and think: *What the hell have I done?* What would his parents be like and would they approve of me? More endless questions keeping me awake as the ship cruised across the Pacific.

As it turned out that cold March day when the ship docked at San Francisco, Tom was still my Tom. The dimple in his left cheek had gone to be replaced by a deep line and there were more lines about his eyes. But in them I saw the same loving expression I remembered and that quizzical lift to his eyebrows was still there too. I saw it when I pulled apart from him to catch my breath. I remember being overcome with emotion so I simply smiled and nodded my head in reassurance.

Thankfully his parents, as I was to find out a few days later back in Wyoming, were wonderful people. Tom's father, John Lockwood became like a long lost father to me and Pamela Lockwood was always kind and helpful, giving me hints on how to do things the 'American' way, supplying favourite recipes of Tom's and suggesting how to furnish our first tiny home, three streets away from their large two storey timber house at Newcastle. Another Newcastle. But of course a very different

Newcastle with numbered avenues like New York, rodeos and a county fair.

In my first year in Wyoming I discovered that biscuits were cookies and scones were biscuits. The garbage tin became the ashcan. It was the living room not the lounge room, lounge rooms were in hotels. *Everyone knows that Peg.* (This was from Mrs Lockwood.) In time, when Sarah arrived, I was changing her diapers not her nappies. When going out with Tom's family people would often turn and stare at me when I spoke, listening carefully to my *funny* accent.

It took me a while to get used to meal times. It wasn't just the way they ate their food. In Australia I used to tease Tom about constantly changing his fork from his right hand to his left and putting down and picking up his knife, but when three out of four people did it then it became a different matter entirely. *My* manner of eating was strange. How English I looked eating like that. *Isn't that how the English cut up their food?* My mother-in-law had asked. As well, there was the way they dished out their food. Not on individual plates but placed in serving bowls and for the first ten minutes of a meal you seemed to be passing dishes back and forth instead of eating.

Minor things really but each of these small things alienated me, undermined my confidence and in my darker moments convinced me I had made a huge mistake. And then often in the same instant, Tom sensing my estrangement, would draw me into his arms or kiss me quickly, while his parents were in another room and tell me, in that generous way of his, how special I was to him.

Holding his letter again, that was what I wanted him to do right now. Pull me into his embrace and reassure me. When I think about him now (without Barbara) that's what I remember, his gentle reassurances. The way, particularly when we first met, he always seemed to be there when I needed him. It's funny but when I recall the two of us together; I have, in my mind's eye, a picture of myself stumbling into his arms. I remember I did that at the dance and at Fenninghams Island.

But in hindsight I can see that it was actually Tom taking the extra steps towards me, when I was unaware, with my eyes closed or looking down, he took those extra steps. He made the extra effort to bring us together. The realisation was painful but I knew it to be true.

Oh, for just one gentle reassurance from him now. But to reassure me of what? My mood plummeted. That whoever she was, she meant nothing to him? That he still loved me? Yet as I imagined him reaching for me, *she* stepped into the circle of his arms and the image of Tom dissipated. Back to that hot summer afternoon, back to the bed and her naked body.

I blew softly on the letter to make sure it was dry, folded it up and without thinking why, or for what purpose, I walked to my bedroom and tucked the letter under my pillow.

Hanging Out Clothes

It was Wednesday, Peggy's day off, and for nearly the whole day she had been watching her mother like a hawk. Well, not really like a hawk. It would have been nice, actually, to be able to look down on this whole scene and circle lazily. But if she was honest with herself she felt more like Peter Rabbit and her mother was Mr McGregor. That wasn't very nice she acknowledged but twice now her blue jacket had caught on the barb of her mother's comments.

'And to what lucky star do you I owe your presence to, Missy? I have a million things to do today and you're under my feet.'

'What can I do to help?'

'Help? Haven't you got a mountain to climb?'

'Not today,' Peggy said in all seriousness.

'Not today,' her mother muttered in reply. 'Well you can peel those potatoes for a start. It's roast mutton tonight and I expect we'll have a good turnout. The boys like a good roast and the numbers are always up when we put one on.' Peggy's mother paused, one of her daughter's white cotton nighties in her hands. 'Oh, I haven't got time to fix that now.'

Peggy studied her mother as she was muttering to herself. She seemed to be staring at the nightie. After a moment Mrs Ashburn recollected herself and put the nightie in her sewing basket.

'Only as many as'll fit in that boiler though.' Mrs Ashburn pointed to an enormous saucepan on the stove at the same time eyeing her daughter suspiciously. Peggy could feel her mother's scrutiny drilling into the back of her head, as she bent over the sink.

'I don't need any extra help tonight, if that's what you're after.'

Peggy turned towards her mother who was closing the lid of

her sewing basket. She felt momentarily lost and it must have showed on her face because her mother spoke in a softer tone.

'I don't trust one or two of those boys with anyone younger than myself. A number of them have been giving Mrs Wallis a hard time lately. That's why we've all decided that for the moment we won't have any one younger helping out. I have Mrs Robinson and Jean Marley to help me. That should be enough. I expect they're at the house now making a start, though what we'll do for vegetables I don't know. Swedes again I suppose.'

Her mother was talking to herself again and Peggy turned back to the potatoes. After a few minutes of straightening the small lounge room, her mother walked past Peggy and disappeared outside.

This CELOPS was certainly keeping her mother busy. It was just a house, next to the school residence, that served as a meeting place for some of the soldiers at Gan Gan but with the arrival of the Navy in Nelson Bay, things were getting busier. Now her mother helped out cooking meals twice a week. And when she wasn't cooking meals she was making scones or biscuits. This last month or so her mother often seemed to be backwards and forwards to the weatherboard house. Once or twice on walking past, Betsy said she had heard someone playing a piano and quite a few voices joining in singing. It sounded like a happy place. She wondered if Tom knew of its existence but perhaps it wasn't suitable for an American officer. Anyway he had the Country Club.

On her fourth potato Peggy sighed and worried that she would never be able to broach the subject to her mother. Well she wouldn't be able to standing at the sink and peeling potatoes. She wiped her hands on her checked apron and went out the backyard looking for her mother. She found her in the fading sunlight hanging up a pair of men's army trousers.

'Are you washing for the army now too, Mum?'

Peggy noticed her mother appeared uncharacteristically flustered.

'I don't normally but a few of the younger boys need a bit of help. I offered yesterday. I'm just doing Teddy's for the time being.'

'Teddy?'

'Yes, he's only eighteen and a bit homesick.'

'I suppose a lot of them are.'

Helen Ashburn turned quickly around to face her daughter.

'Would you like to tell me what this is all about?'

'This?' Peggy stumbled over the question.

'This staying at home and being helpful. It's not like you, Peg.'

'What are you saying? That I'm not helpful.' It was beginning again but she couldn't allow this seed of ill feeling to burst into flower. She pushed it aside and tried for a lighter tone. 'I'm sorry I haven't been of much help lately. I didn't realise you were so busy with CELOPS.'

'It's my own choice to be so busy.'

There was the wall again, Peggy thought but tried not to dwell on the bricks and mortar of it. 'I just felt like staying at home today.' Peggy paused, noticing the quizzical expression on her mother's face. She noticed too that her mother's face appeared softer today, plumper with less lines on her forehead and near her eyes.

Maybe it was just that there was colour in Mrs Ashburn's pale English rose complexion or was there something else? In her busyness she seemed aglow somehow, almost lit up from the inside. The caustic edge to her tone of voice was gone too. Taking in these details, made Peggy glance again at her mother, trying to see her as Tom would, meeting her for the first time.

Her mother always took time over her appearance and today she was wearing her second best dress, mauve linen that looked lovely against her fair skin. She was wearing house slippers now and a pink apron but Peggy knew these would soon be discarded for her navy handbag and shoes. The enormous saucepan would be shouldered and maybe on a second trip to the weatherboard house with the piano and young men lounging around, she would arrive with a tablecloth under one arm and a plate of scones in the other.

Peggy almost wished she could stand inside the house for a few minutes to see her mother as these soldiers knew her. What did they think of her? What would Tom think of her? For a brief instant an unknown woman in her early forties, quite pretty really with dark grey hair was standing in front of Peggy hanging out the washing. Her movements were swift and economical. Here was someone you could trust to get things done. Here was someone practical and clear-headed. Yes, her mother was these things. But approachable, was she that? Was she the sort of person you could confide in or was there just a bit of aloofness in her manner? What some people in the bay called English reserve.

As the last peg was pushed on the line her mother turned and they were again face to face with an enormous distance between them: detachment, pride and wariness were hanging there almost as tangibly as the clothes. But there was something else. It was a new garment. Peggy could sense its presence. It was in the way her mother was studying her carefully. It was visible when Helen Ashburn's attention kept wandering to the clothes on the line, the empty wicker basket at her feet and her daughter standing in front of her.

'You like peeling potatoes do you? That's a first!' Mrs Ashburn said finally.

'I've met someone.'

Picking up the basket, Mrs Ashburn turned to face her daughter. The sun was in her eyes and she raised her hand against her forehead and then wiped her eyes wearily. After a moment she let the basket drop to the ground.

'Who is he?'

'Lieutenant Lockwood and he'd like to come and meet you.'

'Oh he would, would he?'

Her mother was moving inside now, the basket still lying behind them on the small patch of grass. Mrs Ashburn walked to the kitchen and stood looking at the potatoes in the sink.

'You haven't made much of a start, Peg.'

'I *will* do them, Mum, I just wanted to speak to you about this first. He would like to come around Saturday night to meet you. Then we are going on to the pictures.'

'That's the official plan, is it?'

'What do you mean by the official plan?' Her mother's tone of voice alarmed her. 'That's what we are doing, Mother.'

'Don't you "Mother" me! It's precisely because I am your

mother that I know about these things.'

It was beginning again. This dance they seemed trapped in with her moving forward and her mother moving back. But just as suddenly as it started, it was over. Mrs Ashburn slumped against the sink and was looking blankly at the clock on the small mantelpiece. 'Oh, look at the time. There's no time to think let alone do the potatoes.'

'Then we'll have to do them together,' Peggy said.

'It looks like we will.' Peggy joined Mrs Ashburn at the sink and for a few minutes they worked in silence.

Finally Mrs Ashburn said, 'He's an officer, you said? What's an officer doing bothering with a seventeen year old girl and where did you meet him? He does know you're seventeen, doesn't he? I don't want him in this house if he doesn't.'

'He does. And I met him at the dance Saturday before last.' The long practised words were out. Well, nearly all of them. This was what Peggy and Tom decided would be best to tell her mother. She could hardly say she met him near Dutchies. There was still the hard part to come though.

'He's very nice and polite. A real gentleman,' Peggy said, placing the last of her potatoes in the boiler.

Helen Ashburn shook her hands free of water and slammed down the lid of the pot. 'American, is he?'

'How...? Yes he is,' Peggy said, sighing.

'Can you give that boiler a wipe and wrap a tea towel around it while I get my bag and shoes.'

Peggy stood dumfounded for a moment. Slowly she did what her mother had asked, tying a large red tea towel at the top to secure the lid. In her mind the tirade had begun. *I'm not having an American in the house. Have you forgotten about that Private Leonski killing those poor girls in Melbourne and they haven't hanged him yet either! And who's to say there's not more like him?*

On and on it went until the sound of her mother's door closing brought her back to the present. Dully she watched her mother walk across their small lounge room. She had on her blue shoes, and was carrying her navy handbag just as Peggy had envisaged. With her free hand Mrs Ashburn adjusted her hat on her thick grey curls. Meeting Peggy's eye, something her daughter was sure hadn't happened for quite some time, Mrs Ashburn said, 'From America you said?'

'Yes, Wyoming.'

'Then he's a long way from home,' her mother said pleasantly.

Flabbergasted, Peggy watched as her mother picked up the large saucepan. 'I'll be back for the scones and a few other things later.'

'I can bring them.'

'There's no need Peggy. I'm quite capable of a few minutes walk.' Turning slowly near the door, Mrs Ashburn added, 'You'd better ask him for dinner. We'll have tea early so you can still make the pictures.'

With that, her mother was on the porch and down the steps to Magnus Street leaving Peggy in a flutter of emotions – relief, sheer joy and bewilderment spreading their wings in her heart.

The Exchange

I have become my mother, alone in Australia, receiving a letter from my daughter in America. I think some part of me knew, had known for quite a while, that this would happen. Karma, or poetic justice, call it what you will but here I am gazing at the once familiar, now foreign stamp: USA spelled out in red, white and blue with a plane flying under the 21c. No fish, beef or rice for the U.S. Postal Service thank you very much; which is what the Nelson Bay Post Office is selling at the moment – a celebration of Primary Industries. Joan said my mother collected the stamps for her to give to the Red Cross. I would do the same.

Did she worry about the contents just as I am doing now? Did she pray as she started reading that it would contain only good news? My letters always did of course. I wasn't game, under the circumstances (you know about beds and lying in them) to include anything but pleasant chit chat.

I scanned the first paragraph. It was all about setting up house. How she had dragged her brand new husband Richard (never Dick) shopping to help her choose curtains and bed covers. That she was able to do so said more of Sarah's determined character than a supposed affability of Richard's. Light-heartedness wasn't one of my son-in-law's strong suits unfortunately. At the moment Sarah found his seriousness endearing. I just hoped for her sake that over the years it didn't develop into the kind of austere humourlessness that could make life unbearable.

Laughter had definitely played a part in her father's and my romance. How quickly Tom had picked up on the Australian sense of humour, often explaining over the years the slant to an Aussie joke or remark that baffled his parents or our friends. It took me a while to realise that when you were being ironic, Americans invariably took your remark or comment as serious, which could often prove very embarrassing. I don't know how many times since moving to Wyoming I have had to remark, 'I'm sorry, I was joking,' to their raised eyebrows.

Here I am thinking of Tom again. It is strange that he is in my head now, in Australia, so much more than when I was living only half an hour from him. When it first happened (the Barb incident, as I have been calling it lately) I was able to block him out for days, even a week or two. After his betrayal he just didn't exist, for quite some time. Now, here, two months later he is becoming more and more tangible. With difficulty I tried to banish him from my thoughts so that I could return to Sarah's letter.

There was a dinner with her in-laws, a rather wealthy couple living in Stevens Point (who keep themselves very fit walking every day on the many hiking trails nearby.) Then I came to her description of the lake near her new home. Her narrative powers, so evident in College really came to the fore as she wrote about the trees, the lusciousness of their summer growth and of watching a Great Blue Heron standing on the shoreline near their home.

They had bought a small property near Lake Wausau and were both enthusiastic about the wildlife that abounded in the region. Instantly I could visualise Richard with binoculars identifying and cataloguing the local bird life; Sarah just standing and watching a particular bird arcing up into the sky. Wisconsin has thousands of lakes mostly with American Indian names and it gave me a perverse sort of pleasure to realise that both my daughter and myself are now surrounded by water.

Sarah wrote that a neighbour had told her about the flocks of swans and Canadian geese that fly over in the fall and she was looking forward to watching out for their migration south. It was a cheerful, deeply happy letter and I was relieved and happy for her. I folded it up carefully and wished for a nice box to put her letter in. The first of many such letters, I hoped.

I had seen a beautiful carved box on my short stopover in Fiji on the way here but of course I hadn't been in a fit state to even think of buying it, let alone going through with the transaction. I suddenly longed for that box or something similar, when of course there was no such thing to be had in Nelson Bay. Well, in my depressed, negative state, I convinced myself there wasn't.

How restless I have become this last week. I really must think about getting a job although I have no idea of what it would be. I have already made enquires and discovered that the New South Wales Department of Education will not recognise my American diploma and allow me to teach. Beyond teaching I can't think for the moment. The disappointment has weighed me down for days, although it had not really come as a surprise.

For the moment I needed to get out. I grabbed my shoes and leather shoulder bag and strode out into the sunny morning, very warm for August. But then August in Australia was always a strange up and down, blustery month. I made my way down Magnus Street and went inside Maxwell's Newsagency for something to read.

I must have stood looking at the books for nearly ten minutes, quite unsure what I felt like reading. I finally settled for *Love Story*, surprising myself as I generally don't read romances but I wanted to find out if the book's dialogue was as snappy as the film's. Tom and I had seen the movie two years ago and I often liked to compare a book with a movie. After paying for *Love Story* I stepped out into the sunshine again. I stood for a moment and felt the sun on my face and in that instant caught a flicker of movement from across the road. It was Joan waving to me from Proctor's Cafe. I hadn't seen her for a few days and found myself waving happily back. I crossed the road.

Seated at our small table I ordered a milkshake and watched as Joan busily devoured a banana split.

'That looks rather good,' I remarked.

'Go on, be a devil, love.'

I shook my head, holding up my milkshake which had just arrived but Joan wasn't going to be so easily dissuaded.

'I'll help you.'

'All right then,' I said laughing and ordered another banana split.

Joan smiled at my good humour. 'Now you look a lot happier today, Peg.'

'I am. I had a lovely letter from Sarah today.'

'Oh, that's nice, a red letter day. I had one from Angharad too, writing about her travels.'

The waitress delivered our order and Joan asked, 'Been

through the wardrobe yet?'

'No, I haven't. I have sort of been putting it off for some reason but I am counting the days till Mum's solicitor comes back.'

'Waiting's terrible, isn't it? You haven't got your hopes up, have you, love? I wouldn't expect much. I mean she had money but she's left the house to Mrs Wallis. The contents were sold, I hear.'

'Yes. So I can't think what she's left me. I mean I don't expect a thing. It's more the puzzle than anything.'

'Mind, wishing won't make Mr Caldwell come back any faster. But I know something that might pass the time. I've heard that Nelson Bay Public School could use some help. Someone to hear the children's reading and maybe some storytelling to the littlies. It would free our dear, overworked teacher and give him time for the older ones. A couple of mornings a week, is it, Peg? And maybe the odd afternoon.'

I was so overwhelmed by her kindness that it took me a few moments before I could speak. 'You are wonderful, Joan. Was that your doing?'

'Oh well, just a suggestion on my part.'

I grabbed Joan's hand in gratitude. 'This *is* a red letter day. I couldn't see Angharad's letter, could I? And that would finish the day off nicely.'

Joan hesitated. 'Of course you can, love,' she said finally.

I was only partly aware of Joan's reluctance, thinking more as I was on the providence of us both receiving letters on the same day. 'We'll do an exchange. Sarah's for Angharad's,' I told her.

'That would be lovely. Important things are letters,' Joan remarked.

Yes, they are, I mused silently, sipping the last of my milkshake. How important my letters were to my mother, as Joan had told me more than once. And how very important Sarah's letters were to me. From the time she went to college I had waited for them anxiously and now in Australia I would continue to wait for them.

And then there was Tom's lost letter bringing with it the power to rewrite the past or at least my memory of it. To remind me of feelings, emotions that I had felt so strongly at the time but somehow as the years passed, assigned to them a lesser value. Tom's letter had reinstated those youthful feelings of his and mine to such an extent that they had begun to fight for a place in my heart against the angry, hurt recriminations of a cheated wife. *Yours forever, Tom* had been humming inside me for days now.

It was on the tip of my tongue to tell Joan about the strange reappearance of Tom's letter but something held me back. I wanted it to be mine only for a little while longer before I even told Joan about it. I wanted to hug it to me until Tom's words became imprinted on my heart. And then as I pushed my plate away, full up with banana split a sudden thought came to me. Was that what my mother had felt? A desire, for some inexplicable reason of her own, to be closer to Tom by hugging his letter to her? The thought was absurd yet I couldn't dismiss it from my mind for the rest of the day.

Again, a letter from Angharad proved a welcome diversion. I decided to read it instead of watching television. A wise choice as there was nothing decent on the box. I still hadn't written to her. I don't know why but I just hadn't gotten around to it. I would definitely tomorrow and in writing refer to both her letters. I opened up the latest one, thick white paper not thin blue airmail sheets as last time.

> *Prince Llewelyn Hotel*
> *Beddgelert*
> *3rd August, 1972*

Dear Sis,

I always enjoy the run up the coast. Talybont was as picturesque as ever and the clock tower is still watching over Machynlleth. I always forget how dark the local stone is up here and how imposing it makes the buildings look.

I spent the afternoon in Porthmadog, wishing

you were with me to show you around. How I love
walking along the embankment, with the boats in
the harbour and the cob cutting across the water
on its way to Portmeirion. I am saving a visit to
my most favourite of places on the way back. I
know I have written about Portmeirion before,
praising Clough Williams-Ellis for his mad
philanthropy of turning his own personal dream of
an Italianate village into a reality and a reality
that we can all enjoy. But there we are. You can
skip the many pages I'm sure I'll write, if they bore
you.

As you can see from the letterhead I am at one
of your favourite places and forgive me if you feel
it is insensitive of me to be here. It is your place -
yours and Peter's. What right do I have to be here?
I'm not sure. I just felt a pressing need to take this
sweeping route instead of cutting through
Blaenau Ffestiniog, the quicker way to Pentrefoelas
and our old home. When I drove here it was very
cloudy, threatening rain, Aberglaslyn Pass veiled
in mist. Hopefully it will clear tomorrow.

You know how I love the sight of mountains.
Snowdon towering over everything, Yr Aran with
its traditional shape of a mountain peak, and the
gliders, Glyder Fach and Glyder Fawr, not to
mention the lakes too, Llyn Gwynant and Llyn
Dinas. If it is sunny tomorrow I will spend some
time at Capel Curig and sit by Llyn Mymbyr, where
we used to picnic with Mummy and Da. Remember
the roads through the mountains, so narrow with
just low stones walls stopping the car from hurtling
into the valley?

Beddgelert is quiet, despite it being August.
Probably most of the tourists have gone on to
Betws-y-Coed. I prefer it here with my memories of
1940.

Wasn't it a miserable night? Snow falling and

the river iced over. Do you remember how we watched the cars come over the bridge? They were big dark cars in those days, weren't they? All making the drive for you and Peter and that wonderful log fire at the hotel, wonderful warm after the freezing old church.

Do you think of him much? I shouldn't ask this and I don't know what is the matter with me lately, but I seem to be drawn back to the past, to the old places.

So why am I here, I expect you're wondering? Now that's a good question, since you were married here not me. But I just felt the town calling that was all. Maybe Peter too. I can see you raising your eyebrows right now. Or maybe not. Nevertheless I decided to come and stay at the Prince Llewelyn.

I am here looking out across the river and thinking of you. Thinking of Peter too, your first husband. How in love you both were and what a strange place to get married in. But you were happy the two of you, weren't you Sis? Funny I should need to be reassured of that. But I like to think of you here, twenty six and madly in love with Sgt Peter Roberts of the Royal Welch Fusiliers.

How important landscape is in our lives. I think sometimes that it is more than just backdrop. It has the power to influence our lives in ways that are not always obvious. I have come to the point in my life that I can admit this and stop analysing why. I only know now that I am at my happiest wandering through the gardens at Portmeirion or walking through the woods, the Gwyllt, at dusk. No wonder I come to Portmeirion every year now.

We bring associations to landscape: happiness with a grove of trees, mystery in a steep gorge. I do it all the time and can't help myself. The only time we get things wrong is when memory fails us. Over the years, things become jumbled until we visit that place again and there, suddenly, are the feelings and memories given back to us in an instant. Well at least that's the way it has been for me on this trip.

Today whilst driving through this familiar landscape and remembering all our associations with it:your wedding, our family picnics further north, the old story of Prince Llewelyn and Gelert his faithful hound, part of Beddgelert as much as the Glaslyn and Colwyn rivers, I started wondering what you would be remembering. How different your memories would be to mine. Since we can't make the trip together I have decided to make writing my memoir top priority. I've been making notes now and I'll put it all together soon, all of my memories. I expect we'll have disagreements over some of my recollections but then everyone remembers things differently, don't they?

If my map of events gets mixed up, I can always go back and check. I can write to you and say, it was Beddgelert that you were married in not Betws-y-Coed? Or I can even drive there. So when I get home I'll put everything together as I remember it and you can set me right if I have got things wrong.

How is your map reading these days, Sis? Excellent as always I expect. Always aware of your true north, no matter where you are; whilst your older but sillier sister, still living in the landscape of our youth, swings wildly towards all points of the compass. I will go out this evening and stand on the bridge over the Colwyn for you. Me, standing in the landscape of your old life and you, dear Sis, with a very different landscape, in your new one. Even our seasons don't match.

Sometimes life is amazing, isn't it with the sudden turns our lives take?

Thinking of you and wishing for your company.

Your loving sister

Angharad

I glanced at my watch. Nine o'clock. It felt much later. I folded up Angharad's letter, aware now of why I hadn't written to her. The reading of her last letter had churned up so many emotions in me and brought back vividly that afternoon in June and the sight of Tom with another woman. What must this latest letter have conjured up for Joan? I should never have asked to read it. It wasn't meant for a stranger's eyes.

How unaware I am a lot of the time of other people's thoughts and feelings. I saw Joan hesitate, when I asked for Angharad's letter, but didn't stop to wonder why. I knew Tom was drifting away from me but didn't try and reach out to him. Instead I assigned to him emotions, beliefs that in all probability were not his, could never be his because they were mine. Was that what Angharad was doing in her letter? Assigning to Joan, *her* reminiscence of their wedding day?

How did Joan remember that night? Probably the cars and the frozen river were not uppermost in Joan's remembrance. I must stop there before I too add my own version of events. (Peter's happy face, the blissful/disappointing wedding night.) Oh, it was an easy thing to do: assign thoughts and feelings to other people that are in fact your own, to read someone's emotional map upside down.

I felt an overwhelming urge to do two things at once. Rush over and tell Joan how sorry I was that I asked for the letter. And the other of course – check my own map, the map I had been driving by all these years when negotiating the twists and turns in my relationship with my mother, and since her death, as a guide to the woman herself. I expect it needed to be thrown out and there was only one way to find a new one and that was by going through the wardrobe.

Boating

It was still light as Lieutenant Tom Lockwood left the Shoal Bay Country Club. He always enjoyed this walk along the sandy road by the bay, with the strange trees crowding in to the shore on his left and the blue water, a beautiful but indescribable shade of blue, like nothing he had ever seen. On his right, the moon was just visible, low on the horizon and he remembered the other fuller, brighter moon that Peggy had stood under the night of the dance. The sight of her in that white dress! So sad but luminous, slipping from his grasp.

Thankfully he had won her back but it could have gone either way. How different from the Peggy of two Wednesdays ago when they had picnicked on the beach. Three whole hours together! He had done some reshuffling to leave himself free for her but it had been worth it. They had laughed, paddling at the water's edge; his trousers rolled up, part of Peggy's skirt tucked up in her panties. She had done it so unselfconsciously that he felt a pang of admiration.

She was so honest and straightforward in everything that she did, so uncomplicated that it was refreshing. He had remarked as much to Bob Morecroft. The Australian disagreed, saying he preferred a vamp rather than a green schoolgirl. *He didn't have time to put someone in the picture*. That was the way he had dismissed Tom's remark. On hearing those words Tom had been aware that six months ago he would have been in agreement. But not now.

Their picnic on the beach had been the last time he had seen her and boy had he missed her! Things had been hectic since then and it sure was a change after the tedious duties of setting up communications at the Country Club. No wonder he had grasped at the possibilities Peggy presented. He hadn't had much time to himself in the days since last seeing her but he found she was in his thoughts just as much.

God, if he could only take her out in one of the beautiful cruisers that had arrived the other day. A few more were still making the journey up from Sydney Harbour and the arrival of the fleet had meant meetings with the other branches. It also meant a hell of a lot of running around and last minute decisions on how best to employ them and which ones would be suitable for what. Not that he was the one making the decisions, but he liked to keep informed. The engineers and coxswains at the naval base Assault had been like excited schoolboys, inspecting each one as it arrived.

It had all been slightly unreal especially for someone like him, coming from a prairie state and totally unfamiliar with boats and cruising. Twice this week he had walked around to Little Beach to have a look at one or two of them bobbing on their anchors. My word, to have the *Goblin* for a day. He had been there when it cruised in to the dock at Nelson Bay and even he could recognise the superiority, the sleekness of the vessel. To think her mellow timbers were even now being painted with naval grey.

On a boat like that he and Peggy could just disappear down river, away from all this uncertainty. They could play at husband and wife. Tom shook his head and laughed at himself. Was he really thinking this? How many times had he avoided Mary's edging towards such a future?

Maybe it was the war, living in this paradise that was Shoal Bay but the idea of Peggy and himself on that boat was the two of them, but not the two of them. They were different, intimate: another Peggy and another Tom. They had been married for a while and she knew what food he liked, he knew her moods, the way she got up in the morning, all awkwardness between them gone and the war long over. It was just them cruising down some unnamed river, in Australia or America; it didn't matter which. Just the two of them and the rest of the world could go to hell. That's what he really felt deep down. The rest of the world could go to hell.

How he hated the war for turning everyone's life upside down. Not just for the killing but for favouring people like him and dispatching others to their deaths. Plucking Lieutenant Tom Lockwood from his signals company and the 41st division and posting him here. He had lost touch with his buddies and a lot of what represented home for him. Were they still training up north near Rockhampton or had they seen battle in the Pacific somewhere? Maybe some of them were dead. He had no idea.

And where was he? Walking along a beautiful beach on a spring night, while they were doing what? Passing through the chow line? Or perhaps writing letters home in cramped quarters or tents? Maybe even now setting up communication lines on some exposed headland? Being shot at? Stopping bullets with their bodies? Of course that could still be his fate but for the moment he was marooned in this sunny idyll of a small fishing town. And to rub salt into the wound, shine more sun down on this paradise was the friendliness of the locals.

That's what surprised him. They were incredibly friendly. Here they were in a position to be unhelpful, distant, and uneasy and they were none of these things. All the officers had been invited for a meal. He was the last to take up an invitation, but his was the most coveted. Bob had been yapping, he knew, and word had got around about this invitation. He was having a home cooked meal and meeting 'Mom'.

The lighthouse reared up on his right as he cut across the headland and the mess of construction that was Fly Point. Only a few trees had been cleared, the rest left to provide cover. It made road building more arduous but it would leave the camp less exposed. As he walked through the bush he could now begin to see the pattern of roads that would crisscross the base. As he moved closer, Tom caught sight of a few small hand painted signs with arrows. One read *Lofoten*. Another *Tulagi* which sounded vaguely familiar.

Damn, these Aussies could be obscure. What did the signs mean? Sometimes it was like they didn't speak English. Were the signs some sly anagram made by the ratings to poke fun at their officers? The Australian serviceman's attitude to authority had to be seen to be believed and was one of many things that made him feel like an alien. Just as he was about to decide that was probably the explanation, he came upon another sign pointing towards the sea. It read *Guadacanal* and he was immediately flooded with a tide of remorse. Battles of course. The Major had been speaking of the landings at Guadacanal in the Solomon Islands just the other day. Tulagi was nearby, he remembered now. And the battle was still raging with the Coast Guard manning transports.

All the other signs were probably battles too, battles or places that had meaning for the Aussies. He was ignorant of the battles just as he was ignorant about so many other things that made Australians tick.

He had to stop making judgments without having all the facts, or at least a good proportion of them. It was one of the pitfalls of his being here and being an officer. As he came to Victoria Parade Tom put himself on notice – no more assumptions and no more jumping to conclusions. He didn't want to do that, tonight of all nights. It would be hard though. Peggy had already told him quite a lot about her mother, and it was going to be difficult not to let some of this show in his manner towards Mrs Ashburn. Well he'd better watch himself tonight. He glanced at the chocolates and flowers he had brought. Hopefully these would smooth the way. As for his uniform: maybe it was the wrong colour khaki as far as Mrs Ashburn was concerned, but there was nothing he could do about that.

Further up he cut through the bush to Magnus Street and when he reached the road was immediately met by two small boys of about seven or eight.

'Got any change, Mister? Gosh they're nice chocolates.'

'You're a Yank, aren't you?' the younger one asked, gazing up at him wide-eyed.

'Yeah, sure am,' Tom replied.

'Mum said if I saw any Yanks to ask them home for tea. But we've just had tea.'

'That's okay. I'm having tea with a friend. That's who the chocolates are for.' Tea? What the hell was tea anyway? Tom still wasn't sure. He had meant to ask Bob. Was it supper or a sort of Australian version of milk and cookies, something they called afternoon tea. Six o'clock was a bit late for afternoon tea. He was definitely hoping for supper. Here's a few...' he was about to say nickels but caught himself, 'sixpences.' So much change always weighing down his pockets. He was pleased to be rid of it especially when he saw the boys' excited faces as they counted out the money.

'Gee, thanks Mister.'

'Buy yourself some ice-cream.'

'Mum says we can never get any anymore because of the....'
The small boy let out a yelp and clasped his knee.

'What you do that for?' the younger one asked, turning to his brother.

'Keep out a trouble,' Tom said, stifling a laugh.

'Righto,' he heard from the older one as they both headed for a nearby house.

Tom bounded up the porch almost dropping the small bunch of flowers. He changed the chocolates and flowers to his left hand and knocked on the door. Peggy opened it and she appeared flustered, her cheeks pink from helping in the kitchen, he guessed. He smiled in encouragement, at the same time realising, disconcertingly, that she was wearing the white dress again.

She ushered him inside and Mrs Ashburn walked up to stand beside her daughter. 'Mum, this is First Lieutenant Tom Lockwood. Tom, my mother Helen Ashburn.'

As Tom extended his right hand and said, 'Pleased to meet you Ma'am,' he caught a strange look in the older woman's eyes. It seemed to be one of despair and surprise intermingled. For a moment she was quite alarmed and looked down, clasping his hand like a drowning woman. Their eyes met again and she stared into the depths of him. Mrs Ashburn was searching for something, studying his features with frantic dismay. Finally he managed to pull back a little. Slowly the older woman's grip relaxed and Tom was able to extricate his hand.

He didn't know where to look, wondering just what had happened between them and worrying too, whether Peggy was aware of his embarrassment. Had he done something wrong or was it just his presence in the house? Instinctively he felt it was something to do with his name. That was the instant she had recoiled. It was on hearing his name. And Mrs Ashburn confirmed his thoughts when she remarked, quite coolly he decided, considering the look in her eyes a moment before.

'You never mentioned his name was Tom, Peg.'

He handed Mrs Ashburn the flowers and this gave her a moment to recover, as she thanked him and went to get a vase.

'Didn't I?' Peggy asked absentmindedly. She had been straightening the cushions on the lounge.

Tom turned to Peggy to hand her the chocolates but studying her expression was fairly sure that she had missed whatever had passed between Mrs Ashburn and himself.

'Thanks for getting Mum the flowers and for these,' she said holding out the chocolates. 'You shouldn't have.'

Tom glanced behind him and seeing that Mrs Ashburn was out of sight in the kitchen, stole a quick kiss from Peggy. As he pulled away he saw the radiant expression on Peggy's face eclipsed as she glanced down at her dress.

'Mum wanted me to wear it tonight,' she whispered.

'You look beautiful in it. Like you did the other night.'

'You don't think it's bad luck?'

'No, we'll make it a good luck dress.'

'Thank you for your two other letters.' Peggy was whispering again.

'And plenty more to come.'

Peggy led him to a chair and went to help her mother in the kitchen.

Over dinner, a beef stew Tom was enjoying immensely, he was aware of the two women watching him eat. He laughed, having expected this reaction. 'It's the way I cut up my food, right?'

'Is that the American way?' Mrs Ashburn asked.

'That's right, Ma'am.'

'I suppose our way seems strange to you.'

'Some.' He felt the tension at the table ease a little but still found himself glancing at Mrs Ashburn. She was so very different from what he had expected. Obviously he had made judgements from Peggy's remarks, despite his earlier pledge not to, and the woman's appearance had instantly dispelled some of them. She was a little distant, cool as Peggy had warned yet maybe that had something to do with his name. What was the significance of his name? Was it her dead husband's name? He must ask Peggy. He couldn't recall if she had told him her father's name.

She was also much prettier than he had expected. For some reason he hadn't imagined she would be pretty, even though her daughter was. Yet they didn't look alike. Maybe Peggy took after her father. Taking out his plate into the kitchen he observed the photo on a low table. Well, if she did he couldn't see it.

Tom offered to do the dishes but Mrs Ashburn remarked, a little offended he thought, that there was still desert to come. She had misunderstood him. Of course he meant when the meal was finished. She refused his offer saying, 'You'll do no such thing.' Sitting back down at the table, he watched the older woman dish out dessert, apple crumble, he was informed and decided that she seemed a little stiff because she was nervous.

Over their meal he had caught her looking at him rather closely. Both times he smiled as pleasantly as he could. He desperately wanted to make a good impression as her approval of him would make things easier for Peggy.

With dessert over Tom thanked Mrs Ashburn for the meal. At his side Peggy was nervous too. He could feel the tension in her even though they weren't touching. He could see it in the set of her shoulders and a very small frown line across the bridge of her freckled nose.

If only he could grab her hand and give it a squeeze. Instead he did the next best thing. He told the two women of his hometown, Upton in Weston County, Wyoming. He spoke of the school he went to, his parents and his job at the telephone exchange in Newcastle, Wyoming. Gradually he was able to draw Mrs Ashburn out and keep her from the dishes, at least for a while.

He told them of the prairies, his trip to the Rockies as a boy and the two years he spent at the South Dakota School of Mines. He told them about Rapid City, a place of which he was very fond and his last sight of America. After two hours he had what he wanted from Mrs Ashburn: an invitation to come again.

The Wardrobe

Instead of going through the wardrobe, I sat up last night reading *Love Story* into the early hours and was surprised to find that the whole novel is from Oliver's, the husband's, point of view. Around 1.30 a.m. I began to wonder what would Tom's point of view be in regards to our love story. His first letter gave me a bit of an idea, but what of later in our marriage? What were his feelings about that, about the last year, particularly the last six months? Did he even consider it a love story at all?

I brushed the thought aside and closed the book. How feisty Jenny was! I had never been that feisty nor Tom that unfeeling in regards to his family. But we had believed in our love the way Oliver and Jenny did, I was sure of that much. And we had been just as earnest. But then aren't most young lovers? Cynicism doesn't come into it, nor does caution. And that's the way it should be otherwise not many of us would make the leap. But the lack of those two things and a surplus of other factors like enthusiasm and blind faith meant that I and thousands of other war brides had found ourselves on the other side of the world, far away from family and friends. We were tackling a new, unfamiliar life and all for love.

Love means never having to say you're sorry. Corny really when you dwell on it but still reassuring somehow. Does that mean Tom doesn't owe me an apology for sleeping with his secretary? That is, if he still loves me as he swore he did, the last time I spoke to him. And conversely does that mean I don't owe Tom an apology because this last week or so I have slowly and inexorably become aware that I still love him; helped to this discovery by the ghost of his younger, ardent self who has been haunting me since last Thursday. And I know he won't go away until I make some decision in regards to the real Tom.

I have debated the merits of phone versus mail. Both seem wrong. The phone reminds me of our last call when I rang to say my mother had died and that I was unsure of how long I would be staying out here. I can't get beyond it actually and wince now remembering Tom pleading with me to come back. His voice was breaking as he said over and over: *Please, just let me explain. Just let me explain.*

How tense and angry I was. Telling him I didn't want him to justify his behaviour. Nothing could justify or explain such a betrayal. How can I possibly dial his number after such a call? Yet as I go over the conversation in my mind (sitting cross-legged in front of my mother's wardrobe) I desperately want an explanation. *Yes, please tell me why you did it.* Now after two months I really need to know. And more importantly, want to know. But still I lack the courage to actually dial his number.

And a letter? I have always felt at a disadvantage when writing to Tom. His letters had been from the first articulate and heartfelt. My attempts paled to a jumble of words in comparison. How to form them into a coherent whole, into an explanation of how I felt that summer afternoon? It was impossible, especially when, as time passed, it was becoming harder to evaluate my rage and more difficult to explain my behaviour; to justify the fact that I had not let him explain his. If it could be explained.

In truth I no longer felt the same. Did that mean I wasn't the same person? Or had time worked its magic and simply helped me forget my anguish of the moment and reinstated other moments that I had forgotten or pushed aside: the many happy times in my marriage with Tom. They seemed to be surfacing more and more of late.

That wonderful holiday camping in Grand Teton National Park before Sarah was born. We had a long drive there but then seven days of bliss. Boating on Jenny Lake has stayed vivid in my mind not just for the wonderful scenery – the crystal clear water and the mountains reflected in it but for Tom's obvious enjoyment at being out on the water again. Looking back I realise it was one of the happiest times of my life.

Also our fifth wedding anniversary when as a surprise Tom had taken me for a weekend in New York. His enjoyment over my bewilderment at the battered condition of the ubiquitous yellow cabs, the spring beauty of Central Park and his patience while I spent hours trawling through Macy's. What a sweetheart he had been.

I assumed the butterfly position in yoga to still my mind and block out thoughts of his lovemaking. My body had been clamouring for him of late. I had recently started doing half an hour of yoga in the mornings and when possible walked at least an hour each afternoon, finishing the day with a soak in the bath, but I still found it hard to sleep at night and I was aware that as time went on, I would find it harder and harder.

All this wool gathering wouldn't demystify the wardrobe, which from this angle (I was now laying on the floor in the corpse position) had taken on a looming presence. Enough I told myself and jumped up quickly to pull the right hand door of the wardrobe open. I jerked it and in doing so several of my mother's dresses bounced out on their hangers as the door opened. A blue seersucker and a floral cotton I stroked gently. Taking a deep breath and working from the left to the right, I glanced at each article of clothing. Mainly dresses, blouses and some skirts. One or two suits. No pants. My mother had never liked pants. Slacks as she called them. Some dresses I'm sure she wore from the time before I left and I was quite surprised to see them still hanging there.

What had made mother keep them after all this time? She was no hoarder. Well, at least she didn't give the appearance of being one, I corrected myself. I didn't feel up to bagging the clothing now. Instead I just grabbed it in piles and heaped it on my mother's bed. At the bottom of the wardrobe were eight pairs of shoes, ranged neatly in two rows. I opened the left hand door. No hanging space here, instead it was divided into shelves with a large wooden box at the bottom. The shelves contained folded jumpers, two twin sets, mother had looked particularly nice in, some linen on one shelf, hankies, underwear and stockings.

Again I just piled it all on the bed. The underwear I put into a garbage bag. The linen and the rest of the clothes I would sort out tomorrow. But one peep at the linen told me it was worth keeping, particularly a finely crocheted tablecloth, rather fancy that I don't think I had ever seen before.

With the shelves cleared that left just the wooden box. I lifted it out. Now, thankfully, the wardrobe was empty. Taking a deep breath and sitting back down on the floor again, I opened the box. It was full of my letters. I took out pile after pile. Leafing through the date stamps I realised that Mum had bundled my letters up in years. I took each bundle out and grouped them from 1946 to 1972. Even my last few were here. But the box was not empty. Inside was one small bundle tied, not with elastic bands like mine, but with a faded ribbon that at one time might have been pink.

The envelopes were much smaller, the address Mill House, Salisbury Road, Amesbury written in a beautiful copperplate that must be by my father's hand. I pulled the thin rice paper out of the top one and read in the right hand corner: *2nd July, 1916, somewhere in France*. Without attempting to read even a paragraph I looked for the signature and found it on the back, not easy to read with the writing from the other side showing through but I made out: *With all my love, George*.

Quickly I folded the letter back up. I wouldn't read them now. I wasn't up to reading them now, not even one. I would do a Scarlett again and think about them later. But before I put the bundle back in the box, I flipped through each envelope checking the handwriting. They were all the same except for two but like my father's these were marked by the censor. My uncle's letters? Presumably, but there was only two. It saddened me to ponder why there was only two. I put all my letters in the box and put my father's bundle, including those two letters back on the top. I slid the box next to my mother's dressing table and stood up, stretching my calf muscles.

My hips felt sore. Really I was too old to sit on the floor. Stretching again I reached for the suitcase on top of the wardrobe. It was a caramel colour with rather fancy locks. As I dragged it forwards I felt its heavy weight. What was it filled with? Bricks? I would need a chair and was just contemplating whether I could be bothered to tackle it this morning when I heard knocking at the front door. I checked the clock in the kitchen. It was only just after eight thirty. Puzzled, I opened the door slowly. It was Joan and she looked dreadful.

'Might I come in and talk?' She was nervous and timid and immediately I was on the alert.

'Yes, of course.'

'I didn't like to bother you so early in the day but Arthur is away till tomorrow fishing off Broughton Island.'

'Whatever is the matter,' I asked, taking in her tear-stained face.

'Angharad's dead,' and with that she fell sobbing into my arms.

It took some time to find out what had happened but after making a pot of tea and settling Joan into the paisley print armchair, I gradually heard most of it. Earlier that morning Joan had received a phone call from Angharad's oldest and dearest friend, Professor Llewellyn Thomas, a history professor still teaching at Aberystwyth University. He had spoken to the Porthmadog police that evening. It seems that the hotel staff at Portmeirion were concerned for Angharad's welfare after she didn't return from a long walk in the Gwyllt on Sunday evening.

She had told them she would be in for dinner and then when she still hadn't arrived back by 10.00 pm they rang the police. The police came the next morning (last night our time) to find her car was where she had left it and of course her bed hadn't been slept in. Her room was searched for any clues as to where she could be, other than the woods surrounding Portmeirion.

Professor Thomas drove there in the afternoon only to be told on arrival that her body had been found in the Gwyllt and that she had been dead for over twelve hours. The police suspected either a stroke or a heart attack.

'Sitting quiet she was,' Joan said brokenly. 'The police officer thought she was okay till he got close. That's what he told the Professor.'

Professor Thomas had phoned only half an hour ago to explain all this and to assure Joan that he would arrange everything his end, see about the funeral and Angharad's will. He had collected all her things and would take them back to her tiny flat in Penglais

Hill and then speak with Joan again.

At the mention of the funeral Joan had broken down several times.

'I can't go to my own sister's funeral. The last of my family Peggy and I can't go! There isn't the money. I don't know how I'm going to bear it, being here and not able to see her off.'

'The day of the funeral, Joan, I'll stay with you all day.'

'Not in my house, Peggy. I'd rather be here. And what's going to happen to all her stuff?'

'We can worry about that later but I'm sure Professor Thomas will help. Most of her books could be donated to the University. Her personal things can be shipped out to you.'

'But how can I do that from this end? I can't Peggy. I'm too far away.' Joan was shaking her head and crying like a child.

'You can phone from here and keep in touch regularly with Professor Thomas as he sorts through her things.'

'Oh I can't do that. There might be lots of phone calls.'

'I don't care. I have a bit of money. The whole of the money in Tom's and my joint account, actually. He let me have it when I left. It's not enough to send you there unfortunately but there's plenty to pay for phone calls to the professor.'

'I wouldn't hear of it. I can't…'

'Now don't argue with me now, Joan. Would you like to sleep here tonight? I could make up the couch.'

'No, I don't want to trouble you. Is your mother's bed still made up? Maybe I'm morbid but it wouldn't bother me sleeping there tonight. It would be like being near her again.' With this Joan got up and bustled into my mother's bedroom, which was a complete mess.

'Oh, I interrupted you, did I?'

'Not really. I'm sort of doing it in stages. I'll sort it out later. There's plenty of time.' I glanced at Joan who was staring at the disarray of my mother's clothes spread out on the bed. 'Would you rather sleep on the couch?' I said, trying to guess at Joan's feelings.

'Do you know, I haven't told you this, but every time I come here I can feel her in the house.'

'Can you?' I asked, my voice breaking with alarm. I was

startled by the image of my mother watching me these last two weeks, particularly a few of the nights just lately. Whatever would she think of me? More disapproval?

'And she seems very happy. Very calm and chirpy.' Joan said. 'But perhaps I've watched that movie *Blythe Spirit* too many times. Do you know,' Joan turned suddenly to face me. 'Noel Coward wrote the play of *Blythe Spirit* at Portmeirion. Funny I should think of it now.' She advanced towards the bed and touched one of my mother's suits, the tweed one with the box jacket and pencil slim skirt. 'I think she would have disapproved of all this mess. Shall we sort everything out today?'

'Joan, you don't…'

'Oh aye, that's exactly what I want to do.'

'Well then, that's today organised and we have the whole day too as I'm not working at the school,' I said as lightly as I could. I would fuss over her and distract her as much as I could, just as she had my first day back here.

I managed to do just that and after dinner we rang Professor Thomas. There was no more news for the present but we gave my number to him as a second contact for Joan. Later in the evening, I accompanied Joan back to her house where she retrieved a nightdress and a few toiletries and clothes for the morning. We walked back in silence, Joan keeping close to me. It was after ten and we were both tired. I led Joan into my mother's room, now nice and neat and turned down the bed for her. As I stood up and faced her, I felt a like mother to this older woman and gave her a hug. She squeezed me in return. I turned on the bedside lamp for her and left wishing her goodnight but not sleep tight as I knew she probably wouldn't for hours. As I switched off the main light I glimpsed the suitcase like a sleeping tiger crouched on the top of the empty wardrobe, waiting.

The Mirror

Peggy sat in front of her maple dressing table brushing her hair. She had half an hour before Tom arrived to take her to the pictures or movie house as he called it. Behind her she could see her bed with the purple chenille bedspread smoothed over it. Peggy put her brush down and gazed at the reflection of her bed in the mirror.

Lately Tom had become very affectionate and these last few weeks, whenever they were alone, he was becoming harder to restrain. After only a few minutes his kisses would become deeper, his hands would find their way on to her breasts and then move relentlessly, it seemed to Peggy, down her thighs and low between her legs. When this happened she would take his hand and put it back on her waist and he would groan and catch his breath. Sometimes she would tease him. 'Do *all* officers behave like this?' or 'Are you off your pills?' after Emily told her about the bromide tablets soldiers were given to lower their sex drive. He would laugh and shake his head.

Since the first time he had kissed her after the dance, when things had got so crazy, she had been holding herself in, restraining the impulse to kiss him as passionately as he kissed her. This had slowed him down considerably, thank goodness. But like a tidal wave on the horizon she could feel the groundswell building. And what would happen then? A repeat of the night of the dance but this time, it wouldn't be just her breasts. (He touched them, caressed them quite often now and she let him.) This time would it be everything? The bed loomed large in her mirror.

She recalled the night of the dance. Gosh, how frightened she had been. By letting him touch her that way after only their first date, she thought she had lost him for good. Boys like him, boys from good families, her mother had remarked as much, didn't marry girls that let them have their way. She had had the lecture two months ago. *He won't respect you afterwards you know. You're mad if you think he will.*

The talk had been mortifying to listen to but perhaps just as difficult for her mother, whose cheeks had been bright red through most of the speech. All Peggy had been able to do was sit and nod repeatedly. Once or twice she had said, 'Tom would never do that, Mum,' or a similar remark to be met with a contemptuous stare and since then she had become the one to keep things in check although Tom hadn't acknowledged the fact. She needed to talk to him about it. She would have to or she would go mad agonising over how difficult it was becoming and what they were going to do in the future.

Why must she be the one to keep things above the waist when she was barely able to control her own feelings? And more importantly exactly what did men do to women? There had been no specifics from her mother. Obviously it was something to do with that hard part of Tom's body she had felt against her hips on several occasions. Presumably he put it inside her but then what? And would it fit? And when the time was right would she want him to, although lately she guessed that considering the way she had been feeling towards him, she would want him to.

Always when she was with him she longed for the moment when he would first touch her. It didn't matter if it was a quick hug when her mother was in the kitchen, or his taking her hand when they walked to the beach or to the pictures. But after being separated from him for a week or more, her body would almost count the seconds until she could touch his and she knew he felt the same.

He would be polite and serious with her mother and then the moment they were out of the house and he took her hand, he would break into one of his enormous smiles. Or if they had been standing or sitting apart for a little while, when he reached for her, she could see in his face an intense sort of relief that his skin was against hers. When the sweetness of it overwhelmed Peggy, she often couldn't breathe. How she wanted to unbutton his shirt and bury her head against his chest but she didn't dare. She sensed that such an action would be too much and whatever was keeping them both in check would dissolve to retreat briefly like a wave before it crashed on the shore.

Part of her was alarmed and constantly on the lookout for such a wave, the other part wished for it, waited and held her breath. She dreamt of it often, being pulled under by Tom, his body rocking her gently, lulled slowly but inevitably into someone else. Sometimes it was all her doing. She was in charge and Tom submissive but surprised like he had been that second time they met. But how could she be in charge when the details of lovemaking eluded her? She was ignorant. And she didn't like to be ignorant. She liked asking questions and finding answers. Maybe the real threat to her virginity was herself, not Tom.

Surely he must have noticed that last week at their picnic, at Dutchies Beach it had taken her a longer time than usual to remove his hand from her abdomen. He had rested it just below her belly button and as his kisses intensified and they lay back on their blanket, she didn't have the energy to shift it and then just as she was about to, he began moving his fingers gently across her lower abdomen. Even though he was touching her through her clothes, she worried that he must be able to feel her hairline down there, his fingertips were crossing and recrossing it. Could he feel it through her blue cotton skirt and her cotton panties? As she lay thinking this, Peggy noticed she was becoming more light-headed and her breathing was funny.

Slowly she opened her eyes to find that Tom was staring at her intently, almost studying her.

'Why are you looking at me like that?'

'Just keeping an eye on you.'

'On me? Whatever for?' She waited for his reply but he merely smiled and luckily, moved his hand away. She had felt relief she wouldn't have to play warden but last night as she lay awake, unable to sleep she imagined his hand back there, his body next to hers and his breath on her forehead. What had he meant? *Just keeping an eye on you.* It was him, being male that needed watching.

This morning she had found Emily swimming at the baths. She hadn't felt like swimming herself, instead she waited quietly until Emily got out, pushing herself up to the side and then standing on the edge in one fluid movement. Watching her, Peggy wondered how much Emily knew. *Had she done it?*

'How's your cowboy?' Emily asked, grabbing her towel.

'He's not a cowboy. He worked in a telephone exchange straight after high school and did two years of an electrical engineering course at the South Dakota School of Mines.'

'Whew! Impressive. But I bet his parents have a ranch though?'

'Since when have you become an expert on Wyoming?'

'Since last week. My latest beau was born in Montana, that's to the north and he knows quite a lot about the place.'

'Oh, that's nice,' Peggy said, feeling her gaze narrowing as she stared at Emily.

'Is your cowboy teaching you other things?'

God, she was the limit sometimes, Peggy thought and then remembered that because she was the limit, Emily was the perfect one to ask. She was trying to phrase the question in her head when Emily remarked in a conversational tone, 'Getting a bit hot to handle is our Lieutenant Tom Lockwood? How long has it been?'

'How long since what?' Peggy was indignant and confused at the same time.

'Since you met dummy.' Emily towelled herself dry.

Peggy stared at her friend. 'Why aren't you like the rest of us, Emily?'

'What ignorant? Small town?'

'We live in a small town, Emily. There's only a few hundred people here. Well at least there used to be.'

'Don't remind me. That's why I go to the movies. To forget. That's why I like to go out a lot. To forget. That's why I pretend to be something that I'm not.'

Peggy was startled by the other girl's tone. When her expression softened in sympathy, Emily said, 'Don't look at me like that.'

'What are you pretending to be?'

'Sophisticated and ...'

'Above the rest of us,' Peggy cut in. 'Well you are succeeding. You've been like that since second class, Emily. Sort of Ann

Sheridanish but prettier.'

Emily dropped her towel in surprise.

'What are you saying? That I'm prettier than Ann Sheridan?'

'Of course you are. You must know that. Don't all your officers tell you that?'

'Yes, but it doesn't mean anything. It means something from you.'

Peggy didn't know what to say and looking at Emily she realised her friend was upset. Now was not the time to ask Emily what to do about Tom. However, after she sat down next to Peggy, Emily rallied quickly and asked, 'So, how long has it been since you met?'

'Three months.'

'Well then he's probably getting very…'

Peggy cut in again. 'Yes, he is and I'm not sure what to do about it.'

'You'll have to give him the push. Unless of course you want to get pregnant and then find that before you know it, you're living in some backwoods in America wishing you'd never left Australia.'

'I don't want to give him the push, Emily, so that's no solution.'

'Well sorry that's my remedy, so I can't help you.'

'And who taught you that remedy, Emily? Treating men like musical chairs?' Peggy was becoming cold, although it was nearly midday. 'Haven't you cared about any of them?'

'Not really.' The desperation was back in Emily's voice but Peggy ignored it. All she could think about was Emily's cold-bloodedness and thinking about it, made her wish for Tom's arms even more. Peggy got up from the steps by the pool and left without a word. If she had turned around she would have seen Emily crying. But she didn't turn around.

Now, going over the incident in her mind, Peggy was worried by the turn of the conversation. Something had been very wrong. She had the distinct feeling that she hadn't asked the right questions. Well, since Sarah Linden was away in Sydney and Emily had been no help, she would have to ask Tom. Somehow.

Emily and Sarah

'I have been thinking quite a bit about Emily,' I remarked to Joan. 'And a conversation we had at the pool.' It was a Sunday, two days after Angharad's funeral and my Welsh neighbour was doing better than I had anticipated, thanks to a number of things. The major one being that the day before the funeral, Professor Thomas had phoned and told Joan that evidently Angharad had died very quickly from a massive heart attack and hadn't suffered. Also that she had been found near her favourite part of the Gwyllt, in a gazebo overlooking one of the lakes.

This information had cheered Joan up a lot and was comfort against the ordeal of missing her sister's funeral. The other thing was that I had been her constant companion for four days now and would continue to do so until Joan felt ready to spend more time on her own. In the meantime we had simply been enjoying each other's company, with me doing most of the talking.

In a way Joan had also been a comfort to me because today and yesterday I had begun to talk more of the time when Tom and I first met. This afternoon as I answered Joan's question about what the bay was like in 1942, I remembered a strange conversation I had had with Emily at the pool.

'There can't have been too many girls around your age,' Joan commented.

'No, just a handful. I was friendly mainly with Betsy and Emily. Emily was so different from the rest of us. She spent a lot of time going to the movies and she would see a movie over and over. I think, looking back, that she must have really studied some of the actresses. She adored Betty Davis but she looked more like Ann Sheridan without those bedroom eyes. Emily's were big and a bright clear blue. She was so graceful but she could be very catty. Funny I should think of her now.'

'What happened to her?'

'She became engaged to a young American, one of the thousands who came during '43 to be trained here. Talk about whirlwind! Mother was horrified, in typical Mum fashion. I mean at least Tom looked like staying for a while. The servicemen from the 32nd Division were here only for an average of two to three weeks,' I stammered into silence at the memory. 'So many of them died,' I said finally.

'Killed was he?'

'Yes at Saidor, I think it was called. In New Guinea.'

'Awful for her.'

'Yes, it was. She took it really hard from what I heard. I was married by then and totally wrapped up in Tom and when I wasn't seeing him or looking forward to seeing him, I was working or helping out at CELOPS. I think she fell out with her father over the whole thing. He didn't approve of course. He was a widower and from the old school. He had an oyster lease around at Little Salamander.'

'Emily never talked about her GI,' I continued. 'She left soon after he was killed, got work in Newcastle and I totally lost contact with her. And when I left for America I eventually lost contact with Betsy too.'

'But your mother used to get letters from Betsy, didn't she?' Joan remarked.

'Yes, she did. But it's years since she has written. Mother gave up hoping for a letter. About fifteen years ago, I think it was and I didn't come across any when I cleaned out Mum's wardrobe.'

'Could be some in the buffet,' Joan said, pointing towards the teak buffet on the other side of the room.

'Yes, maybe. I'll have to go through it sometime I suppose.' I was silent for a while thinking about Emily's sadness that day at the pool. I looked at Joan sitting in my paisley print armchair and recognised her, in that moment, as probably the best friend I have ever had.

'I haven't had much luck with girlfriends or women friends,' I told Joan. 'The girlfriends moved away or I did. And with the women friends there just didn't seem to be a connection.'

'That's the way of it sometimes.'

'I suppose, but I still feel I should have picked up on how sad Emily was instead of realising it thirty years later.'

'Well, what did she say, love?'

'I can't remember the conversation exactly. I was aware of something but I couldn't work it out. I was more concerned with the fact that Emily hadn't been able to help me and that I would have to approach Tom.'

I glanced at the bay through the lounge room windows. It was a typical August day with the wind tossing the tops of the trees. Whitecaps rolled across the bay. I was silent for a moment and Joan waited quietly for me to continue, tactful enough not to ask me what I had needed help with.

'In those days I used to think that all Emily wanted was to escape the oyster lease and find some wealthy officer. Tom thought so too. At the time of the conversation I was sure that Emily was following some carefully laid out plan and by then she was onto her third officer. Now of course it's much more obvious. If she had been simply looking for a way out she could have at least ensnared one officer. Australian if she didn't want to go to America. She was pretty enough to carry it off and she could be witty too. But she didn't. Who did she become engaged to? A young private in the American army.'

I paused for a bit and drank the rest of my tea. 'Now it's so obvious. She wasn't looking for money. She was looking for love. But knowing her and talking to her, you wouldn't have known. Or perhaps I have a habit of just completely misreading people.'

'And who else are we talking about,' Joan asked.

'Other than Mum?'

Joan nodded.

'Sarah Linden. Did you know, Joan, that she was a lesbian?'

'Yes, love. Everyone knew.'

Ignorant again, I told myself and paused to collect my thoughts. After a moment I said, 'I couldn't believe it when Mrs Marley told me the other day when I ducked out to the shops. Did Mum know?'

'Yes, your mother knew. But didn't say much about it, mind. None of her business as far as she was concerned.'

I got up and walked to the window to watch the whitecaps

dancing.

Joan spoke from behind me. 'Did you know she wrote children's books? I expect your mother never told you. After the war and when the communist threat subsided, it all came out. They used to have a thing about writers,' Joan explained.

'And in America,' I cut in.

'Oh aye. Well, when the time was right she gradually let it be known what she actually did. You know, allowed one or two things to slip in her lovely efficient way and left the gossips to do the rest.'

'You liked her I can tell.' I was smiling now.

'Yes, I rather did.'

'She was very beautiful when I first knew her.'

'So I've heard.'

Joan sounded a little bit dismissive so I added, 'More than skin deep but sad. And was she in love with Mrs Wallis?'

'With Nancy Wallis?'

'Betsy's mum,' I said.

'Oh yes, for years.'

'What about the man Mrs Wallis was seen with in Newcastle?'

'All gossip, it was. Sarah's publisher as it turned out. Nancy was dropping off Sarah's latest manuscript. Sarah couldn't be bothered with Newcastle or Sydney for that matter. Not after her divorce. I spoke to Nancy about it once when she was visiting Sarah. She said it was one of Sarah's rituals. She didn't like to post her manuscripts. She always had them delivered. Mostly by Nancy and occasionally by someone else. Mind, Nancy loved visiting Newcastle and going to the shops, buying pretty things so the arrangement worked out well. Nancy visited Newcastle, sometimes Sydney and Sarah got to stay here. I don't think the locals really appreciated how much she loved the bay.'

'I can't believe I don't know any of this. So that was her income? The money from the children's book?'

'I think there was some other money too but I don't know the details.'

'I wish I had known she was a writer, I could have taken some of her titles to the States with me.'

'She was a very private person so she kept a lot of this to

herself. I only know as much as I do through Nancy and I think that was because Nancy was aware of me being friendly with your mother. Nancy said that Sarah had told her more than once how fond she was of you.'

I was overcome with emotion. Finally I asked, 'What were her books like?'

'Mainly set in the bush they were and really for older children. What we now call teenagers.'

I came to sit back down near Joan. 'It's funny Mum not mentioning it. It's the sort of thing she would have loved to put in her letters and I could have given them to Sarah. She is such a reader, more than me really.'

'No reason why you can't still have a look at them. Why don't you speak to Nancy when she comes back from Newcastle next Wednesday?'

'I will.' I paused. 'However did they keep their relationship going?' I asked after a moment. 'With Sarah at the bay and Nancy living in Newcastle after her marriage breakdown?'

'They managed somehow. You do if it's really important, mind. You just manage. Lots of letters I expect. And then Nancy visited the kids regularly and Sarah too. In the last ten years or so, with the kids well and truly grown, it has been more obvious but by then everyone had got used to seeing them together so it didn't seem to matter so much. But then if it had all come out during the war, it might have been a different story.'

I sat quite still, absorbing all this. 'The solicitor comes back tomorrow.'

'Have you got an appointment?'

'Yes, I have. Will you be fine if I don't see you much tomorrow? Arthur's back this evening, isn't he?'

'Yes, he is,' Joan said with a smile.

'I'm just worried because the appointment's in the afternoon and I'm at the school in the morning.'

'I'll be fine, love. I've been letting you mollycoddle me enough as it is. I've got to start getting back into things again. I expect my house will need a total spring clean by now, I dread to think. It's best if I keep busy, isn't it?' Joan finished her tea. 'Anything I can do for you? To repay you like.'

'Perhaps there is one thing.'

Joan leaned forward in anticipation.

'Could you go to the library for me tomorrow and find out if any of Sarah's books are there? I'd love to read at least one.'

'Of course I can, love.'

I took the tea tray into the kitchen and Joan insisted on helping me with the dishes, which included plates and cups from lunch. I was washing and Joan drying. Looking at the clothesline I said, 'Since coming back here, I have begun to realise to what extent I make judgements about people and then won't be budged from those judgements. My mother, in many ways, is a mystery to me. I misread Emily and now I discover that I was completely ignorant about most of Sarah's life. And that's someone I adored and wrote to for a number of years. I don't know why our letters petered out but then I am not the best of letter writers.'

Joan threw her tea towel on the kitchen bench. 'I think it's about time I set you straight, Missy. You have to understand that a lot of this is not due to some fault in your personality. It's time and distance, Peggy, for the three of them. For your mother, Emily and Sarah and others from those days. Yes, you probably made judgements about them but don't forget, love, you didn't have the intervening years with them to correct your assumptions. That's the sad part of course and that's no fault of yours. You went to live in America with a wonderful man and that meant you couldn't really get to know what the other people were like, the ones you left behind. Only just learning about understanding others aren't we, at seventeen? Who knows that much at seventeen I ask you?' Joan was laughing heartily. 'I didn't.'

'I did,' I said, surprising myself. 'I knew I loved Tom and that's something I've only recently remembered: that at seventeen, I really did love him.'

Slowly Joan put her hand on my arm. 'By leaving, unfortunately you lost the chance to get to know your mother better.'

'I did, didn't I, Joan?' I brushed a stray tear away.

'But, mind, there still might be a way. How did you go with the wardrobe? Anything at all?'

'There was nothing there, just some letters.'

'You've done her whole room then? Sorted through it I mean,' Joan qualified.

'Yes. All that's left to go through is the suitcase on top of the wardrobe and the buffet drawer.'

'Early days though. You haven't been back a month yet and Nancy was a good friend of your mother's. I'm sure she'd love to have a chat with you when she arrives. I have a feeling some things will gradually come to you.'

'Maybe, you're right, Joan,' I said, putting plates away.

'I've been thinking a lot about Angharad lately.' Joan smiled weakly. 'But I've also been thinking about your mother. You have a lot of questions that need answering, that's obvious. I adored your mother but the one question I often used to ask myself about your mother was: Why was she such a prickly person? I am a widow too. Well, used to be, until I married Arthur. Your mother and I had both lost a husband and I think that's why we got on so well, in some sort of way. She knew I understood at least that part of her life.'

'But my question has stayed with me. Why was she so prickly? Sometimes it seemed as if it was some sort of outfit she had put on and couldn't get off. You know like the fashion of twenty years ago. One of those dresses with the tight bodices, cinched in waist and circle skirts and all the tiny buttons at the back. She just couldn't get out of it. And if she tried, her slip would come away too and she'd be left almost naked.'

The image was so palpable that I smiled in acknowledgement. 'Oh, Joan.' I went over and hugged her. 'Oh, Joan, you are a darling.'

'Silly really, but there we are. Don't suppose that is any help but I just thought you should know.'

'Thank you, Joan and it is a help.'

'Let me know what Sarah left you, won't you?'

'I will.'

Practice Run

Finally Tom was sitting in the boat with the wind up, the sea a little rough and waves curling away as he headed for Nelson Bay. One of the sappers, part of the engineers section from Little Beach, had given him instructions on how to handle the boat and keep up the revs. No questions asked of course, he being an officer. They were just a little curious and as he headed off, making a slow arc around the headland, he heard one of them yell out, 'Have a good day, Sir.' And then laughter. Better than Bob Morecroft's comment as he left the Country Club: 'So, Miss Peggy Ashburn is going to get hers well and truly.' Tom never bothered to reply.

Of course they all knew at the Country Club, knew that he had worked hard to reschedule a day off in the middle of the week and moved heaven and earth to borrow a small boat (not much bigger than a dinghy, but at least it had an engine and a canopy of sorts). But by God he didn't care. He let the wind take some of his troubles away and watched as the azure blue water opened out on all sides. Hell, this was nearly as good as making love. But making love with Peggy? Now that might be a whole other matter.

Unfortunately on their last date they hadn't parted on good terms. Saturday night at the movie house, as she sat next to him, he could feel a sort of tension in her. She was quiet too and twice removed her hand from his. She mentioned something at the beginning of their date about wanting to talk to him and then it had all gone wrong when they left the movie house.

They were outside holding hands when that funny little foreigner starting playing his accordion. He was pretty damn good too and he'd gone to tip him when Peggy had shook her head. *He just does it because he enjoys it, silly. You are a bit of a cowboy.*

The way she said it had hurt and her tone had reminded him of Mary. But more than anything else he was aware that the term had brought back memories of home and the struggle his parents had, trying to keep the ranch. The depression years had been very lean and in 1940 they had finally lost the struggle. He wondered how they were doing with the hardware store in Newcastle, Wyoming. Had his Mom been able to buy a few new dresses? How was his kid brother doing at school?

When he was with Peggy, he seemed to experience everything to an acute degree. Feelings, emotions were heightened until sometimes it was unbearable and he couldn't understand why she had this affect on him. He only knew that she did.

She had the power to make him see things through her eyes; to understand the way the residents felt about the Americans who were living amongst them. He could now accept that open-heartedness, could and did, go hand and hand with wary speculation. He was also beginning to grasp this Australian concept of continually questioning authority. No longer did he flare up with astonishment when it occurred but was beginning to realise that in certain circumstances (particularly in the field of war) it could prove invaluable, even life-saving.

Peggy looked at life very differently from other girls and it wasn't just because she was Australian. It was because of who she was: adventurous, thoughtful and definitely not shallow and it had cut him to the quick to hear her sound so superficial, to hear her call him a cowboy.

He raised his voice in an angry denial and then quickly apologised. Peggy apologised too and he said maybe it was time he told her something of his life back in Wyoming, but not today. Despite her agreement, things had been strained after that. They walked around the bay for a while then he took her home.

He was lucky she was coming today but he wrote a pretty persuasive letter, well two in fact and he'd taken some trouble over things. She was bringing a picnic basket. He had blankets, some brandy, and flowers – white daisies he had brought from the woman in one of the cottages near the club. He closed his eyes for a moment. He couldn't wait to see her and she would be his for the whole day! The whole day and not just for a few hours. His, no matter what happened because he'd make her his.

He'd tell her all about himself. He'd tell her about home and how hard it had been to watch his parents gradually face the prospect of losing their ranch. How the money he sent home, while working at the telephone exchange, had been nowhere near enough and how the bank had foreclosed while he was away at training camp. He would explain his restlessness. He would explain everything.

Right this moment, however, he wanted to just look and feel. The breeze was on his skin and to his left was Fly Point, the camp finished now and full up with ratings and officers. Through the trees he could see men walking about, getting themselves acquainted with the layout of the shore establishment, as some called it, HMAS Assault to the rest. He was glad they were all finally settled. He had got sick of hearing about the impending move.

Between Fly Point and Nelson Bay, huts and tents were springing up along the shoreline. He passed the new naval boatshed and wharf, next the old wharf and the long, low structure of what would soon be the engineers shop and beyond that the main wharf. There were more huts on the shoreline and if JOOTS went ahead Tom was sure there would be more again. If it went ahead.

The other month there had been talk from the American end about shutting it down but the Australian Navy had held their ground. They had invested too much to put a halt to it all just yet. But as far as Tom could tell it was still up in the air. There was, he felt, the distinct possibility he might be reassigned. He just had no idea what lay ahead. For now the 20 day officer training courses kept him busy.

The curve of West Point was now on his left. In a minute or two he would be with Peggy. God, he hoped he could pull this off. He wanted her today and he hoped that it would be today. Their special day. It was what they had agreed upon.

Last Sunday night after she got his letter, they met secretly on the beach, Peggy explaining she felt it was all becoming too much, he carefully telling her he was sorry that she felt he had been pushing her. After Peggy had a little cry in his arms, she shyly told him she didn't want to break up with him and he explained he couldn't ask her to marry him at the moment with everything up in the air. Finally they resolved that they needed to take it further and Tom assured her he would take care of her in every way. They agreed to wait until after her eighteenth.

But unfortunately her eighteenth birthday was the eighteenth of December and on the Monday he found out it was the day of the mock landing with HMAS Allenwood as the first Assault Landing Ship. It was going to be bedlam. There would be no way for them to meet for days beforehand. He would be jumping around like a cricket, bouncing from one thing to another.

No, the time was now. Today. He wouldn't be able to see her again until after her birthday and he had a terrible need to claim her before then. He wrote her again Monday night and told her about the mock landing and how long they would have to wait. She couldn't get away to meet him but she wrote a letter back, which Sarah dropped in to him yesterday morning, agreeing to meet. He just hoped now she hadn't changed her mind.

Hell, he must love her. He had never in his life worried so much about it before. Here he was worrying if she could handle it and worrying about how she would feel. And what did he have to offer her in return? Nothing. At least nothing concrete – tangible. Only his love.

As he rounded the bluff he caught sight of Peggy's yellow dress by the red tent. Feeling a smile break out on his face at the sight of her, he cut the revs down and swung the boat in to the beach.

There he was looking serious. In her excitement to see him she dumped down the heavy picnic basket and ran to the boat. He was dragging it into the shallows, the bottom of his trousers rolled up, his legs brown she noticed through the silvery blue water lapping around them.

'Can you hop in from here?'

'Course I can.' Quickly she jumped in and sat down on the wooden bench under the canopy. He retrieved the picnic basket and after stowing it safely towards the back of the boat, he was sitting beside her. He did something to the engine and they were off again towards open water.

'Where are we going?'

'Near Banks's Farm, I think it's called.'

'That far?'

'Not so far. You'll see.' Tom consulted his wristwatch. 'It's only nine now. We have the whole day.'

The whole day. There would be time to talk, she realised. Definitely time to talk. Time for a lot of things. The thought made her nervous and Tom must have noticed this in her expression because he asked, 'Are you okay?'

'Yes, I'm fine.' She almost had to yell her reply because the wind was up as they headed out towards Salamander Bay. Holding hands, skimming over the water, the large bay gradually opened out before them. Today it seemed enormous with only a few small boats anchored there.

Peggy moved closer to Tom to ask him, 'Where's the Westralia?'

'Gone for a refit I think. She'll be back.'

'The bay looks so much bigger without her.'

Tom nodded.

Further ahead were two very white beaches separated by a small rocky point of land. As they passed the second beach several dolphins swam near their boat.

'Wow, will you look at that! Heard a lot about them but never seen them this close.'

Peggy smiled at his excitement. And they were wonderful, the dolphins. The sight of them was like a blessing. She trailed her hands in the water and found herself smiling happily. A blessing. That was a nice thought.

The dolphins followed their boat around the point but disappeared as Tom made his way between two small islands.

'You know the way,' Peggy said gaily.

'I had some instructions,' Tom said with an inscrutable smile.

As they motored further down into the bay, keeping to the right, they passed what seemed like an endless line of mangroves on their left until the bay closed in again. They were entering a channel formed by an island on their right. The wind dropped and Tom motioned Peggy to sit closer to him on the wooden seat. Behind them was the wind and the water sparkling with the sun, in front now a wide channel that appeared to fork into two up ahead. On their left Banks's Farm was merely a few holiday shacks scattered close to the shore. Further down beyond the shacks, the vegetation became dense. Tall gum trees covered the hillside with mangroves growing at the water's edge.

Tom was looking in the other direction. She followed his gaze as he studied the opposite shore to their right, Fenninghams Island. At that moment both of them caught sight of a clearing between the mangroves. Grabbing Peggy's hand, Tom steered the boat off to the right to cross the channel.

The breeze was lifting her hair and cooling her neck. Tom's touch was firm and she didn't want him to ever let go. He lowered the revs and they cruised into the beach. The mangroves were larger than she expected up close. There was a pair leaning towards each other, long roots extending across the beach. They pulled the boat in under the shade of the trees and sat down on the beach to take in the view north across the water, another expanse of water glittering in the sunlight and another stretch of deserted coastline in front of them.

They were completely alone, but the thought didn't make Peggy nervous, just wakened a few butterflies in her. After a little while sitting in silence Tom got up and tied the boat to one of the mangroves. It was so nice under the shade of the two rather majestic trees that Peggy decided to lay the blanket on the sand. While Tom wandered off, she checked the picnic basket. There was some cold beef and lettuce sandwiches, a bottle of cordial, some apples and cake. She covered everything with a tea towel and put the lid back on the basket.

Tom had returned from scouting around. He was standing above her with his legs apart, looking down on her. Suddenly he took his shirt off, unbuttoning only the two top buttons and pulling it over his head. He smiled at her but she didn't know what to say. Instead her eyes were drawn to the sweat glistening on his chest and to the dog tags around his neck.

She hadn't expected his chest to be so muscular. After all he wasn't a big man and she was thinking this, thinking what a nice chest he had when he began to unbuckle his belt. She looked away in embarrassment and a breeze played across her back, bringing with it a feeling of unease and disappointment. Just like this, she wondered. He undresses and expects it all to happen! She crossed her legs in annoyance.

This is what she had worried about the last time she saw him at the Arcadia picture theatre. That it would all turn out to be a big disappointment and that really she should have waited until she was married. But there was the catch, Tom hadn't asked her yet. He said he couldn't at the moment and she didn't want it to be anybody but Tom. She couldn't imagine making love to anybody but Tom. She reminded herself of this now as she sat feeling annoyed.

'Want to go for a swim? The water looks pretty clear.'

'A swim?' She looked up at him in enquiry but he was about to take his underpants off and she averted her gaze.

'I don't think so. I forgot my bathers.'

'I'm not swimming in bathers.'

She couldn't stop herself from giggling and burying her head down. 'No you're not.'

'Come in your bra and panties then. We can lie on the beach to get dry.'

'With you with nothing on?'

Tom simply smiled mischievously. He turned away and was walking towards the water, searching for a patch clear of mangrove shoots.

She hadn't anticipated this! Or had she? Was this why she had somehow forgotten her bathers, hoping that they would swim naked? Well now that the opportunity had presented itself, she was self conscious.

With a quick intake of breath her eyes wandered over his

body. He looked slender and strong at the same time. And he was so brown. All except for his bottom and upper thighs and the whiteness of both only inflamed her curiosity more. What did a man look like? What did Tom look like? Betsy had whispered to her once that they looked funny. (She had a younger brother and had bathed him many times.) But then she probably hadn't seen a man unless she had caught sight of her father naked.

Now she wished she knew so that she could be more prepared when she saw Tom. He turned but not completely and when she was about to cover her eyes again he winked at her. 'Are you coming, sweetheart?'

'Why don't you go in and I'll think about it.'

'Come closer then and watch.' He was standing in the water and lowering himself in. Crouching low he turned and faced her. 'It's not too cold.'

She moved to the water's edge and stood wondering what to do. Unwittingly her gaze fell on his groin and she squinted in the sunlight. She couldn't see a thing, just the pale green outline of his body under the water. He was moving his hands and they seemed to beckon her in. With the water lapping at her ankles, she was about to follow when she realised she still had her yellow dress on. With the task of pulling it off, she retreated back to edge of the blanket.

Sitting with her legs bent and leaning on her knees she watched as he dived, arching himself up over the water and then disappearing for ages. He splashed about, ducked down again and broke the surface like a silky sea creature. Mostly though he dived under water and swam below; on one occasion for so long that she stood up in alarm. But then he surfaced and waved. After a moment he swam close and stood up, the water coming to his waist. He held out his arms but didn't smile this time. She didn't move. Couldn't. He still held out his arms as he walked closer to her, his eyes never leaving her face, the water receding to his thighs.

She studied his body in the sunlight. All she could think was that he looked lovely. Could you say that about a man? But he did. And she wanted to be in his arms. Whatever else happened she wanted that more than anything.

She took another quick glance as she moved closer to the water's edge again. Finally that part of him was a mystery no longer and she was relieved. His body wasn't intimidating but then it wasn't hard either. And even when his groin had been hard against her those other times, his embrace had never been intimidating: gentle, passionate but never forceful. He had never forced himself on her and he was certainly not going to do that now, she realised. He was waiting for her to join him.

There was such longing in his face that Peggy couldn't bear to have hers unanswered another minute and she pulled the bright dress over her head and threw it onto the beach. In the next instant her feet hit a rock and she nearly slipped. Peggy bent her head to try and glimpse the bottom and unseeing walked straight into his arms. She felt them close about her and pull her next to his smooth body. They floated for a little, the water not deep but just to their shoulders.

'Not scared now?'

'No.'

'Nothing really is it, a man's naked body?'

'It's your body and it's lovely.'

'Lovely?' he asked, pulling her closer. 'I don't think my body's ever been called that before.' He was laughing nervously.

'But it is,' she told him and when she looked up at him to try and read his expression, he kissed her deeply. She still had her bra on and he was feeling for the clasp but struggling. She unclasped it and threw it toward the shore. Her breasts were revealed but she bobbed quickly below the water line.

'Now, fair's fair.'

Slowly with her eyes closed, she stood up. Almost immediately, before she could become really embarrassed he embraced her again.

'Now that's lovely.'

'You hardly looked.'

'Enough to see. I knew they would be.'

'How?' Tom and Peggy were both drifting in the water, in the green shade of the mangrove trees.

'From touching them.'

She was embarrassed now. 'Now, we're even,' she told him firmly.

'Oh, no we're not,' Tom said, moving close suddenly and with one swoop, picking her up in his arms. As they reached the shore, she felt him duck down to retrieve her bra. Grunting, he carried her to the blanket and laid her out in the dappled shade. He sat up beside her. He was talking conversationally now to amuse her and distract her too, she decided, but didn't mind. 'It's like this. I get to take one thing off and that's me. But now you have to take two things off.'

She glanced down at her French panties. They were thin silk, that now wet revealed quite a lot, but somehow she couldn't part with them just yet.

'Can I keep them on a bit longer?'

He ducked his head for a moment and she couldn't see his expression.

'Sure you can.'

He lay down beside her, both of them stretched out on the blanket. In the half shade the summer sun felt just right and for a while they didn't speak. Peggy was drowsy and languorous; every part of her warm but her hips, her wretched panties, damp against her skin. She was about to take another peak at Tom when he pulled her hand across and put it on his body. His member was hard now and smooth and he curled her fingers around its warm thickness. Tom's hand was gently but firmly holding hers in place. She wanted to draw it away but when she rolled on to her shoulder to look into his eyes, they were closed and his head was thrown back in pleasure, in such a way that she no longer wanted to move her hand.

'Please hold it for a little while and I'll be happy,' he begged.

Keeping her hand still wrapped around him, Peggy moved to sit across his thighs, unsure of what to do next. She was staring at him now. Slowly he opened his eyes and looked at her.

'And then what happens?'

He laughed and said breathlessly, 'Always asking questions, Miss Peggy Ashburn.'

'I mean it,' she said. 'I don't know.'

'I know you don't,' he said tenderly. 'But nothing will happen that you don't want to happen.'

'But what do you want to happen?'

Her hand fell away as Tom moved to prop himself up on his left elbow and stroke her face with his right hand. 'You are so pretty and sweet. You are lovely.'

'You didn't answer my question.'

'I want to be inside you. Of course I want to be inside you.'

'Did you bring any of those things.'

'Prophylactics?'

She nodded, touching his face.

'Yeah I did. But do you want me?'

'Yes, I want you closer than we've been before.'

'But maybe not. You don't seem so sure.'

'If I knew what happens I wouldn't be so nervous.'

'Do I make you nervous?' Now he was stroking her face and brushing at the frown lines above her eyes.

'No, you don't. It's just not understanding exactly…'

Tom paused. 'I don't know that I do neither. It's not something you should analyse. But how about a practice run?'

Peggy got off him and Tom sat up, looking about him and at the blanket they were sitting on. 'Not here.' He picked her up again and stooped for the blanket. Gently he set her down under the she-oaks a little way in from the beach. He cleared the ground of a few twigs and spread the blanket back down. He seemed embarrassed and walked back to where they had left their clothes and the picnic basket. Tom retrieved something from his trousers.

After a moment he was cursing. 'These damn things.'

Before she could speak he was on top of her, the full length of him and it felt blissful to have his weight on her body, to feel their legs and arms touching, their bodies so close.

'I still have my panties on.'

'It's a practice run,' he said smiling and shaking his head. 'Keep them on.'

He nudged her legs apart with his knees and settled himself in closer and with the weight of his body on his arms, he began to move softly against her. His body was hard, his movements gentle and Peggy began to feel the rocking motion take over. His hips were moving slowly, rhythmically and she found herself responding. Drifting at first and then rocking too and after a little she hated the barrier between them.

'Are you sure?' Tom asked brokenly as she bent down and yanked her French panties off. For an answer she drew his body in to hers and within minutes she was grabbing at his shoulders and gasping for breath. She was drowning and it felt wonderful. Tom was wonderful. He was the sea, caressing, pulling, and dragging her away up to a great height. She was flying and floating. She sighed and felt a long sigh from him and then his body was still.

Provisions

The sun blinded my eyes when I walked out of the Solicitor's
office. I had quite forgotten about Mum's will. I knew from a few
years back that it existed but strangely had not thought about it
since my arrival. I think something was mentioned at Mum's
funeral by Mr Caldwell's secretary and that was all. I had come to
find out what Sarah had left me but first I had to sit through the
reading of my mother's will. Very simply and there was no other
bequests – the house was left to me. The solicitor handed over the
Certificate of Title and other documents and advised me to lodge
these with the bank.

Sipping coffee, Sarah's will was read out: everything to
Nancy, which included the house in Magnus Street and money in
the bank. There were also some legacies for a number of nieces
and nephews and a few small bequests. *My hand carved keepsake
box to Peggy Gay Lockwood.* The box was handed over, wrapped
up in brown butcher's paper. I tucked it quickly under my arm,
thanked Mr Caldwell and walked out. The deeds were in my large
crocheted bag. I would call in to the bank tomorrow. For now all
I could do was stand in the stillness of midday and blink stupidly
at the horizon.

The sun was illuminating the water and throwing Nelson Bay
into a bright hard glitter that made the town look small and tacky.
Immediately the old allure of escape returned: the wish to climb
away from all this and widen my personal vista; to look down on
everything and in doing so gain a measure of calm and in a funny
sort of way, confidence. *See we're all just specks down there.
What do any of us matter?* I recalled the view from Tomaree. The
beautiful semi-circle that was Shoal Bay mattered, the lumps of
hills decreasing in height from Zenith Beach mattered, the rest
were tiny boxes of houses that would fall over in the next wind
and in the distance we, the people of Nelson Bay, were

inconsequential.

I walked down the road and crossed the street to the park. I felt disorientated and unsure of what to do next. I gazed up and to my right towards Fly Point. Out of sight beyond the headland was Tomaree. I closed my eyes and visualised it as I had seen it last week on one of my long walks. The enormous mass of it!

I remember when I climbed it at twelve years old; it took me hours, half a day of scrub lashing my face, of dirt under my fingernails, of gripping, pulling and dragging myself up. My knees I recall were shaking on the way down and scabbed with grazes. Yet an incredible feeling of exhilaration had filled all of me. I did it! All by myself, I did it! For the rest of the day I floated languorously. Nothing touched me. Everything was beautiful and I was calm, the calm arming me against my mother's tearful rage and lectures. *How could you do this to me? Didn't you think I'd be worried sick? Why did you do it? Why? Why? Just to make me worry. Is that it? None of the other girls would dream of doing something so stupid and pointless. Betsy or Emily have never given their mothers the worries you have given me with your climbing and your wild ways. Going off for hours on end and then I hear later you were sitting up on top of some cliff somewhere.*

I could hear her yelling now. And as a mother it was all very reasonable. Everything she had said was reasonable. It was my behaviour that had been unreasonable. I really had given her many causes to worry. But why? Another question I didn't have an answer to except the vague feeling that accompanied my memories of being quite young, a feeling as tangible as the wind on a windy day. It was the sense of being shut in, suffocated by her presence.

Often I seemed to be at the window looking out, wishing for some sort of escape. How old was I? Five or six? I did go to school of course but never walked by myself for the first few years until I reached the age of nine or ten when she could no longer, within reason, accompany me. And with that first taste of freedom I yearned for more. I began disappearing after school. Climbing, walking for hours on end. I can still feel the excitement and relief of those early expeditions. I was as free as the wind. Well until I got home anyway and faced my mother's wrath.

A lot of these memories, the ones carrying feelings of confinement, came back to me for the first time when Sarah was little. I recalled a number of them when I fussed over Sarah's clothes and hair and worried over her too. As difficult as it was, I promised myself not to restrict Sarah's freedom unnecessarily; not to hover over her or to make her feel trapped. And sure enough Sarah didn't disappear for hours without telling me where she was going and she didn't climb any cliffs either. Not that there were any to climb in Newcastle, Wyoming.

I looked at the parcel in my hands. I could take it back to the paisley print chair where I had sat these last two weeks and thought about many things, but the heights beckoned. It was too beautiful a day, despite the glare, to be inside. Well, Tomaree was out of the question so the small hill by the old post office would have to do. I made my way up there and sat down in the shade of the camphor laurels. Taking a deep breath I undid the butcher's paper to reveal an exquisitely carved wooden box.

Just as I thought. I recalled it now. It had stood in Sarah's study on her writing desk, sometimes with half opened letters on top of the lid. At that moment I could see in my mind Sarah's beautiful hands tucking a letter back into the envelope, slowly putting it in the box and then turning her attention to me.

Being seventeen and wrapped up in my own world the thought never crossed my mind to wonder who the letter was from. I was aware though that she kept other letters in piles on her desk. Only a few found their way into the box. Now of course I'm guessing, or at least like to think that they were from Nancy. Once I remember the box was missing from her desk – perhaps taken to her bedroom to read the contents over again in comfort.

Tentatively I traced the line of the engraving with my fingertips. Inside a rectangle formed by an exotic flowering vine were tiny stylised birds, fruit and more flowers: nature in abundance. I traced the outline of a small bird. Taking a deep breath I flicked the catch open and lifted the lid. There was a letter inside for me. I opened the envelope.

15th July 1970

Dear Peggy,

I hope you like the box. I think you admired it once and I (wherever I am now) like to think that you will shortly put your most precious letters inside it, just as I once did. Nancy has her own, in case you are wondering why I didn't give it to her.

With this letter comes my wish that you are happy now but by writing this letter I may put that happiness into jeopardy. You see, I have long had some information about your family but have never found the right time to talk to you about it. Obviously, since you are reading this letter, I have left it too late to tell you personally so instead I am letting you know that if you wish to find out, then Nancy will tell you. She is expecting you to call, so please think about it. If you decide not to speak to her about the matter, then expect no reproach or censure from Nancy. She is the sweetest, most open-hearted creature I know and will respect your decision.

If you don't mind my saying we have just had the most enlightening evening discussing the provisions that this letter has necessitated. For instance, we both had to write a letter (and organise our wills of course). Nancy writing one that I would give to you if she died first and me writing this one. Both of us sitting in front of the fire debating how the cards will fall and therefore which letter you would read. What a pair of old goats! I hope you are still reading Tom's. I would just like to add that in all my life I have never seen a man so much in love as Tom that day you were together in my house. God speed my darling Peggy.

Love

Sarah

It seemed that fate was playing card games with me, forever withholding the trump from my grasp. Slowly though and inexorably Jacks, Kings and Queens were being laid out, even if I chose not to pick them up. (I still hadn't gone through my mother's suitcase, written to Tom, called him or even written to Betsy.) Did Nancy hold the trump? Well, I would have to wait another two days until her return. If I chose to ask her what she knew, wouldn't it put her on the spot despite Sarah's assurances? Placing Sarah's letter back in the box I wondered: *What did Nancy know?*

At home later in the afternoon, I took a look again at the Certificate of Title, registered now in my name. So the house was mine but it still didn't feel like it. Early days though. Unbelievably I had only been back just under two weeks. Yet I felt I had travelled months, even years emotionally. Joan had too.

Night was closing over the bay. I drew the lounge room curtains and turned on a lamp. Empty corners gnawed at my peripheral vision. The room was a bit bare, I thought for the umpteenth time. I liked a bit of clutter. I surveyed the lounge room, really looked at the lounge room. It just needed a few more things – pictures definitely, a writing desk perhaps, an old trunk maybe, over in the far corner. Another lamp to light the room would be nice. I hated overhead lights.

I walked into my bedroom – bare again and the white bedspread was beginning to get on my nerves. Talk about utilitarian! Without stopping to really think about what I was doing but nevertheless fully aware that I should be doing the same thing with another suitcase on top of another wardrobe, I pulled my suitcase down. It was light with just a small weight fallen in one corner. I opened it and took out the pile of Tom's letters.

The bundle contained every single letter he had ever written to me, except his first still under my pillow. Around twenty letters mainly from the first few months of meeting and then the rest were from the last few years of the war. Once we were reunited, there were no more letters. How I longed for one now!

I'm still not sure how I came to bring them. I think that when I packed, I was aware only of the fact that I couldn't possibly leave them behind. I will read them again soon. Not yet, but soon. At this present moment that first letter is enough for me. The amazing reality of it: to have it back and to read again the words of my husband as a young man. And how long has it been since I read the others? Too long most probably. I walked back into the lounge room and put the bundle of letters in the keepsake box.

The Plains

Tom felt like he had been shot. His body was aching, his heart bruised and his soul lost. He was fairly sure it was in Peggy's keeping. But that was okay, she could have it. He just wanted something in return. He propped himself up on his elbows again and looked at her. Peggy's cheeks were flushed, her eyes appeared cloudy and she barely had the energy to raise her hand. But she did slowly to touch his face. 'I love you,' he told her.

Peggy just smiled dreamily.

'Do you love me too?'

'I do.'

'We're not at the altar yet,' he quipped more for his benefit than hers.

She didn't seem to hear him but said instead, 'I do love you.'

He moved closer to her. He was worried now about her reaction to what had just happened between them. 'How was it?' he asked.

'Like climbing Tomaree.'

'How do you mean?'

She traced the outline of his lips and touched his forehead. She was the one now to smooth the worry lines. 'Very steep but the views at the top...' She paused. 'Were wonderful. That's the only thing I can think of that it compares to, but it was so much better.'

'I think you're still up there,' Tom remarked, feeling a lump in his throat and relief that she had enjoyed his lovemaking.

'Yes.'

He stroked her flushed cheeks. 'Take your time,' he said, laying his head against her breasts and feeling the quick rise and fall of her breathing.

A few moments later she asked, 'Where are you?'

'At the bottom. I came down pretty fast.'

'Slid down?' She was laughing. 'I can see you have.' Peggy

was looking at his groin.

He rubbed his eyes to hide his embarrassment. 'You learn fast.'

'You didn't slide down did you? That wouldn't have been nice,' she said absentmindedly.

'No, more like parachuting. Not that I've done it before but heard about it.'

'The lovemaking or the parachuting?'

Suddenly he was annoyed. 'Couldn't you tell?'

'Yes, I was only teasing. I could tell that you knew so much more than me and that you knew exactly what to do. You were gentle and patient and very loving.'

He gripped her tightly in his arms, afraid for a moment that tears would come like the night three months ago but they didn't. He moved away from her then and rummaged through the pockets of his trousers that lay in a heap nearby. 'Damn, I forgot my cigarettes.'

'Are they essential?'

'No. Being close to you is though. How's your descent going?'

'I'm with you now, looking up.' She stretched out her arms and he fell into her embrace. Within minutes they were both asleep.

Later, after they had dressed and eaten all the food, Tom said, 'I want to apologise for the other night at the movie house.

'The Arcadia?'

'Yeah.'

'When I called you a cowboy?'

'That's right.'

'I'm sorry but I thought your parents owned a ranch.'

'They did until a few years ago.'

'And you didn't like it? Living on the ranch, I mean, 'Peggy asked, looking at him intently.

'No, I hated it. It took me a few years to work that out. I can be slow,' he joked. 'You know,' Tom rubbed his hand through his hair, 'everybody around me loved it. My Dad, even my little brother, all my friends loved being a ranch hand but not me. I don't think Mom was that keen but she'd didn't want to let on to my father.'

Tom sat up to lean his elbows on his knees. 'I don't know how to explain it exactly but the living was harsh and it used to get to me. Pa would say: *It's just the weather, boy.* But it was more than that. It was the whole way a life. The wind that never stops blowing, the enormous sky. Some days it sure feels like it's bearing down on you. And then there's stock frozen where they stand in bad winters and often the snow not melting till June and before you know it the heat's upon you. The red dirt, grasshoppers jumping about, driving you crazy. The wind, the dust and winter again.'

'Don't get me wrong,' he continued. 'The plains can be beautiful but they're harsh too. Just the same though, Wyoming is in my blood. A part of me probably for the rest of my life but I just don't want to be right in the middle of that wind, on a ranch.' Tom paused. 'Upton's a nice town. You'd like Upton. Real friendly people and Newcastle's not too bad neither.'

'The other Newcastle,' Peggy said.

'Funny we both live near a Newcastle,' Tom said. 'Well my folks do now. And then there's the Black Hills and they are beautiful. I'd like to take you there. The hills kind a remind me of the water here. You know the way you catch it in the corner of your eyes. Always there, waiting. Maybe that sounds stupid but...'

'No, it doesn't,' Peggy said, shaking her head. 'I know just what you mean.' Her gaze was far off for a moment. 'And where else do you think I'd like? I bet there are lots of places.'

'There sure is! The Devil's Tower, a sort a strange rock formation. There's some climbing for you. Straight up and a sheer cliff on all sides.'

Peggy laughed. 'Sounds beyond me now but it must be wonderful to look at.'

'That's for sure. And Mount Rushmore. I went in '39. You should see what they're carving into the cliffs. I hear it's finished now. I'd love to take you there and to the Rockies.' He reached for Peggy's hand. 'After the war,' he added.

Peggy grasped his hand firmly. 'I'd love to see it all.'

Tom smiled. How excited he was when he spoke of home but he hadn't been that first time they met. 'You didn't mention so much beauty when we met in the valley,' Peggy said after a moment.

He nodded. 'I know. All this was strange to me then and more beautiful than the grasslands I'm used to. These other places we'll have to drive to see. Upton and Newcastle are grasslands and ranching country. But even the grasslands have their own kind a beauty. I've realised that lately.'

Tom spoke more of the grasslands, prairie dogs and the antelopes in Campbell County. He made her see it all in her mind and she longed to see it in reality. She was dreaming about all the strange places he had mentioned when she noticed Tom had gone quiet. She studied him carefully. His head was bowed and he was rubbing his forehead. Peggy tightened her grip on his hand and he looked up to meet her questioning gaze.

'Peggy, I just wish I could see ahead. See what was going to happen with this war and me. And then I'd know what to do.'

'To do? About what?' she asked gently.

'About us.'

Peggy didn't know what to say to this. Was he thinking about marriage, about her going over there or was she just letting her thoughts run on, spurred by his talk of home? 'We'll just have to wait till the war's over,' she said as cheerfully as she could.

For once he didn't touch her face gently or smile in reassurance. Overcome with worry, she grabbed him close and rocked him in her arms as tenderly as he had rocked her just a little while before.

Tomaree

Two days later Nancy Wallis was sitting in my lounge room.

'You haven't made any changes yet, Peggy? Too soon I expect,' she said, answering her own question.

'I've just started to think what I'd like to do.'

'That's a good sign,' Nancy said, gazing at me sympathetically. She was a very attractive woman; well preserved some would say, with beautifully permed chestnut hair. She looked lovely in a peach coloured pant suit. Nancy was quick on the uptake because she added, 'I turn out all right, don't I?' I was relieved to see she was laughing quite happily. 'Sarah's doing of course. She would have loved this little get together. We talked about it you know.'

I nodded. I had, just moments before, brought the tea tray out laden with cups, saucers, the teapot with cosy, a plate of biscuits and sandwiches. As I began to pour the tea, I realised Nancy was studying me closely. 'The whole works just for me!'

I handed her cup and saucer over. 'I thought I'd start doing it again. Afternoon tea with style,' I joked. 'My American friends used to love it. They'd go ga ga over it all. I'm sorry but there's no sponge cake.'

'Don't tell me you can make sponge cake. Like your mother?' Nancy added hesitantly.

'Actually I can. I think it's the one thing I've been able to master of her cooking.'

'She was a wonderful cook, your mother. I'm sure attendance doubled at CELOPS when word got around that it was your mother's night to cook.'

I laughed. This was exactly what I needed. Talk like this about my mother. I was dreading to break the spell and I think Nancy sensed this because she said, 'You know I wish you could have seen her, Peggy, just once more. Well both of them really,' Nancy was blushing with embarrassment. 'I really meant Sarah but your mother of course too. It was 1967 wasn't it, the last time you were out?'

'Yes.' I sipped my tea.

'We were both up at Surfers Paradise. Sarah dragged me up to peacock watch, as she called it, all the tourists in the beer gardens of the Surfers Paradise Hotel. The two of us would giggle over their awful clothes and garish bathers. She loved wandering around the shops, watching people and buying trinkets. I think she bought some lovely bangles at one of the new shops. Turquoise, if I remember rightly.' Nancy trailed off. 'I'm sorry.' She took a biscuit and ate it looking out the window. (Nancy was sitting in the paisley print.) 'Do you know, she was so much fun? A lot of people didn't know that about her.'

I must have been looking at Nancy with surprise because she added, 'Yes she was, but not in the way you are thinking. No practical jokes or constant joke telling or laughing all the time. It was me doing all the laughing. She was so witty.'

'I didn't know.' I put down my teacup.

'Oh, how could you, Peg? You were only a child, barely twenty one when you left. And her jokes were of the intellectual kind, if you know what I mean. People fascinated her. She would study them very closely. She loved living here and often called Nelson Bay her goldfish bowl. She liked to think of herself as looking in and watching all our antics. Sometimes she would say, *Now why do you think she did that, Nance?* Or, *Whatever is that old so and so up to now?* I called her a gossip once and we had a dreadful row but that was a long time ago.'

'You were happy?' I had the courage to ask.

'Yes, very happy. We suited each other. And now I have to get her house in order.'

'Yours now and I have to do something about mine.' I was looking around me. 'Perhaps we can give each other tips,' I suggested.

'I expect I won't change much. I still have all of Sarah's furniture. It's in storage. Actually I have way too much furniture. When I move in I would love you to come and take a few pieces off my hands.'

'Nancy, I couldn't.'

'Yes, you could. You see, I have some of my brother's stuff. He died recently you know.'

'Yes, I know.'

'And I even have some of my ex husband's things. That's the trouble when you get older. Everybody has a habit of dying around you.'

I must have looked grief-stricken because suddenly Nancy came over and sat next to me on the two-seater lounge. 'I'm sorry I can be so tactless sometimes. Sarah was often complaining.' She paused. 'And Joan's sister died recently too?'

'Yes.'

'But I bet you were a comfort to her.'

'Yes, I think I was.' I wiped tears from my eyes and sat up a little.

Nancy poured me another cup of tea and continued. 'Do you know Sarah could really be fascinating, particularly the way she observed things? She really had some original ideas. She believed in signs. That's what she called them. She'd say, *It's a sign, Nance, I'm sure of it*. A sort of divine intervention. You know like: Have you thought of this? Of course you have to notice the signs first. But the point is that since she died, I have been noticing things more and wondering about them too.'

'How do you mean?'

Nancy had my attention now and became more animated as she explained the theory. 'Well it works something like this. Things have a sort of second meaning or else they point you in a certain direction.' Nancy looked at me closely and remarked, 'you're frowning, Peggy.'

'Yes, I'm sorry. It sounds fascinating. Go on.'

'For instance, now that I am moving back here, I have taken stock of all my furniture and I've discovered that apart from everything else I have three writing desks and four rather lovely table lamps. No other objects have doubled up or at least I've found that I want to keep similar objects. Why the writing desks and the table lamps? I can't say any of this to anyone else here because they would just tell me I'm a bit odd and should have a large jumble sale. But I keep pondering on them. The writing desks are easy. One is obviously meant for you.'

'Why do you say that?'

'I'm sure you are at a stage in your life when letters are very important.'

I studied Nancy's face. Of course there was no way she could know of my estrangement with Tom. I was sure Joan wouldn't have told her. 'In what way,' I asked.

'Well, you have a daughter and husband back in America, don't you? When you are away from loved ones, letters become a lifeline don't they? Something that wasn't so important, except in wartime of course, becomes the object you wait for every day. I should know. I still count the days to Betsy's letters. I end up phoning her of course. She's a terrible letter writer.'

I smiled in relief. 'I have been meaning to write to her for ages.'

A shadow crossed Nancy's expression. 'I've been meaning to ask you for years. Did you and Betsy have a disagreement over Tom?'

'I'm afraid we did,' I told her.

'Don't tell me she didn't approve of Tom.'

I nodded and Nancy continued. 'I thought it was something like that. She could be so pretentious and her marrying Nigel, a Pom, eighteen months later.' Nancy paused. 'Which is probably why she did marry him.' Nancy laughed.

'All the more reason to write. We have a lot in common.'

'Of course you do.' Nancy recrossed her legs. 'Well, Peggy, you can try with your new desk but you'll probably end up putting a trunk call through instead. I always seem to.'

'It doesn't matter which and the desk would be lovely.'

'Remind me to give you her address and phone number. Now where was I?'

'The importance of letters.'

'That's right. You don't think about letters much, do you, unless you have someone overseas? I mean everyone telephones now. And here I am with three writing desks. I am meant to have one, I'm sure. You are meant to have another. I just can't think who should have the third. But I expect it will come to me.'

I felt better now and cheered by the turn of the conversation. I would have to steer our talk back to my mother but the thought didn't scare me now. 'And the table lamps?' I asked.

'Illumination obviously. Sarah did that for me. She opened my mind to so many things. Sounds odd but I think I'll keep all of them. Since I don't have Sarah,' Nancy added after a pause.

'You can read more,' I told her.

Nancy looked blankly at me for a moment.

'You know, illumination,' I explained.

'Oh yes, yes I can. Once I get Sarah's house....'

'Your house,' I interrupted.

'My house,' Nancy smiled. 'In order. Then I'll have plenty of time.'

'I can recommend some reading. When I was studying to be a teacher in the States I met a lot of women doing some very interesting courses. I can write to one or two of them and get their reading lists.'

'Would you?'

'Of course.' There was a pause and finally it was time to broach the subject. 'About my mother...'

'Yes.' Nancy put her teacup down and took my hands. 'It was Sarah who made me think of an incident in your mother's past. She told me it was very important and that she felt you should know. Sarah made me realise that you had a right to know.' Nancy looked around nervously and rubbed her eyes. 'I don't know where to start.' She paused for a moment. 'When your mother first came to Nelson Bay you must have been about nine months old.' Nancy paused, staring into space, thinking.

'Yes, you would have been that, because the first time I saw you and your mother, it was September. Right after my birthday, I recall. You were sitting up in your baby carriage, very alert, watching everything. I had Betsy in mine and I thought I could welcome her and offer to introduce her to a few of the other mothers. Not that there were many of us. Anyway, we stopped near the bakery and your mother told me her name and that she had moved here the week before.'

'At that time, I must explain, my husband Len and I were backwards and forwards. I had a brother in Newcastle as you know and Len's family were here. For a time Len worked with my brother Harry at a dairy out on Ash Island but then they lost the delivery contract. Harry found some work at BHP around this time and Len came here to take up an oyster lease, his father had been running. I was coming here checking on Len and then going back to Mayfield to wait for our house to sell.'

'Well all this meant that I knew most of the news from the bay and from Newcastle.' Nancy paused. She was looking uncomfortable and I tried not to stare, simply willed her to continue. I busied myself straightening the tablecloth and checking the teapot.

After a moment she said, 'You see I knew the name straight away when your mother said Ashburn. I recalled that a baby by that name had drowned and that a week later the baby's father had died in some sort of accident at BHP. I can't recall the details only that Harry had gone on and on about how stupid it had been, sort of unnecessary. I mean the accident and the other death. Well, my heart went out to that mother.' Nancy had reached out to hold my hand again.

I wanted to burst into a flood of tears and if the woman sitting next to me had been Joan, I knew I would have. But it wasn't. It was Nancy Wallis. Something to do with her knowing me as a child, her being Betsy's mother, or the fact of her being beautifully dressed, made me want to hang on to even the smallest shred of dignity. 'The baby drowned,' I said finally.

'Yes, he did. A little boy.'

'Oh, my poor mother.' I began to sob then, all self-control gone. Nancy put her arms around me and held me tight for a few minutes. After a little while I was able to pull away and wipe my eyes.

Nancy, seeing that I had recovered a little, patted my hand and began talking again, 'It's terrible to think of, I know. I was very upset when I read it in the news. I don't think it reached Port Stephens.' Nancy said this as lightly as she could. Tentatively she glanced at me and must have been reassured because she went on. 'So I knew the name straight away as I said, and there was a baby in the carriage.'

'I was confused you see and your mother knew that I knew

and immediately a sort of wall went up between us and it stayed there. Oh, she was polite of course and we were often thrown together because of you two girls but I could never get close to her.'

'I thought maybe that it was something that Sarah knew.' I was feeling a little better now and oddly relieved. Finally my mother's demons had a shape, a recognisable form. I had always felt that there was something between us but had never been able to fathom out what. Now that I knew and was beginning to comprehend the terrible cruelty of my mother's loss, I could see the pattern behind her erratic and often frightening behaviour towards me. Here was the reason behind her over protectiveness when I was little; here too the reason for her bitter view of life. Finally things were becoming much clearer.

My attention had wandered. I had to ask Nancy to repeat her question.

'Why would you say that, Peg? That it was something Sarah knew.'

'It sounded like it in her letter to me.'

'Oh, of course. But really it was just that she felt *she* should be the one to tell you.' Nancy paused for a moment. 'I nearly told you the week before your wedding when you were asking a lot of questions about your mother. Do you remember?'

I nodded.

'But of course it wasn't the right time, or I felt, my place to tell you.'

We were both silent for a moment, then I said, 'Thank you for telling me, Nancy. Sarah couldn't have done it any better.'

'What a lovely thing to say but I think she would have. She had such tact.'

Now it was Nancy who needed comforting. I gave her a hug. 'I don't think my mother liked Sarah,' I remarked after a pause.

Nancy perked up like I knew she would. 'She didn't understand Sarah. That's probably what it was. Sarah didn't arrive in the bay until 1934 when you girls were ten and I had forgotten about your mother's tragedies. Well, put it out of my mind, I should say. I had to, you see, to be able to...' Nancy was lost for words again.

'Cope with my mother.'

Nancy grimaced. 'Not exactly. But it seemed necessary to treat her as if nothing like that had happened. It's what she wanted and I went along with it. Sarah picked up on it though. She knew there was something and she puzzled over your mother and didn't approve of the way your mother...' Nancy paused again. 'Tried to rein you in,' she said. 'And then of course I remembered, and that's when Sarah started to take a special interest in you.'

'It was because of that and nothing else?' I was disappointed and couldn't hide the fact.

'Oh no, Peg. Only at the beginning and then she adored you and said, quite often, that you reminded her of herself at the same age.'

'And she wrote children's stories,' I asked, trying desperately not to think of my drowned brother.

'Yes. Very clever and chummy too. You know girls together.'

'They sound lovely.'

'They are. Would you like a few to read?'

'I would love to borrow some. I asked Joan if she would find out if the library had any.'

'Oh, they don't have any there or at the school.'

'Well, I'll have to do something about that,' I said, feeling a little better, although a million thoughts were swirling around in my head, demanding attention.

'I think that would be a good idea. No good me trying. That would really get them stirred up,' Nancy laughed. Once more she put her hand on mine. 'If there's anything you need. Anything. If you want to talk some more or just feel like coming over to the house, please don't hesitate...'

'I won't,' I told her. I was thinking of the baby, my little brother again, pondering what might have been. My older brother by the sound of it. I didn't know. I would have to try and get my head around it all. And what of my father too? How did his death fit into all of this?

Nancy was standing up. 'Don't forget,' she said, kissing me on the forehead. 'Anytime.'

'I won't forget.'

By midnight I had been sitting on my bed for over two hours telling myself over and over that I was a moral coward. When did I stop asking questions? At seventeen I was always asking questions but gradually I had stopped. Why? Because I was afraid of the answers obviously. Today I had asked a very difficult question of Nancy and she had answered as best as she could. But the answer could have been mine almost eight months earlier, I'm sure of that; at the very least in June when my mother was still alive.

You see I had a foreshadowing of this knowledge that has come to me today but as per usual I ignored it. I shoved it away. It was late November last year, only two months after I started teaching at the school. Little Jessie Schultz had been off sick for nearly a week. Finally when he returned to school his mother insisted he wear his coat in class. I agreed watching the way she fussed over the child. The way she did up the top button tore at my heart. It was so painfully familiar. I smiled and reassured Mrs Schultz yet there remained a strange light in her eyes. The answer was there for the taking but I pushed it aside. I kept busy and carefully didn't ask after Mrs Schultz.

When I finally asked Mrs Fairchild, the principal, that hot June day, she apologised and said she forgot to warn me about Mrs Schultz but it was understandable of course – the woman having lost a baby daughter from double pneumonia the previous winter.

I think I knew then, deep down that my mother had lost a child too but that day I lost my marriage and the discovery became just one more thing I couldn't cope with. I realise now how much it has preyed on my mind. Not just from the June but from the November before. If I had only asked after Mrs Schultz then, discovered the truth and found the courage to talk to Tom, I feel certain he would have made sure I was on a plane home for Christmas. But me being me, I put it off and by that hot June afternoon there was no discussing it with Tom; there was no discussing anything with Tom.

Some time in the early hours of the morning I dreamt I was on top of Tomaree again but this time Tom was with me. We were both sitting there with the sky our horizon, and the dark green mass that was Yacaaba to the north, the islands grouped nearby. We couldn't stop smiling. We were euphoric and I knew we were both in some way reliving that first time we made love.

I kept looking at him. He was Tom but he wasn't Tom. He was my drowned brother, all grown up, smiling at me. *See, everything's okay,* he seemed to be saying. *I'm here. When you're the happiest you can be, I'm with you.* I woke up shivering and couldn't get back to sleep until dawn.

Sea Change

In late January Tom's mother wrote, desperate for news of him. She had read reports of the 41st Division's activities on the Papuan Peninsula and was deeply concerned for his welfare. He had written in September last year to say he had been detached from his division and was in Shoal Bay. He didn't write again, waiting to hear from her.

By January when he finally received her redirected letter he realised she mustn't have received his last one with his new address. He wrote again, reassuring her that he was fine and that he had remained behind in Australia. Since that time he had kept up a steady correspondence and in his last two letters he had begun to mention Peggy, knowing that his mother would read between the lines and guess the depths of this young girl's importance in her son's life.

By March 1943 JOOTS had become the Amphibious Training Centre, nineteen Higgins landing craft had arrived and Tom was busier than ever training a forward contingent of 32nd Division troops. By the first week in May he was lucky to see Peggy once a week, usually at the movies. He and all the other members of the training centre were gearing up for the arrival of the first large influx of American troops expected to roll in soon. This meant more co-ordination with the Australian and US Navy and the RAAF and days spent preparing the training syllabus. The syllabus included 29 hours of practical flashing, semaphore and buzzer and it was the best that could be offered under the restraints of the centre.

His days sure weren't his own any more. Last September seemed like another world, another Port Stephens. He barely had the chance now to get away, not just to see Peggy but to walk along the beach on the mornings when there was no training. He looked forward to his early morning walks, sometimes going as far as Nelson Bay, to the small beach where he had kissed Peggy for the first time.

Last week he had stood under the shade of a she-oak at Shoal Bay, his cigarette burning against the early dawn light and watched several small boatloads of Aussies, in the charge of two elderly Militiamen barking orders.

He had seen the LCI heading out earlier and after a time watched as the rubber boats, unloaded from the LCI and made their way to shore. As they closed in, Tom could see, by the way the young men were rowing, what they were up to and he couldn't help chuckling to himself. He was starting to get a handle on the Aussies' attitude to authority. The boys, no more than eighteen or nineteen, timed the waves to perfection and as the boats hit the sand both Lance Corporals, in two of the boats, were soaked to the skin.

Not stopping and hoping to set an example, the Lance Corporals walked up the beach in imitation of a reconnaissance, pointing the way, both failing to see that no one followed. Instead the young men scrambled back into the boats and yelled, 'We're off!' and began to push off from the beach, only allowing the middle-aged men to board at the last minute. Tom hadn't stopped laughing for some time. He sure had to hand it to them. They had spirit and he had to admit he was warming to their strange ways. Peggy helped of course but living here did too.

He knew if he recounted the story back home there would be cries of disapproval and more examples thrown in of undisciplined Aussie soldiers. Many of his compatriots wouldn't understand but at least he did and was pleased he did. And then there had been another incident.

Only yesterday he had been smoking a cigarette outside the Country Club when a delivery van pulled up. It was some distance down the road and the driver hopped out and began to look under the bonnet. Tom was about to offer his help (although his mechanical skills were limited) when he noticed a young Australian private taking something from the back of the van. It was a large green cylindrical carton. Ice cream, Tom guessed, for the Country Club. Quickly he cut the young man off. When approached the young private faced him boldly and saluted in an exaggerated fashion. The smart ass Tom thought, but decided to ignore it. Instead he enquired about where the ice cream was going.

'Thought I'd take it back to me mates.'

'What at Gan Gan?'

'Yes, Sir,' he replied and Tom let him go. If the guy was determined to walk all that way carrying such an awkward load then the private and his buddies deserved a treat, although he knew there would be complaints back at the club when the shortage was discovered. Lucky for the Aussie that this American wasn't overly keen on ice cream.

When Tom thought about both these incidents he realised how much he had changed these last few months, particularly his attitude to Australian servicemen. Puzzlement, and ignorance had slowly turned to understanding and often admiration.

Nelson Bay too been transformed. Apart from Fly Point and Gan Gan there were now camps at Nelson Bay, Shoal Bay and Anna Bay. A truck and vehicle depot now took up part of Magnus Street and the bay itself was bursting at the seams with people. Officers were everywhere and dances were held every week, sometimes at the old hall and now at the new workshop on the waterfront.

Tom had noticed recently that the boom gate at the corner of Nelson Bay Road and Soldiers Point Road was finally being manned in earnest. There was now a milk bar at the bay run by a pretty blonde who managed to keep all the young GIs in line, all the while frantically serving milkshakes and hamburgers and answering their snappy one-liners. He had been in once or twice and had to admire her for her restraint under difficult circumstances.

Some of the guys could get out of hand. During the last month Tom had given more than one lecture, squeezed into his course, on doing the right thing by the locals. Not coming on fast to the local girls was the key bit of advice. Word had finally got around to the residents about how fast these Yanks were. He knew it would and frankly, it didn't surprise him. As far as the Aussie males went they seemed to prefer the pub to a date out with a pretty girl. The 18th Battalion could have the pick of the local girls but women just didn't seem to be on their itinerary and when his fellow countryman began to move swiftly on the Newcastle or Nelson Bay girls, the news had spread.

Of course this development was making things difficult for him with Mrs Ashburn. Over the last two months he had noticed she had cooled towards him. In her eyes he used to be that nice young American officer from the Country Club, now he was sure she just thought of him as one of the Yanks. But that wasn't all. The last time he had dinner with Peggy and her mother, the older woman kept talking about his plans after the war. Was he definitely going back to live in Wyoming? Had he thought about living in Australia?

Her questions had taken him completely by surprise. Live in Australia? He had never thought about it and couldn't see himself living here, no matter how beautiful it was. America was his home and that's how it was. But he hadn't told her in so many words. She was probably already alarmed by the news of a young girl in Fly Point engaged to a naval officer from Chicago. She had put her name down for the next ship out and would be staying with his folks to wait until her young fiancé could join her.

Tom's thoughts shifted back to Peggy. He couldn't ask her to marry him. Not now. Not yet when he didn't know what lay ahead. His Dad had always called him cautious and stubborn and he was right. Tom couldn't imagine changing his mind. It just didn't feel right. It was best to wait until the moment came when he was sure. Right now that moment hadn't come.

No, they couldn't marry yet. If he was posted to the fighting, they would write and if he made it through the war, then he'd come and get her. They'd make the trip back to the States together and hopefully with Helen Ashburn's blessing.

In the meantime he would ask her to wait for him. He was sure of that much. If he was posted out tomorrow, he wanted her to wait for him. God, he couldn't bear the thought of her being with anybody else. She was so different from all of the girls he'd known. But in a strange kind of way she was like him. He had picked that from the start and his gut feelings of the kind of girl she was, had been proved right. Time had proved him right and it was as if they were made for each other.

He thought about both their personalities. Both he and Peggy were active and liked to keep busy and boy did she like puzzling over things even more than he did. She asked the darnedest questions sometimes, did Miss Peggy Ashburn. She often had him beat! If only he could marry her right now! But he couldn't. Not when he didn't know what lay ahead after Shoal Bay. More active service most likely and would he make it through that? Two of his buddies hadn't. Members of the 163rd Infantry Regiment, they had been killed fighting in some place called Sanananda. Another buddy Lyle had written to him of their deaths. Unfortunately he had no word of his signals company. Lyle didn't know where they were.

And where was he? He was enjoying one of the most beautiful views he had ever seen in his life. He had just finished smoking a cigarette and having a quiet coffee. He had slept in a decent bed last night and his uniform was clean and dry. Ever since he'd got the letter from Lyle, guilt and a constant need to justify his own existence here in Shoal Bay had been eating away at him. Hadn't he been working hard since January? Didn't he have skills to offer? Sure, there were a lot of guys that could have done this job, in different companies, in other divisions, but his name had come up and here he was. Just as well he didn't have too many quiet moments at his disposal these days. All this worrying was getting him nowhere.

If he was really honest with himself, then he had to admit that he was looking forward to the troops arriving. Thank God he would be exhausted at night soon and not have trouble sleeping like he regularly did. And while training the men, he would be doing something useful for the war. He could stop whipping himself constantly for sitting pretty out here because he would finally be paying his dues.

Tom rubbed his hands through his short blonde hair and leant against the window of the small internal landing in the centre of the Country Club. It was his favourite spot. Standing here, he was a few steps removed from all the activity below him and in front of him was the bay glittering blue and silver, like a picture postcard. But did he deserve it?

Hell, he would miss this place when he left. It was starting to get into his blood: the whiteness of the sand, that sweep of beach on the other side of the bay, the occasional sight of dolphins, nosing in and out. And those spectacular peaks, the headlands guarding the entrance to the harbour. At this moment the sun was beginning to climb and sunshine was speckling the water. A pleasant northeaster was blowing gently on his face. Almost winter but it was a beautiful day.

He had a sudden vision of Peggy in her yellow dress running down the beach to meet him and throwing herself into his arms. In his mind she was a part of this place. She was as sunny as the weather and as beautiful as the sweep of white beach in front of him. If he could only run to her right now but he wouldn't be seeing her for a week. He had codes to write up and a meeting to attend.

Only very late at night would he let himself think about her, really think about her. Lying in his bed, in the small room behind what was once the reception area of the club, he often tortured himself with the memory of her naked on the blanket at Fenninghams Island. It was the only time they had made love in daylight. How many times had he replayed that day in his mind? He had lost count. No wonder he couldn't sleep.

Wishes

It didn't take me long to find the tiny article in the paper, 24th April 1925. 'Infant son of Mr and Mrs Ashburn, Tom, aged two drowned in the bath yesterday. It appears the child slipped and hit his forehead rendering him unconscious.' A week later there was a report of my father's death. I had copies made of both and came down the steps from Newcastle Library to sit in the green shade of Civic Park. Both reports were folded up in my shoulder bag. Brushing tears away I took out the photo I had retrieved from the album in Mum's suitcase, which I finally investigated yesterday.

He was a lovely looking little boy and he looked like my Tom in quite an amazing way. The same shock of blonde hair, the same dark eyes. How I longed for the two baby photos of Tom that Pamela gave me when Sarah was born. To lay the three photos side by side and be reassured of the likeness. Instead the photos were in storage along with all my stuff from my life with Tom.

Half my life was in storage! The American half and now what was I doing, but opening up box after box of my Australian life. Little by little I was becoming reacquainted with my past, making discoveries about people, about love and loss.

Oh, the heartbreak of my mother's life! It was too painful to contemplate. Surely there can be nothing worse than losing a child and one so young. What agonies my mother must have gone through and then to lose my father so soon afterward.

It was a wonder that my mother had kept her faith in God. She must have been cursing the heavens for her losses and of course hanging on to me desperately, for as long as I can remember; clutching at me as the one thing left to her, stifling me with her worries and her desperation that I might be taken too.

More tears came when I thought of that time in my mother's life – her husband and son snatched from her. What sort of woman would I be now if I had lost Sarah? And Tom too. Bitter and withdrawn like my mother? Quite likely, I thought now, sitting on the cold steps.

I mourned the death of the father I had never known but there had been 47 years to get used to the fact of his death. This other bereavement: the death of my older brother preyed on my mind. What sort of brother would he have made and what would he have looked like at twenty one? He would have been four years younger than Tom.

Was that why my mother liked my Tom so much? Because she could see the resemblance? She must have seen the resemblance just as I was seeing it now. Yesterday going through the albums in Mum's suitcase I had cried for all the lost years: for my Mum and Dad, happy and on holidays; for Tom playing with his grandparents in what must have been their home in Mayfield, the one with the rose bushes. Joan said I should try and chase them up and see if I have any cousins. Sitting now gazing at the Town Hall, I decided I would.

I really was on a quest just like Joan said nearly three weeks ago. I have been since I got here. I just didn't realise it till now. Well, I have found my brother, I have come to realise the magnitude of my mother's loss and also to understand why she tried so hard to keep me close to her when I was little. If I could only take back all the worries I gave her! All the times I disappeared walking for hours or climbing cliffs. How agonising it must have been for her. Sometimes it must have felt to her like I was doing it on purpose. But I wasn't. I just wanted to break free.

My tears had finally stopped and the trees and grass were no longer blurred. I blew my nose and brushed my hair. It was nice here in the filtered sunshine. Joan's EH Holden that I had borrowed this morning, was not far away, parked in King Street. I could see it from where I was sitting. I glanced at my watch. Time to get a move on. As I stood up I noticed a blue beetle parking in front of Joan's car. The colour was beautiful, a soft powder blue and there was something so cheerful about the shape of a VW. As different as a car can possibly be from the Studebaker, the Nash and the Chevrolet that I have driven these last twenty six years.

At that moment a plump, middle-aged woman got out of the powder blue car, locked it and bustled towards me. Joan! God, it was wonderful to see her! I got up quickly and threw my arms about her.

'Did you find what you were looking for?' Joan asked me gently.

'Yes.'

'And you've had a bit of a cry?'

'Yes.'

'Feeling better?'

'Yes.'

'Well, there we are then. I've come at the right time. Timed it beautifully, if I do say so myself.'

'You have Joan.' I couldn't help but laugh.

'How about a gin sling at the Clarendon?'

'Gosh, I haven't had one of those in years.'

'Well, it's about time then.'

'I'd love that, but I'm paying.'

'Right you are then.'

This is nice, I thought, looking around the glasshouse, a very trendy area at the back of the hotel where Joan told me bands played on the weekends. Thankfully it was quiet this afternoon: only a middle-aged couple and a man sitting at the bar. I gradually felt myself relax. The drink was helping of course. After a little while I said, 'Oh, Joan, I meant to ask you. Whose car is it?'

'Nancy's brother and it's for sale.'

'Well then I'm going to buy it,' I told Joan. 'I need to salvage something from this day.'

'You've gained a lot I think.'

'No, Joan. I've lost so much.'

Joan put her hand over mine. 'I'm disagreeing with you, love. You lost him a long time ago. You can't wish him back. I expect you have a lot of wishes at the moment.'

'I do. I wish my brother and my father had never died.'

'Nothing you can do about either of those, love.'

'I wish I never left my mother.'

'I thought we dealt with that a while ago, Peggy.'

'Yes, I know we did.' I rubbed my forehead.

'Constructive wishes,' Joan said firmly.

'Philosophy again?' I asked peevishly.

'Just being practical.'

I stared around the glasshouse for a moment and finally said the words that had been humming around in my head for a week now. 'I wish I'd never left Tom.'

Joan smiled. 'You forgive him then?'

'Yes.'

'And what about his affair?'

'I haven't really been in the marriage for quite some time. Well I have been,' I paused, 'behind a large wall that I started building after my last visit here.'

'Thought it was something like that. I had a hard time of it when the boys left home. And where are they now, I ask you? David's in Canada and Paul's in Poland.'

'And Sarah's in Wisconsin.'

'There's always letters,' Joan said.

I had a sudden thought about Nancy's third writing desk. I would speak to her about it. Tell her I had a candidate and also a buyer for her brother's car. Me. I felt better already.

'Any other wishes?' Joan cut into my thoughts.

'Other than moving Lake Wausau into New South Wales?'

'Other than that, my dear.'

'No, but I need another one of your lists. I want to find my father's relatives and don't know where to start.' Biting back tears I showed Joan the photographs and newspaper clippings.

'What a lovely little boy. He's like a little angel. I bet he's been watching over you all these years.'

I cupped my hand quickly over my mouth to stifle a sob. 'Do you know Joan, I think he has been.'

'There we are then.'

We sat in companionable silence and discussed the merits of gin slings as opposed to Harvey Wallbangers. As we were both driving back we decided it was best not to have another drink and instead bought a big bag of peanuts from the bar and ordered a lemon squash each.

After a little while Joan said, 'Well let's see about that list. Did you find your father's death certificate?'

'Yes. His and Tom's were with my mother's will in the buffet.'

'Well then that will give you the address.'

'Yes, but that's only my parent's address. There's no way of finding out where my grandparents used to live. I mean I don't even know if my father had a brother or a sister.'

'The phone book. You could go through all the Ashburns.'

'Yes, I think I'll have to. But of course if he had a sister who's married…'

'She won't be in there,' Joan finished.

We both sat nibbling peanuts and thinking.

'Your father's letters,' Joan said suddenly.

'Of course. I mean they're from the time of the Great War but some of them should mention his family.' I sat staring into space for a moment and then said, 'Time to go through them and Tom's as well.'

'You brought Tom's with you?' Joan asked.

'Yes, I did. And I didn't tell you but I recently found Tom's first love letter he wrote me.' I didn't want to explain where and Joan sensing this merely congratulated me and didn't push for details. 'You know, I think I might ring Tom on our anniversary.'

'I thought you were married in June?'

'We were. This is the anniversary of when we first met.'

'Now that should go to the top of the list.'

'Yes,' I said feeling light-hearted for the first time in days.

'Do you know your mother used to say something about wishes.'

'Did she?'

Joan was frowning, trying to remember. Suddenly she burst out with, 'If wishes were fishes most would swim free.'

The following day I bought a large supply of paint, drop sheets, brushes – the works to finally paint the house. It would be wonderful to get rid of the dirty off-white colour of most of the walls and I had actually been itching for years to paint over the lime green in the kitchen, not to mention the grey of the bathroom and laundry.

I had chosen *moonshine* for the lounge room walls. It was a soft pinkish beige. It wouldn't go with Mum's old furniture she bought in the thirties but I would worry about that later. There was a very pale aquamarine for my bedroom, Mum's old room. I had chosen yellow for my old room because it was at the back of the house and had always been dark from the trees overhanging the backyard. It desperately needed brightening up. *Clotted cream*, a very nice, slightly yellow tinged off white would do beautifully for the kitchen and the laundry. I still had no idea what to do about the old purple tiled, grey walled bathroom. Retile it most probably but as I hadn't even considered what colour tiles would be best, there was no point in worrying about painting the walls at the moment.

I set to work mid morning starting with Mum's room first, at times cursing her for not telling me about my baby brother; at other times crying over her losses. All her losses. She had done what I had done: left her country of birth because she had fallen in love. It should have brought us closer together in the months before I left, but somehow it didn't. That's just the way she was, I told myself. But I couldn't go on living my life the way she had, so closed in on herself. I *had* closed down these last few months. It would be hard but I must start to open up again. I pulled Mum's heavy backed curtains down and let the sunshine into the room. I had seen some white cotton material advertised in a shop in Newcastle that would do nicely.

By Wednesday I was painting my old room in *halo*, a bright sunny yellow and the cream paint opened up the kitchen and made the dark green tiles above the sink glow. It was good to bring colour into the old house. By Thursday afternoon the house was transformed. I felt better, lighter somehow despite all the hard physical work. With thousands of brushstrokes I had painted away grief, anger, guilt and finally the last to leave, regret.

The Weather

For a while now Peggy had been watching her mother carefully like she used to do as a child. Since the age of ten or so when she started to assert her independence, Peggy gradually began to learn to read her mother by the way she walked, moved or went about her housework. She could tell even before her mother said a word whether her mother was just tired or that an outburst of her mother's wrath was about to rain down on her head.

It wasn't that her mother was bad. She knew she wasn't, even as a small child. It was just that she had an awful temper. A lot of things made her mother tired and angry. She wasn't good with strangers and had little patience with life's pleasantries. *Things were the way they were and that was that.*

Life had been very unkind to her mother. Betsy's mother Nancy had assured Peggy of this fact numerous times whilst she was growing up. It was almost as if she was helping Peggy to make allowances, trying to help a young child understand the unfathomable.

Well she was eighteen now, not ten. A grown up woman but that made no difference. She was still wary of her mother's moods. A storm was brewing. Dark grey clouds had been hanging low over their house for days. And in the still before the inevitable storm, Peggy felt like she was going to suffocate. She was praying for rain, no matter how hard it fell or for how long.

It was something to do with all the Americans. When they arrived last week there had been an enormous convoy of trucks and troops marching six abreast stretching from the Sea Breeze Hotel to Fly Point. Talk about making their presence felt! Almost choking the small town with their large numbers. It was hard not to feel intimidated except for the fact that they were so friendly, waving and smiling as they passed. Peggy had received the odd whistle too but was thankful her mother hadn't been there as she would have been horrified.

And last night it had been hard to sleep. It seemed like one truck after another was rumbling down Magnus Street right past her window. Lying awake she could hear other noises too, a more distant, deeper rolling sound of maybe a whole convoy moving towards Fly Point. She tossed and turned for ages thinking of Tom, wondering how he fit into all of this.

It was Wednesday night and she hadn't seen Tom for nearly a week. *Wednesday used to be our day,* Peggy thought to herself, standing by the window but not looking out. There was nothing to see. The town was draped in the sleepy dark grey of blackout. How she missed their long walks up and down the beach, picnics near Spiro's tent where they would kiss sometimes for nearly an hour, kiss after kiss intensifying until their lips were numb and they couldn't stop looking into each other's eyes.

That had been last year before Fenninghams Island. This year they had only managed to make love twice and the last time had been months ago now. She longed for those kisses again. But when or how and for that matter where? With winter coming it had become impossible. But they must find a way. Somehow, despite the weather and her mother's moods, they must find a way.

At that moment the gate slammed shut. Her mother was home from CELOPS and obviously, judging by the sound of the gate and her mother's heavy footsteps, the evening hadn't gone well.

As her mother shrugged off her coat she exclaimed, 'I can't believe you didn't tell me about Jimmy. I had to hear it from Pat Marley of all people.'

Peggy approached her mother as the older woman sat wearily down on the lounge. 'What news?'

'What do you mean what news? You know perfectly well what news. He was killed at Atherton last week. In a training accident. Marjorie had the telegram on Monday.'

'Killed?' Peggy sat down suddenly on the small chair near the window, away from her mother's speculations and accusations.

'What? Doesn't Betsy talk to you anymore?'

Her mother's tone was bitter and Peggy could feel lightning in the air. 'Not much,' Peggy added, after a pause.

'I'm not surprised, given the circumstances.'

'What circumstances?'

'Being invaded by thousands of Yanks.'

'They're here for a reason Mum, a good one and we just have to make do.'

'Yes, here having a good time while our boys are being killed in New Guinea.'

'That sounds like Mrs Marley,' Peggy remarked, staring intently at her mother. With each of her mother's moods lately Peggy was becoming aware that there was a pattern to them. Firstly there would be an outburst triggered by something she found intolerable. This time Jimmy's death obviously. (When she was a child, coming home hours late.) But strangely the true nature of the incident would never be discussed or resolved. Instead worn out phrases and old grudges would be dragged out.

Some things her mother remarked at this point were often without reason or intelligence and could not be answered by Peggy or rationalised away. They were simply angry words flying out of her mother's mouth to be hurled at Peggy. Yet still her mother required an answer and Peggy was tired these days of trying to work out exactly what answer to give. 'I'm sorry about Jimmy. I'll try and see Betsy and Mrs Hartley tomorrow.'

Clouds momentarily drifted higher and her mother moved into the kitchen. Peggy relaxed back against the chair. So he was dead and all she could think about was not Betsy and how she must be feeling but how in heaven she was going to be able to endure the rest of the evening with her mother.

Jimmy was part of another world, the world before Tom. Maybe she would cry about him tomorrow but right now, she just felt numb and full of dread at how her mother would react.

When Harry Matthews died at Singapore last year it had been excruciating. The heavy silences, the sighs and worst of all the things that her mother muttered under her breath, just loud enough for Peggy to hear. *It's all to be endured again. And I'm supposed to be grateful I haven't got a son in the war. Back to waiting again for bad news.*

Peggy sat wondering what lay ahead: heavy silences or a

sudden rush of fury lashing at her as fast as lightning. If only she could dash out on the pretext of seeing Betsy; to run out into the cold, dark night to Dutchies and into Tom's arms. But Dutchies was out of bounds now. Communication lines had been laid to their special part of the beach for the sentry on permanent watch in Salamander Bay. Nelson Bay was so busy this year and Fenninghams was completely out of reach. Impossible now for Tom to get a boat. In fact even half an hour alone these days was almost out of the question.

How she wished her and Betsy hadn't fallen out. She could go over there and comfort her friend. Talk to her and try and take her mind off Jimmy. Quickly words of condolence began to form in her mind and just as quickly she mentally tore them up. What could she say that would be of any use? What could anyone say? Her presence, with Tom still alive and very much American would be like an insult to Betsy. No, she couldn't go over to Betsy's. Oh God, if she could just see Tom!

Peggy paused in her thoughts and gazed for a moment at her mother. In a year from now would a letter arrive for her to say that Tom was dead? She couldn't bear thinking about it. Would she hear at all? Hopefully nothing like that would happen. If he did have to go away she would have regular letters from him and he would return from the war.

But would he return here? Probably not. He'd return to Wyoming and what would happen then, to the two of them? Would there just be no more Peggy and Tom? Just Tom with someone else possibly and Peggy probably by herself. Maybe she would move to Newcastle... Her mind running on was brought to a halt by the sound of the kettle whistling.

With relief Peggy realised her mother was making a cup of tea. How long had she been sitting like this, Peggy wondered. She looked down into her lap. There was a handkerchief in her hands. She didn't remember getting it out of her pocket. With surprise she opened the crushed cotton to find it torn in several places. She must have pulled and pulled at it after her mother told her the news. She threw it onto her sewing basket in the corner of the lounge room and walked into the kitchen.

'I suppose you think it won't happen to you?' her mother said, swinging abruptly around to face Peggy.

'What do you mean?'

'It's just happened to Betsy. It could happen to you.'

'But I'm not engaged like Betsy is...was,' Peggy finally got out.

'Well if I know our Lieutenant Lockwood, I'd say he's working towards that.'

'He's not sure what is the best,' Peggy said, trying not to look at the intent, almost hostile expression on her mother's face. Why did she get like this sometimes, Peggy asked herself. Where did all this anger come from? Her mother was leaning towards her now, her mouth was set hard and the whole of her body seemed to have shifted from resignation to a terrible stance of intimidation.

'You are not going to marry him, do you hear? I won't have it,' her mother continued. 'If you marry him now and go over there, what will happen to you if he gets killed? His family mightn't bother with you and the odds are you won't have your fare home. At least Betsy's mother is there to comfort her. How will I get to you? And you won't get any money from the Yankee government. I've been hearing all about that. You'll have no rights over there. Not like you do here. Is that what you want? Is it? Is it? I won't have it do you hear. I won't!'

Finally her mother's appalling speech ceased and Peggy was left stunned, shivering. Here were more of these stupid meaningless words. And that's all they were, Peggy told herself. There was no point in answering. She had found that out as a child. Don't answer them, her mind throbbed.

But this time it was different. She was no longer ten and late home. She hadn't been found out climbing Tomaree. She was eighteen and Tom, the man she loved, was involved.

Peggy took a deep breath and stared her mother down. 'I'm eighteen and I'll do what I want and if you continue to treat me like this, to say such things then I won't consider your feelings. Tom and I will get married whenever it suits us, not when it suits you. Which it obviously doesn't.'

Mrs Ashburn turned away from her daughter then and made towards the back door but Peggy cut her off and stood in her way, facing her mother squarely.

'I used to take this as a little girl, Mum, but I'm not taking it anymore. I know you're worried, but your thinking is all messed up. You see if I hadn't met Tom I might already be in Betsy's shoes. I could have met someone last year. Maybe the year before and he could be still rotting in some prison camp. Or this so-called Australian soldier I might have fallen in love with, could be dead. Maybe he died last week. Maybe Tom will die next year. I don't know, Mum. You don't know,' Peggy said this, pointing her finger at her mother, as her mother had so often done when she was a child.

In that moment Mrs Ashburn seemed to rally and straightening up said, 'How dare you speak to me like this? I didn't bring you up to speak to me like this.'

'But you have, to me, lots of times. And that's all right, isn't it? I know you are worried and have been worried all through my childhood but if I want to marry Tom, I will.'

'And if he survives the war, what will you do? Live in Wyoming, thousands of miles away?'

'It's his home Mum. I thought you liked Tom,' she said after a moment.

When Peggy's tone softened with her last words, her mother frantically tried to push Peggy away from the door. This time she wasn't afraid of her mother anymore. She didn't shrink away from her mother's nearness nor look away from her mother's distraught face. As she leant against the door, the seconds seemed to slow down to a long pause and Peggy was able to grasp the whole moment clearly in her mind. It was obvious. Something that she had never thought of before was now so clearly evident. Her mother was scared. Her mother was really scared.

Was that what had plagued her mother all these years? Not anger but fear? 'I thought you liked Tom,' Peggy repeated, and with the words Mrs Ashburn collapsed against Peggy crying.

'I do like him. I do very much. But don't you see,' Mrs Ashburn sobbed. 'If you go you'll have your Tom, but I won't have you.'

There was nothing to say to this. All Peggy could do was hold her mother until the crying stopped.

White Horses

Since my flurry of painting I have spent the last two days shopping for new furniture. I have ordered a brown leather lounge suite, quite simple in design and not too large for the lounge room. The brown was a very soft mid brown that I hope will go with the walls and will be delivered next week. I've also bought a new pine table with four chairs, not too big for the kitchen and disposed of the terrible vinyl covered table Mum managed with for years and the disreputable chairs. Along with a bookcase and a nice standard lamp, the two main rooms should very shortly be transformed.

Having made a real start on the house, it was definitely time to start on my family. Last night I read Dad's death certificate carefully. My name was on there and Tom's too with a 'Dec'd' beside it under the column of issue. Obviously Joan had been a bit confused. If I wanted to find out Dad's brothers and sisters it would seem that I needed either his mother's or father's death certificate. I *would* apply for both somehow but not until the next time I was in Newcastle.

My eyes lingered over our two names. I wondered what sort of a brother and sister relationship we would have had. Images of the two of us together haunted my dreams again last night, as they had nearly every night since finding the newspaper article. He was climbing Tomaree with me but he was up higher, shouting down instructions. *Walk around that bush, Peggy. Watch out it's slippery this way.* In my dreams he was always up ahead, just out of reach, but often turning back to make sure I was following.

Somehow it was reassuring and hopeful too. And there was something else. He often seemed to be pointing things out to me. *Did you see that, Peggy? What a beautiful sunset. Told you it would be worth the climb. Look at that view!* He had the childlike sense of joy in simple things. Something that I had lost quite a while ago. And hadn't he always been by my side when I was in touch with it? Of course he had.

As I picked up his baby photograph, now framed, from its place on the buffet, the teenage boy in my mind regressed to a two year old with dark eyes, an angel at my shoulder. So there was another Tom in my life. But in reality he was the first Tom. I must do something about the second, but first I had a family to find before I could think about awkward phone calls and apologies.

Momentarily I was stabbed by the recognition that I was continually putting my husband in the too hard basket. Wasn't that what I had been doing this last month since my arrival? Constantly finding things to divert me from the real issue at hand which was: *Did I still want to be married?* As each task had manifested itself – Mum's funeral, the snapshots, the wardrobe, Angharad's death, my mother's and Sarah's wills, my lost brother, the possibility of family which I was now investigating – I had experienced and was still experiencing a feeling of inevitability.

Maybe not in the beginning if I stopped to analyse it all but definitely from the turning out of the wardrobe on. It was a sort of: *Yes, of course* feeling; of things long blurred coming into focus. The black and white bird I had caught sight of in my mind that night on the porch was gradually hopping nearer. Its wing beats were slowing to a steady pulse and it was choosing to perch closer and closer to home. I must phone my husband soon no matter how awkward or painful it would turn out to be.

I put Tom's photo back down and looked through the phone book. For a moment I was startled to see my mother's phone number there. It was a jolt but stupid really because of course she was there. It's just that I have never had cause to look her number up, knowing it by heart as I do. I phoned the other two listings. The first was a young couple that had recently moved from Perth. I apologised to the wife for bothering her. The second was an elderly gentleman from Karuah who turned out to be no relation to my father but he thought he had heard of a Maisie Ashburn who lived in Swansea. I thanked him profusely.

Well Maisie wasn't on the phone but she wasn't far away. I would visit her soon. I made myself a cup of coffee and took it into the small backyard. It was nice here in the shade of the gum trees and near Mum's yellow, white and purple garden of snowdrops, daffodils and the irises – spears of dark purple not yet unfurled.

I hadn't done much in the last week since my visit to the library in Newcastle. It was school holidays so there had been no morning or afternoon reading to the littlies. I had managed to write three letters to Sarah and finally one to Betsy but that was all. I have been licking my wounds for the most part, taking long walks and having endless cups of tea with Joan. Not much to show for a week but a progress of sorts as my Welsh neighbour assured me. However, there was still so much to do.

Drinking my coffee I stopped to feel the breeze on my face. It was surprisingly warm today. On a sudden impulse I walked inside and changed into my short-sleeved shirtmaker dress. It would be nice to feel the sunshine on my bare arms, I decided. It had been a long cold month. After brushing my hair and tying it back, I fetched the large box from the wardrobe and sat down again in Mum's small garden.

With the sun on my face and arms and a warm breeze blowing softly, I read the two letters written to my mother that I had found in the bottom of the box. They were from her brother as it turned out and his name was Bertie.

It was obvious from the content of the letters that they were not the only ones, just the last. I wondered where the other letters had got to. Perhaps lost in a move. The first one dated 22nd July, 1915 described conditions at Gallipoli as part of the 5th Wiltshire regiment.

Dear Helen,

I had to ask Pat the date and was surprised when he told me. This week has flown as I've been working in the fire trenches. I'm doing all right so I don't want you to worry. We were issued with a new blanket and waterproofs last week which has made life easier and because of the hot weather lately, the trenches are dry. The Turks have been on the attack today, the 39th from what I've heard but they're not close to where I am. I'm tucked up right now with my new blanket but there's no moon, thank God. That'll keep things quiet. The boys seem to think the Turks are planning another raid. Well it won't be the first time they've tried to drive us into the sea and we've got more men now. How's the garden going? I hope you are well.

Your loving brother,

Bertie

The second letter, dated 9th August was altogether different.

Dear Helen,

It's late and I'm running out of light, so please excuse if my handwriting is a bit of a mess. My asthma has been troubling me a bit but I don't want you to worry. These last few days I've been thinking a lot about the white horse at Westbury. It's a funny thing to think about when you consider where I am. We are all crouched here so tight and there's that horse spread over the hillside. I remember it as being so white, very white. Perhaps that's just because you and I were kids and it looked like something from a fairy tale. I don't know if you have the train fare but I would love you to go take another look and write to me about it.

I just wanted to say, Helen that I'm so proud of you and grateful too for the way you made a home for the two of us after Dad died. I know it wasn't easy but you did a wonderful job and I'm *looking forward to getting out of the trenches and seeing you again. And when I come back, I'll be taking care of you for a change.*

Till I see you again,

Love

Bertie

Tucked inside this letter was the telegram announcing his death on the 10th August. I brushed tears from my eyes and put the letters back. After a little while I studied again the address on the envelope of both letters: Mill House, Salisbury Road, Amesbury, Salisbury Plains, Wiltshire. Miss Helen Endicott. I said the name over to myself. What was it like Mum, living in Mill House at Amesbury? Things must have been hard on brother and sister. No father and presumably no mother for quite some time.

There was no mention of a mother in either of the letters. No wonder my mother could be so grim on occasion. Was grim, I corrected myself and her temper! It seemed now to be more a case of flaying at life, than being angry at a particular person – me mainly. Another darling brother lost, killed at Gallipoli the day after his last letter and what of her father? Had she mourned him when he died? Presumably she had, but there was no way of knowing now.

Very carefully, I put my father's letters in order. Immediately I fell in love with the cheerful and fun loving tone of the letters, so different from Bertie's. He spoke of their meeting at a dance in Amesbury. He made fun of the parade ground antics at Lark Hill Camp where his battalion, the 34th was being trained and in the next paragraph mentioned his dread of leaving Salisbury Plains and being posted away from her, his sweetheart.

Well, whatever happened, he was coming back, he assured her. She had to take him to see this horse she kept talking about. And which one were they going to see? He'd heard there was a few in Wiltshire. And of course there was Stonehenge. He had seen it from the sports ground at Lark Hill but wanted to walk over it with his sweetheart. He couldn't leave England without doing that.

In his letters from France he began to write of his home in Mayfield (and to my excitement) of his family.

'As you know there's just Mum, Dad, Maisie and Henrietta at home now in Ingall Street. Maisie is a bit eccentric. Not sure what you'll think of her but I'm sure you'll love Henri as we call her. Everyone does. She's so full of fun and sort of old for her years. We'll stay there for a little while , love and save our money for a place of our own. Things will be tough at first but you know about that. You've been through a lot and you understand about how difficult life can get at times. About working and saving towards what you want. I'll take good care of you sweetheart. You know I will....'

The letter went on with more terms of endearment, as good as Tom nearly at expressing his feelings. Mum and I had been lucky there I acknowledged. I continued reading, virtually without pause, all of my father's letters. While writing about his training at Salisbury Plain, his first encounter with trench warfare at Armientieres, France and the following year the attack on Messines ridge in Flanders, the tone was fairly light-hearted. My father was obviously trying hard to make the best of things, continually mentioning only positive aspects (not that there were many) for my mother's sake. There were frequent comments of quiet days at the parapet and spells behind lines. No mention of comrades dying beside him (although there must have been) or bodies on the parapet and the horror of No Man's Land.

By September 1917, however, the tone of his letters had changed.

Dearest Helen,

The mud that I've been writing about for weeks has really begun to get us all down. It's a terrible dark stain that invades everything - the trenches, our boots, our uniforms and blankets. Rainwater has turned into cesspits all over Ypres, making it almost impossible for the supplies to get through the Menin Road. It's like muddy quicksand that can drown a horse and wagon. I've seen it happen. And the misery of walking through it, I just can't describe. Sometimes my clothes are so sodden with mud and ice that I can't put one foot in front of the other. And it's not easy to stay dry. I bet you've already guessed that. You asked me not to spare you and I'm trying hard not to but there's some things I won't be writing to you about. I'd better end this letter. I don't want to depress you any more, only know that you keep me going and I can't wait to see you again.

All my love,

George

Daylight was fading in the garden by the time I came to his letter dated 13th October 1917 after the first day of Passchendaele. I went inside, taking all the letters with me. Sitting down in the paisley print chair I turned on the small lamp nearby and began to read again.

With these last two letters I could feel the desolation behind his words. His sad questioning brought a lump to my throat.

Dearest Helen,

I have been going through it in my mind, sweetheart and can't honestly say why I'm still here. Fellows, good men falling all around me and somehow I've managed to make it through all those other hellish battles I've written about and now the start of this new offensive.

We lost our C.O. yesterday, Captain Jeffries, shot down by machine gun fire. His death has affected me badly and a lot of the other blokes in my

company. None of us spoke for the rest of the day.
He had always seemed invincible. The bully beef
back behind the lines almost choked me. I didn't
want to have any of it at first. You know, just
didn't feel I should somehow. But you know Cooper!
I've written of him often enough. He gave me a
shove and said, Come on mate. Get into it! And so
I did. That's all you can do, isn't it?

They're coming round the trench with our
rations. Will write again soon.

Love

George

The last letter in the pile contained details of his 'Blighty' wound
and to what hospital he thought he might be sent. How wonderful
it must have been for my mother to receive. With what joy had she
made arrangements and rushed to be by his side? They were
married two months later at the Methodist church in Amesbury. I
had found their marriage certificate in the drawer of Mum's
dressing table when I first went through her room.

The house was in darkness except for the small light beside
me. I got up and turned the main lounge room light on and drew
the curtains against the lights winking across from Hawks Nest
and the long stretch of darkness I knew to be Windi Woppa. I
placed the pile of letters on the coffee table in a vain attempt to
dismiss them from my mind, at least for a while until I cooked
myself dinner but it was no use. I paused in the middle of the
room, looking at the pile of letters. I couldn't help but wonder
what effect that penultimate letter had on my mother's
sensibilities when she read it.

I was aware it wasn't as simple as likening my reaction to hers.
In her case there were many contingencies. Distractions. The
letter may have arrived, days, weeks even after she read reports of
the battle in the newspapers and she would have received it with

such relief that nothing could take her thankfulness away. Perhaps she noticed the tone and worried about the sadness in his writing but only until his next letter arrived when it would have all been forgotten in the joy of his impending return. As for me standing in the lounge room of a house that was never his home I found myself left with his cry of: *Why was I spared?* reverberating through my soul until it reached a resounding echo. I stood still for a moment gathering strength to ask the inevitable: Had Tom ever asked such a question?

The Wind

On the morning of the 24th May, 1943 First Lieutenant Tom Lockwood took his coffee up to the small landing inside the Country Club. He had earlier smoked a cigarette outside and because of the cold had come indoors to finish his coffee. Now he leant sideways against the window and cradled his coffee for warmth.

What a miserable day. It wasn't raining. Not yet but it was overcast and a south easterly wind was churning up enormous waves in the centre of the bay near the sand banks. This side of the harbour it was calm but across the bay a number of fishing boats were seeking shelter from the wind. They'd be stuck there for a while, he guessed.

As Tom sipped his coffee he noticed a Higgins boat powering into view. It had left Little Beach and seemed to be heading towards the other side of the bay. Another appeared soon after from the direction of Mile River. Tom glanced towards where they were heading. At that moment he saw a PBY Catalina approaching the bay from the northwest. What the hell was it doing out there, Tom wondered, peering at the choppy waves below the Catalina.

The aircraft's vast wingspan dipped from side to side as it approached the bay. It was an enormous seabird limping home, the wind buffeting it as the craft headed for safe harbour. Tom couldn't hear the drone of the engines – the wind had blown the sound away. His heart was pounding as he watched the Catalina dip lower towards the waves. The pilot appeared to be attempting a forced landing. 'Bring it in. You can do it! Bring it in. Bring it in,' Tom chanted over and over. But the Catalina never made it. Just short of deep water the cat suddenly dropped down and ploughed through the waves. It emerged briefly, struggling for the sky, only to crash back down with such force that its tail snapped off.

Momentarily, it bobbed in the waves and the sight of the stricken aircraft gripped Tom with a terrible incomprehension. He was unable to move, almost to breathe. It couldn't have happened. Not here! Not so quickly. He shook his head to free his vision of the partially submerged Catalina. But no, it was still there, a little lower in the water. He leaned against the window and bowed his head. His feet felt rooted to the spot, his whole body heavy. As he raised his head to look again there was nothing but choppy waves, the familiar bay transformed by white horses.

Had it really crashed? Finally after a few more moments he forced himself to move from the small landing and make his way to the scurry of activity below. Slowly he walked out the front of the club and stood, scanning the windswept bay.

There were steps behind him and Bob Morecroft yelled, 'Jesus fucking Christ! Tell me it didn't go down, Tom.'

'I wish I could.' Tom was breathless. Dazed.

'Well! What the hell happened?' Bob had grabbed him and was shaking him by the shoulders.

'I thought for a moment it was going to make it and then it suddenly dropped down, bounced and crashed. The tail broke off.'

Bob covered his face with his hands and was pacing up and down near the entrance to the club.

'Jesus fucking Christ!' he repeated. 'I think it was the A24-39 with Tubby Higgins, our best bloody pilot. If he couldn't bring it in...' Bob was speechless. He studied Tom's face as if searching for answers, an explanation to what had just happened.

'It didn't look good did it? I can tell by your face,' Bob said.

'It floated for a few moments.'

'Well it's not fucking there now!'

'No.'

'To hell with this! I'm not standing around here. I'm going to see what I can find out.' Without another word Bob walked quickly away in the direction of Little Beach leaving Tom feeling bruised and battered as if from a gale force wind.

For the next hour Tom walked up and down the beach, watching the Higgins boats and other navy craft converge on the crash site. He wondered if any of the crew had survived. He doubted it. The sight of the impact still throbbed behind his eyes. No matter how he tried to get his mind around it, he was unable to come to grips with the tragedy he had just witnessed.

How had it all gone so terribly wrong? He was no pilot so he wasn't in a position to speculate, but was pretty sure that this was the Rathmines base's first loss of a Catalina. He had heard a number of PBYs had gone down in active service off the coast of New Guinea but none in Australian waters in front of a sleepy fishing town. The whole of the club would be talking about it for weeks. Bob would come up with his own theory pretty quickly, if he knew Bob. Tom could only stand around and blame it on the weather and fate.

He had listened to enough stories from Bob and his mates about Tubby's brilliance in the air to rule out pilot error. So what had gone wrong? Were they all dead and why? Here in this paradise? Here, he had thought they were all safe – everyone in the club, the people of Nelson Bay, Peggy. All of them but they weren't. No-one was safe. Not completely.

Slowly he left the beach and walked across the road to return to the club. He discovered the clubhouse and grounds were all but deserted. Right now he wanted to run to her, along his favourite route, past the lighthouse and Little Beach, past Fly Point and all the tents camped by the water; up the steep zigzagging path to Magnus Street and along to the Ocean View Guest House where Peggy was probably making beds right now; run in this wind and expunge the vision of the Catalina from his mind; run until he couldn't catch his breath.

Maybe with the wind buffeting his body, as it had the Catalina, he would be able to clear Bob's angry words from his head and the idea that Peggy, his darling was no longer safe. But he knew he wouldn't feel she was safe until he could see her again. It was stupid, inexplicable but he needed to see her, hold her in his arms, to know she was safe. The sight of her would reassure him and hopefully stop the vision of the Catalina crashing again and again in his mind.

As people began to return to the Country Club and Little Beach, Tom stood outside the clubhouse for another half hour, staring across the bay.

Close to eight thirty that night there was a knock at the door. Unable to turn on the porch light because of the blackout Helen Ashburn, a little flustered, invited an immaculately dressed Sarah Linden into her home.

Her mother was annoyed, Peggy could tell. She didn't like being caught with her apron on in her own home and there was Sarah looking beautiful in a dark brown jersey dress.

'Sorry to bother you Helen, at this late hour, but could I borrow your daughter for an hour or two? I'm working on a project for a Sydney newspaper. Some reviews of children's books and I really need Peggy's help.' Sarah spoke so confidently and with just the right amount of condescension that there really was no refusal that could be put forward to sound reasonable. For a brief instant Peggy felt sorry for her mother.

'If it is absolutely necessary, Mrs Linden but I need her back by ten o'clock.'

'I'll make sure she is, Helen.' Sarah's smile didn't reach her lips. She turned from the older woman to Peggy. 'Well then,' she laid her hand on Peggy's shoulder as they walked out the door.

Peggy waited until they reached Sarah's steps before she spoke. 'Tom?'

'Yes, it is. I just want to tell you that he's had two whiskeys. I gave them to him and they've gone to his head a little. He was very distressed when he first came and I've spent an hour trying to calm him down. I told him I wouldn't get you, until he did.'

They had reached Sarah's front door. 'I've put him in the study. I'll be in the lounge room.' Together they walked into the house, down the short hall and with a gentle push from Sarah, Peggy found herself in the book-lined study, staring at a very distracted Tom.

In the instant before she ran to his arms Peggy noticed that Tom's hair was a mess. It looked as if he'd been running his hands through it all day and his khaki uniform was crushed. She laid her head against the coarse material just like she had the night of the dance. As he put his arms around her she could feel a difference in him. He was hugging her tighter than he normally did and he was moving a little from side to side. For a moment she thought he was sobbing but when she glanced up at his face, he smiled a little sheepishly and looked away, begging her silently not to look at him too closely. She closed her eyes and wondered why he was so different tonight. It must be the crash.

Finally he loosened his hold on her and when she looked up at him, Peggy could see Tom's focus was a little blurred.

'Sorry, I've had a few. Don't normally but Sarah was offering.'

'She said you were...'

'Yeah, I was. I'm okay. Now that you're here.' He was stroking her hair back from her face. 'Did you hear about the crash?'

'Yes. Did you have something to do with bringing...'

'No, I never,' Tom cut in abruptly. 'But I saw it. Don't want to talk about it though. The whole clubhouse has been all day. I had to see you. I was worried about you. Where were you when it happened? At Ocean View?'

'Yes.' She laid her head back down on his shoulder.

'Making the beds?'

'How did you know?' Peggy raised her head again.

'Just a lucky guess.'

They were swaying a little, Tom's balance obviously affected by the alcohol, but it was pleasant, as if they were at sea. One of the wall lamps shone directly behind Tom and it illuminated his blonde hair to a halo of white. Peggy felt like she had been drinking too. She was intoxicated with the sight and feel of him. Swaying with him, enjoying the feel of his body under his uniform and happy at seeing him so unexpectedly, Peggy didn't want the moment to end. Neither did Tom. He was holding her tight again and every now and then, murmured in her ear. 'I love you so much, baby. I miss you. I love you. I miss you when I don't see you, Peggy. I really miss you.'

Occasionally she would murmur back. 'I love you too, Tom. I wish we could be together all the time.' But mostly she let his words flow over her. Tom's mood had set the sails and they were drifting slowly in their own happiness. The lamp was the sun and Sarah's study their boat that would take them far away. Suddenly Tom pulled the boat in to shore. He moved away from Peggy and began to dig in his trouser pocket. He dragged out a small ring box and shakily got down on his knees.

'Will you marry me, Peg? I love you with all my heart and want you to be my wife.' He held out the ring box.

Peggy took it and both his hands, in her own. She pulled him to his feet and as she did so, found that she was crying. She threw her arms about him and said quickly, 'Yes, yes, yes. I want to be with you forever.'

He smiled then. 'That's good,' he said simply. 'It's not much,' he added, as she opened the ring box. 'All I could get in Newcastle but it's blue like the sea.'

It was too, almost the exact colour of the bay most days. The ring was a small turquoise in a delicate silver setting. 'I love it,' she assured him and put it on her finger.

He was still worried about the ring. 'I can get you a nicer one in the States.'

'I don't want another one. I love it. Don't you dare think of getting another one.'

'Your Mom doesn't know I'm here, does she?'

'No.' Peggy frowned at the mention of her mother.

'I thought we could go to the dance at the Quonset on Saturday. I'll come home with you and ask your Mom for your hand. There's no one else to ask is there? Guys I mean, like an uncle?'

'Not that I know of.'

'Well I'll have to ask your Mom then.'

'I do love you very much,' Peggy told him, overcome with emotion.

'I know, baby. I know.' He began kissing her then, deep long kisses that Peggy wanted to go on for hours. They lasted for ten minutes until Sarah tapped lightly on the door.

'You two lovebirds, it's nine forty five. You've got five minutes to straighten up before I see if Peggy will pass inspection and you too for that matter Lieutenant Lockwood.

'I want to tell her, Tom,' Peggy said, stretching her left hand out to gaze at her ring.

'Why not? She can keep another secret,' Tom said.

Shadows

All Monday night I spent reading Tom's letters. Near the end I found what I guessed to be my husband's Passchendaele, a place called Wakde Falls. It was May 1944 and he was attached to a signals battalion. I had only read the opening sentence when it all came back to me in a rush. This was the letter, the one that had bothered me for ages. I remember desperately wanting to talk to him about it after our reunion, but somehow we never did. I know I raised the subject more than once but Tom must have evaded my questions and the letter was eventually forgotten like his first, becoming submerged in the busyness of our first few years in America.

I sat down slowly, gripping the letter in my hands.

Underground telephone cables had been laid prior to the landing. The leading wave of men landing on the mainland encountered heavy surf which made things tougher for the troops. There was also fierce enemy fire from the flanks. A number of coxswains and boat operators were killed. One of them Tom knew, from way back. His letter went on:

'The beach strip was unprotected and all we could do was scramble ashore and crouch under a rock shelf. We were trapped there for hours.'

I closed my eyes. I could see it now.

Tom glanced behind him at the seven men of his section and back out to the beach straddled by gunfire. He checked his watched. God, they had been trapped here for three hours but he didn't want to send any of them out. He'd have to though, but not yet. His section had been cut off and he needed to regroup the signals platoon. They couldn't sit here all day, but as far as he could tell the gunfire hadn't eased. Where the hell were the Japs hiding? They must have underground access to the caves. Throw a hand grenade in and they just disappeared.

'Lieutenant!'

'What is it, Turner?'

'How much longer?'

Tom was about to answer when he heard a low, grinding, revving noise from the beach. Before he could stop him, Private Billy Wilson was off, crouching low through the scrub and dirt, elbowing his way to a clearing nearby. The kid was a worry, so keen and hot-headed that Tom had to keep a constant eye on him. Billy was popular in the section. He looked no more than sixteen and still didn't shave but he had been with the division since Buna so it was anyone's guess as to how old he was. Tom was relieved when Wilson was back in ten minutes to report that the tanks had landed. The boys whooped in excitement and everyone was off, edging forward for a look.

Tom glanced about him as his men lay low in the scrub. The machine gun fire on their position had eased and was now arcing back towards the beach. Tom followed the line of fire to the tanks. Even on the ramp, the tanks were laying down machine gun and cannon fire and his men were cheering and then cursing when one of the three tanks disappeared in the water. The other two hit the beach working together so magnificently it was a sight to see and now the allies had the upper hand.

It was time to move further inland to find the lines and begin the long task of repairing them. Hell knows what the Japs had done to them! As his section set to work, Tom kept an eye out on what was happening near the beach. Company A had control of the ridge and the remaining tanks were moving to support Company B. After more than an hour of fixing the cables, things got pretty hectic. More LSTs and barges were landing with marines and sailors getting in the way. And still the telephone cables refused to work.

Taking Billy Wilson with him, Tom moved up the dry creek bed to check the last part of the cable when there was a whooshing sound behind him. Tom turned to see Billy's neck blossom into red. Within seconds his uniform was soaked and the young boy was drowning in his own blood. With both hands on the boy's neck, Tom tried to stem the flow of blood but it was useless. It kept seeping from under his fingers. Billy made a gurgling sound and then he was still.

Oh, Tom, Tom. How did you bear it, I wondered? I desperately wanted to talk to Tom about it. I had this mad desire to phone him right now but it was nearly midnight, the wrong time to ring. And I knew too with our estrangement, such a conversation would be difficult, if not impossible. Sitting with his letters spread around me, I kept muttering to myself, *Why didn't we talk about it, Tom? When we were together again, did it seem as if I wouldn't understand?*

Maybe it had, I thought now. I did ask him more than once though; I was sure, definitely more than once. But he hadn't talked to me about Billy's death just as I hadn't talked to him about the depths of my guilt over leaving Mum. We had both bottled things up.

I stood up and walked around the room. How many things had I kept locked away since Sarah went to college in Wisconsin? Definitely my resentment at never having a real job and finally, when I got into teaching, feeling that I was too old to offer much. My worries when Sarah was young, of smothering her with over protectiveness just as my own mother had done. And my resentment of Tom's long hours working at his company, bringing in a lot of money to be sure but not allowing the time to make it to Australia and missing both those trips. That had hit me hard. Had I expressed any of this? No, I'd just bottled it up. Thrown the odd sly hint maybe, but that was all. Just kept it all locked tight inside me.

As I put all of Tom's letters away it was easy to think that the letter would have been bothering me more than it actually did. When I saw him again after years apart, standing below me at the wharf in San Francisco Bay, I am certain it wasn't uppermost in my mind. In fact I'm pretty sure I was thinking how good he looked and how much I had missed him.

But there had been so much to think about. There were decisions to be made, such as where exactly we would live. I wanted to know when his electrical engineering course began;

how far away the Black Hills were from his parents' home in Newcastle. He wanted to tell me about all the places he would take me, when he had semester breaks. There was so much to decide and plan, plans for the rest of our lives in fact. It was an exciting time.

When I woke up this morning all I could think about was our early married years at the South Dakota School of Mines. I don't know what started it all but while I moved about the house, my mind was alive with memories of the Black Hills.

Those first few years really were the happiest and simplest too. For the first six months after my arrival we lived with his Mum and Dad in Newcastle. In the fall when Tom's course began, we moved to the Black Hills and lived on campus very cheaply. It was just veterans housing, a bunch of old buildings thrown together on the lawn of the North West part of the campus. But it did us. We had two rooms and a bath.

What a beautiful place! The dark hills on the horizon, almost breathing, it seemed sometimes. And when I was very depressed and feeling lonely whilst Tom was studying, I sometimes imagined the beautiful hills were creeping down towards me, to overtake my whole life. But mostly I just loved the aspect of them, the knowledge that as you came closer and closer the black turned to the dark green of Ponderosa Pines, those majestic trees marching up and down the landscape in rows like a quiet army.

Tom was studying on the GI Bill and not long after we moved there, I found a part time job working in the reference library on campus – shelving books mostly but it helped us money wise.

Tom's first class would start at 8.00 am and I would get up to see him off, waving to him as walked towards the old prep building or some mornings the Engineering building where he took classes in trig and calculus. I was left with the house to tidy (five minutes), a bed to make (two minutes) and two pots of red geraniums to water.

Needless to say, I was bored much of the time, and if Tom was having lunch in the old building where I couldn't visit, I would take a walk to Rapid City, heading west down St Joseph Street or St Joe's as we called it. I liked to browse through the bargains at Woolworths, or J. C. Penney's, which I preferred. Sometimes I would walk down Sixth Avenue to gaze up at the Hotel Alex Johnson, an imposing building, very swish with a wonderful chandelier in the lobby.

Often, though, he would come back for coffee and bring some of his classmates, veterans like himself from the 41st and that's when I just loved to sit and listen to them all talk about how they won the war. Sometimes Tom would tell the guys about Nelson Bay and pull me into the conversation. Those were the times Tom and I wished one of us had had a camera, so that we would have been left with something tangible of the bay, something that could be passed around. It was a small regret but it rankled with me, particularly over the years. When we were married there just hadn't been any money for something like a camera.

The South Dakota School of Mines and Engineering. How I loved the sense of purpose of that place! Six hundred students working hard towards a goal. There were six female students, Tom told me. I had envied them their determination. They had to be determined because they came up against a lot of prejudice, being females taking engineering or science. Sometimes I asked, how the two were doing, that were in Tom's classes. He said, *Fine, they were doing fine*. A small part of me would have liked to ask them where they got their confidence from.

A few young couples like Tom and me, we saw quite often. Ruthie married to Ed had twins, so she always seemed to be up to her knees in diapers but Larry's wife, Lola, from North Dakota was fun to be with. In the first year or two we often went shopping together in downtown Rapid City. We lost touch with the four of them after Tom graduated in 1949, and we moved back to Newcastle.

Right now, sitting out in the garden with the smell of wattle on the breeze, I missed that little shack of ours. We made love a lot then, in the mornings usually. We had a little window right above our bed that we always left open. Sometimes after we made love, a cool breeze would blow in over our naked bodies. We'd hold hands and just lie there feeling the breeze and our hearts and breath slowing down to a normal pace.

I tried to will myself to a place like that, a moment in time when we both felt at peace. It could even be here, now, in this house. The breeze was blowing on my face, my heart was beating fast and I imagined him beside me. We had just made love and the incredible feeling of closeness was still with us. That was the time to tell him everything.

I would take his hands in mine and say:

Tom, I never really explained how difficult things were between my mother and myself; that I grew up with a woman whose moods were as unpredictable as the weather, who could suffocate you with concern and worry one moment and the next flay at you with a temper that was truly frightening.

I never told you how heartrending it was leaving her and how distressed she was at the docks that day; that she was so bowed down with grief, that I didn't recognise her as my mother. Perhaps if I had, you would have understood the depths of depression I seem to have sunk into since Sarah left for College.

Darling, I have never stopped feeling a terrible, wrenching guilt at leaving her and part of me has been so angry with you for not realising and for not coming with me to see her. And now it feels like I'm being punished. Sarah has grown up, married and moved to another state. I know she's happy but how often will I get to see her?

But more than anything I want to tell you about Tom, my other Tom, my older brother who drowned. You see he's the reason behind it all. His loss defined my mother's life just as leaving her, has defined mine. But I'm back now where I feel I should be and I want you to be here too. I want you to come back and remember and more than anything, to sit and talk to me. We could talk about my brother and you could tell me about Billy Wilson and what you really lost that day. And finally explain to me, where you think we should go from here? Which landscape should we choose?

For a moment, just one moment, it felt as if he was by my side.

In the afternoon I got stuck into the gardening. About time I did. I've been here just over a month and haven't weeded, mowed the lawn or planted a single thing. It's winter of course but spring was only a few days away. Back home the trees would be starting to turn and Sarah would be looking out for those Canadian geese. The thought made me smile.

I surveyed the front garden. I had been watering regularly because, although it's been cold and windy, there hadn't been much rain. The cineraria were looking a little ragged and the roses looked like they could do with another trim. While I worked, I chatted over the fence with Joan and asked her what annuals my mother put in along the front strip this time of year to replace the cineraria.

'Stocks, love. She always put in stocks. That doesn't mean you have to though. Delphiniums or Canterbury bells would be nice to colour co-ordinate with your car,' Joan said, nodding towards my blue VW parked out front.

'What a great idea.' Trust Joan to think of something like that. I laughed as I worked. Joan could always make me laugh. So could Tom.

'Was that Nancy's son who dropped it off last night?'

'Yes, baby Charlie. That's what we used to call him as he was the baby of the family.'

'He looked to be thirty five to me.'

'I suppose he would be,' I said. 'She's moving in tomorrow.'

'That'll be nice,' Joan said absentmindedly. 'When are you taking the car for a spin?'

'I've got the furniture arriving in the morning, so I thought I might drive to Swansea Thursday and door knock for Maisie Ashburn.'

'Should be interesting, love. Any idea how long it will take you?'

'How many houses are there in Swansea?'

'Half the day,' Joan replied.

I got up from digging and stretched my back. 'No, I thought I'd just speak to a few of the shopkeepers. Would you like to come?'

'No, Peg. I've got Arthur home all tomorrow. Next time you

go to Newcastle give me a yell though. Meant to say to you,' Joan said, leaning on our dividing fence.

Something in her tone made me go over to stand near her.

'I've been hearing all about the little fancy tea party that you put on for Nancy the other week. Feels like I've been left out of the picture. I mean yes, you made me tea but the last time I was over I didn't get the lemon slices and the cucumber sandwiches or the teapot if I remember rightly.'

Laughing, I told her, 'You got the teapot, Joan.'

'Did I get the white linen tablecloth?'

'No,'

'Well, there we are then.'

Still laughing, I asked, 'How does four o'clock sound? That would give me time to make Mum's sponge.'

'Oh, that would be lovely.'

'And iron the tablecloth.'

'Oh yes. We have to have the white linen tablecloth. I'll bring welsh cakes.'

Joan was prompt and brought treacle scones, as well as the welsh cakes. It was a celebratory afternoon tea. We have both turned very windy corners, a strong wind trying to knock both of us off our feet, but we were still standing and life was getting easier. After Joan left I did the washing up and found a small note folded under Joan's teacup. It read:

'Sometimes life's shadows are caused by our standing in our own sunshine.'

Ralph Waldo Emerson (1803-1882) American essayist, poet and publisher.

Underneath this Joan had written: 'P.S. this is not a gardening tip.'

Oh, Joan! She had done it again. Given me what I needed when I needed it. How timely this quote was. I've been thinking along these lines the last week or two in regards to my relationship with Tom that somehow I couldn't see what was right in front of me. I read the note again, laughing at Joan's P.S.

It was time to do a stock take. No, I haven't phoned him once since I left him. No, I haven't written either. Yes, I have forgiven him. At least now, after being here for a month and doing a lot of thinking. Yes, I have actually brought all his letters with me on this trip home and something else too. I walked into my bedroom and pulled down my battered suitcase – ex Newcastle, ex South Dakota School of Mines, ex Nelson Bay. I opened it up on my bed and fishing in the right hand corner, pulled out a small jewellery box that contained two rings – my plain silver wedding band and the turquoise engagement ring Tom had given to me at Sarah's.

I hadn't been able to put them in storage with all the furniture. That's what I told myself. Yet I could have left them in my safety deposit box at the bank in Newcastle. But no, quite simply I couldn't bear not to have them with me. I gazed at the rings. It was too late to catch him at work now. I would have to sleep on the decision.

The next morning, even before I had my coffee, I made a trunk call to Lockwood Electrical Engineering. I worked out it was around three o'clock Wyoming time and I couldn't wait to speak to him any longer. Young Amy answered, all excited, and asked how Australia was. 'Sunny,' I told her. I asked for Tom.

'Oh, I'm sorry Mrs Lockwood but he's out at the moment. I'll put you through to...'

I spoke quickly. 'No, Amy, I'm sorry, but I don't want to speak to my husband's secretary.'

The line was bad and I missed the first few words of Amy's reply, something about knowing all of Tom's movements. 'Thanks anyway.' I hung up thinking I bet she does know his movements, all his moves. I couldn't bear to think about another woman's body pressed against Tom's. I didn't want anyone but me knowing what his lovemaking was like.

I was furious at Tom for not being there; furious too at having to think about Barbara again and angry with myself for calling. I shoved both rings back in the box and snapped the lid shut.

Transformations

Around mid morning Nancy's van arrived in Magnus Street and I popped over to see if she needed any help. She greeted me at the door, wearing a headscarf and overalls but still managing to look chic. We kissed and she exclaimed, 'It's lovely to see you, Peggy.'

'Is there anything I can help you with?'

'No thanks, Peg. I have both my boys, Bill and Charlie. And of course I have the two boys from the moving van. So I'm going to bark orders to the four of them all day.'

'It's not going to take all day!' someone yelled from inside.

'Oh yes, it is!' Nancy whispered to me. 'By the time I arrange everything. Come over at five, Peg, for cocktails!'

'Cocktails!' I exclaimed.

'It's a tradition from Sarah, which I am determined to keep up. It's very decadent. I have this rather snazzy little cocktail book and we can try something new from it.'

'Can I bring some sandwiches over for lunch,' I asked, still feeling that I should be doing something to help.

'No, that won't do at all. I don't want you coming over in the middle of it. I want you to see it transformed.' She drew the last word out.

I smiled and felt truly happy for the first time in ages. This attractive woman in her late sixties had become an amalgam of my two favourite people. She was still herself, my surrogate mother but she was Sarah too.

'At five o'clock then.'

'Yes, Peg, at five,' she replied and walked back inside the house to answer a yelled question from Bill, it sounded like.

I laughed and walked home, wondering how to fill my day. As I stepped back inside my home I realised there was still so much to be done. I pushed the hideous orange curtains aside and peered out. Sitting down on Mum's old couch I decided that no one from the street could see me and feeling excited, I pulled down the curtains and bagged them up to drag out into the laundry for now. Perhaps Mrs Marley, who did odd sewing jobs around Nelson Bay, could make use of them.

I decided to ring her to find out if she would like to make up the white material that I managed to pick up last Saturday, into curtains for my room. I was aware that she would need to come over and measure up. I'll have to listen to her chatter for a few hours but it would help pass the time. When I rang her she sounded quite pleased that I had thought of her and in fifteen minutes she was knocking on my door. She exclaimed at the colours I had chosen and, from what I can gather (beyond politeness), actually liked the changes to the house. I ended up making us both sandwiches for lunch as she wielded her tape measure.

By three thirty when Mrs Marley finally left, I had discovered what had been happening with the Radburn Estate. I finally had the courage to walk there last week and the devastation was heartbreaking. It appeared that the estate had been planned for a housing development but when the land behind Halifax Park was cleared of every single tree, leaving an arid stretch of sand, not surprisingly the blocks of land didn't sell and were still not sold. The residents were appalled and to make matters worse, it seemed that finally building would take place in the near future, but not single homes as had first been planned, but as high rise. I decided I must contact the council to see what was really happening.

I also heard all the local gossip regarding people I could barely remember. I ummed and ahhed in response for about half an hour and then I was saved by the noise of a van outside: my furniture. Luckily Mrs Marley took the hint and left, with the orange curtains.

Half an hour later the van was gone taking away the old furniture (for a small fee) and I dashed back up the stairs to my living room to survey the changes. The brown leather lounge suite really did look good against the *moonshine* walls and the kitchen was lighter and more open with the new tables and chairs. I decided I really did need new kitchen curtains though, possibly a pale yellow wouldn't look too bad. I took the old ones down and looked back at the lounge room and through to the glistening bay beyond. I could tell by the light that the sun was about to set and realised I had only ten minutes to get ready to see Nancy.

At five o'clock I was standing on the porch looking through the stained glass windows of what used to be Sarah's living room. As I straightened the hem of my black cocktail dress, Nancy answered the door. She was wearing a silver long sleeved top with a turquoise skirt and looked stunning. Smiling with excitement, she ushered me inside.

It took me a moment to realise that Nancy had transformed the living room into a bright sitting room featuring a cane lounge suite with pink and orange coloured cushions. There were pot plants everywhere and the chairs were arranged so that they were facing the bay. Behind this room was the old dining room, which Nancy had obviously made into a television/family room. The old dark cupboards in the kitchen had been replaced and Nancy's room, once Sarah's, had been painted in peach with a new cream bedroom suite.

'It's wonderful, Nancy. I didn't even realise you'd painted the house.'

'I got the boys to do it last month but I understand you've been painting too.'

'Yes, how did you know?'

'Oh, you know, the local grapevine. Now what can I offer you?' Nancy asked me, leading me back to the new sitting room where a tray of nibbles had been laid out. 'I'm going to have a *Golden Dream*. I'm rather partial to Galliano. Would you like a *Blue Hawaiian*? It's pineapple juice with rum, blue Curacao and crème de coconut. Very summery.'

'Sounds wonderful.' I watched as Nancy made the drinks, standing over Sarah's old sideboard.

'How are you getting on? I mean really getting on,' Nancy asked me as she gave me my drink. It was an amazing coloured concoction and tasted divine. I thanked her and exclaimed at the taste and she sat down next to me.

I said, after a moment, 'Everything makes sense now, of course. Her over protectiveness and her not wanting me to marry

Tom. The only thing I really can't get my head around was her temper, her prickliness. I mean, I keep wondering was she always like that? Or was it only after my father and brother died?'

'I wouldn't know the answer to that, Peggy. As you know, I met her after they had both died, but I did know how bad her temper was and how frightening she could be.' Nancy sipped her drink, considering. I waited for her to speak and then she told me, 'The two of you must have been about eight, I think. One day Betsy came running home in a state. She wanted to go over and see you and ask you something. I can't remember what now but within five minutes she was back home, quite in shock. It took me ten minutes to get it all out of her. You must have arrived home late and Betsy overheard your mother screaming at you.'

'Peg, I'm not one to call the kettle black. I spent about fifteen years yelling at my four but this did seem...' Nancy hesitated. 'Much worse.'

'She could be very frightening,' I commented bitterly. 'And yes,' I said, returning Nancy's gaze. 'It is the one thing I am having trouble coming to terms with.'

'She lost a lot of people in her life, Peg. That would be enough to send anyone bitter. And angry,' Nancy added, after a moment.

'But to take it out on me? A child?'

'You were the last one left to her.'

'Yes, I suppose so,' I said, staring at my drink.

'I mean how many people did she lose?' Nancy asked.

'Both her parents when she was fairly young, her brother at Gallipoli and then ten years later her husband and her son.'

'A lot of people to lose in one lifetime, Peg. A lot of people.'

'Yes, it is,' I replied, staring out at the fading light over the bay. 'Too many people. And then of course I left her anyway.'

'Now Peg, what is this?' Nancy said. 'You can't go blaming yourself for falling in love.'

'That's what Joan said.'

'Well there you are then,' Nancy said, doing a fair imitation of Joan's Welsh accent. 'How about we go for a stroll? I would love to look at what you've done with your house. Oh, and don't let me forget. You must choose which writing desk you would like and I think I have a spare occasional table as well. Come over on the weekend and I'll have them out for you. All the extra furniture is crammed into the spare room at the moment.'

I was amused by the image of the cluttered spare room in contrast to the immaculate interiors we were just leaving. Nancy closed the door behind us and we strolled up the street to my house, arm in arm. I felt so much better for her company. The light of understanding was beginning to shine down on me. It really was all making sense now. I smiled. The moon was out and we sipped our cocktails as we walked.

White

The next day after seeing Nancy, I spent thinking about Tom rather than my mother. It really was time to think about Tom, about his gentleness and his strong physical presence – two of the things I loved about him the most. At times during the day I kept wondering what he would think of the transformation of this old house. At other times I was just wishing I could talk to him. After a sleepless night dreaming about his lovemaking, I got up around eight o'clock this first day of spring, made myself a coffee and put both rings on – the turquoise and the silver wedding band. I contemplated their slim, delicate beauty. With them back on my finger, was I standing in my own sunshine now?

Gazing out at the windswept stretch of water, I really felt as if I had shed layers, thrown off the mantle of years to finally touch base with the young girl I had been. After nearly a month of being immersed in the past I had become the past. I was eighteen year old Peggy Ashburn and the day of my marriage was before me like a banquet, ready to be devoured, detail by detail. But just as I felt ready, (me the betrayed wife) to face one of the happiest days of my life, my wedding day, I was also aware that this was the day that Peggy Ashburn ceased to exist. The irony in the realisation had the ring of truth about it. That echoing: *Of course, of course.*

Could I somehow keep her inside me this time? Not lose her to the passage of years, the accumulation of all those experiences and events that separate a teenager from a middle-aged woman. I hoped so. The elements, offering their support, had ensured the weather and the bay were very much the same as on that blustery afternoon. Smiling to myself, no longer working from the known to the unknown, I went back to that day.

Peggy Ashburn and Lieutenant Tom Lockwood were married

at the small Methodist church on the hill above Nelson Bay. It was an overcast and windy day in June 1943. Tom wore his full dress uniform with the dark green jacket, dark cap and light grey trousers and Peggy wore Tom's favourite dress, the white voile with the lace neckline.

Nancy had run up a beautiful turquoise cape that came to Peggy's waist, as a wedding gift and her mother had given Peggy her best white gloves with the pearl buttons. The gloves completed all the requirements. The cape was something blue, well almost. She had borrowed a white satin garter from Mrs Marley, who volunteered it quite happily a week before. (Peggy had been dying to ask what she was doing with one but in the end hadn't the nerve). The gloves were old and her white shoes were new, from Sarah.

It was a good turnout with Emily as bridesmaid and Captain Morecroft as best man. A lot of Peggy's school friends turned up, a few officers from the Country Club and about half of the bay as spectators, standing around outside the church, the wind blowing the odd hat away. Thankfully most were more curious than disapproving. There were lots of comments about the weather. *At least it hadn't rained.* And more comments about how beautiful Peggy looked. Pale, but beautiful. Helen Ashburn was subdued throughout but accepted all the congratulations with good grace. Tom couldn't stop smiling till well into the reception at the CELOPS hall.

Peggy was overjoyed to see Betsy early in the evening. She had missed having her at the church but it had all been a bit awkward as Betsy refused to be bridesmaid. (Still mourning Jimmy she had explained.) There were stacks of food of course and a crush of people. It was unseasonably warm that evening and very damp. All Peggy wanted to do was run away with Tom, just take his hand and run with him down to the beach. But there were all the wedding presents to open and people to speak to. No honeymoon unfortunately. Tom couldn't get leave but the new owners of the Ocean View Guest House, Mr Ben and Mrs Norburn, saved their best room for the night for Tom and Peggy.

Peggy changed into a new peach jersey dress for her going away outfit. *Going away just up the road.* But it didn't matter.

Betsy caught the bouquet and they waved goodbye. At the door Peggy caught her mother quickly in her arms. She held her tightly. So tight that at first Helen Ashburn resisted and in a moment tried to pull away. Still Peggy held on and whispered in her mother's ear. 'I love you, Mum. Please don't forget it.' She thought she heard a sob from her mother but decided, as she moved away, that she must have been mistaken.

It started to rain on the short walk to Ocean View.

Tom asked, 'How is she?'

'She'll be all right.'

Inside their room Tom began to take off his clothes, stripping down to his boxers. He said, 'You were fighting yesterday.'

'Yes, sort of and today. She's afraid of losing me.'

'But she said yes when I asked for your hand.' Tom sat down wearily on the bed and took Peggy's hands in his 'I thought when she gave her permission everything would be okay, that she'd be happy for us.' He was stroking her fingers.

'We put her on the spot and she couldn't refuse you even though she wanted to.'

There was a crack of thunder and the rain began to beat heavily on the roof. Peggy closed her eyes for a moment. She was so tired, so worn out after almost two long days of placating and consoling her mother's last minute fears, beginning yesterday morning. *I'm not leaving yet, Mum. Tom could be here for another year. I'll still be living here with you; Tom will stay maybe one night a week. I told you that Tom said it was better this way. If we aren't married he's heard it can be very hard to bring me into the country. Yes, his parents are happy. They are writing to you. I think a letter is already on its way. No, Mum, we just couldn't wait.*

And finally when all her assurances seemed to have failed she yelled in exasperation. *Why all this now when you gave your consent nearly a month ago?* Bitterly Helen Ashburn had replied, 'How could I not under the circumstances.' There was no answer to such a remark and Peggy's white voile dress laid out on a chair in her room, seemed like a reprimand. She stared at its pale shape in the darkness for over an hour before falling asleep.

Now she faced Tom in the light of a small bedside lamp and

said, 'She couldn't refuse you. You see, Mum's English, don't forget. And in 1915 she met this big friendly Australian who swept her off her feet and asked her to marry him. He asked for her uncle's permission and they married in her home town two years later when he was invalided back to England. Her brother and her father had died by this time.'

'I thought you didn't know that much about your mother's past.'

'I didn't. But I became so frustrated last week with Mum's moods that I went and saw Nancy Wallis. She told me the little she knew. So you see it's very like what has happened to us. Her uncle said yes, so how could she say no, when she did exactly the same thing? She married a soldier from half way around the world, left her home and went to live in another country.'

'Yeah, I see what you mean,' Tom said after a long pause. 'And I just thought she was happy for us.'

'She is. It's just these old fears of hers have returned. About losing me I think. Like when I was little. I used to think she was angry with me when I came home late from running around on the beach or climbing Tomaree or Stephens Peak. Not so long ago when we heard of Jimmy's death I realised it's fear than makes her like this, not anger. It's fear, Tom. And there's nothing I can do about it. I told her I wasn't giving you up. That I'll never give you up.'

'She'll come around. She just needs some time to get used to things the way they are now. If she sees how much I love you, she'll soften up. She'll be happy for us.' Tom took Peggy's face in his hands. 'I was worried about you during the service. You looked so pale, I thought maybe you were having second thoughts.'

'Second thoughts about marrying you? No, it's what I want more than anything, to be yours. To be your wife. Things are different now. They have been since that morning the Catalina crashed. I don't exactly understand why. But they are, aren't they?'

'Yeah. I don't know how to explain it but afterwards I needed to know that you were mine, whatever happened.' Tom began to unbutton her dress. Peggy pulled it off tiredly and lay down beside Tom. He held her from behind, wrapping his arms around her, his body finding the outline of hers. Together they listened to the rain.

This was the moment that had kept her going all through yesterday and today, Peggy acknowledged: this first real embrace as husband and wife. 'That day, I knew you were safe but somehow I knew that you were worried about me. How did I know that?'

Tom pulled her closer. 'Because you love me and you know me. You understand me too.'

'Yes, I do, don't I? And you understand me. You know what I want and need and now, finally, I understand my mother.' Peggy turned a little way towards Tom. 'Do you know when I hugged her?'

'Yes.'

'I told her I loved her.'

'I'm glad, sweetheart.' Tom moved over and switched off the light. Against her back, Peggy felt the cold metal of his dog tags.

'You're too tired and I'm too tired for anything but this. Let's sleep for a little while.'

Although my wedding day was grey, in evocation it shimmers white with illumination. It was on that day I fully understood my mother and her fears. I kept that knowledge for a while but then misplaced it. Did it slip away in the two and a half years living without Tom or was it lost in the depths of the Pacific on the voyage to the States? Somewhere, somehow it disappeared, the white truth of it.

But of course that wasn't the complete truth – my understanding of my mother's strange moods and dependency. As I have since found out, it was only part of it. The rest I now hold to treasure and mourn: my brother Tom. He was the missing piece in the jigsaw puzzle of my mother's behaviour and the knowledge of his death made my mother now a complete person and a tragic one.

If I could only hug her now and say I'm so sorry, Mum. I'm

so sorry that you lost nearly everyone you loved, but you didn't lose me. I'm so glad I gave her that hug on my wedding day.

I remember my wedding day so clearly and my wedding night. I was pale that windy day. White-faced I heard Mrs Marley say to another woman. I didn't care, Tom was mine. And when, just before I drifted off to sleep, I said to Tom, 'I'm glad it wasn't sunny. It wouldn't have been right, you know what I mean.'

'I know exactly what you mean, Peg. But I didn't marry you because of the crash. I would have married you anyway but because of them we were married this month, this day. That's how it worked out from my asking you on the 24th May. We still would have married, just not now.'

'Not today,' I murmured.

'Another day,' Tom answered.

'I love you,' I told him.

'I love you, Peggy Lockwood.'

I can still hear him say it, almost thirty years later, and the exact tone of his voice, his deep, gentle voice that I miss so much. It was raining now. I stood looking over at Jimmy's beach, at the place where the aircraft still lay. Oh, the sound of the rain on the roof! I was mesmerised listening to it, just like on our wedding night.

A crack of thunder woke Tom and his caresses woke me. I thought he would turn on the light but he didn't. He seemed to be all over me. So urgent, so impatient. He was inside me quickly. Still half asleep, I just held on to him tightly and let his passion, the wild fever that had taken over him, burn itself to a dim flame. He cried out and I stroked his back.

'I'm sorry, Peggy.'

'Don't you dare say you are sorry,' I told him and closed my eyes. I must have dozed because sometime later I woke to see he had turned the bedside lamp on. He was leaning on his elbow, gazing at me. I smiled at him. He was so gorgeous, his blonde hair and strong compact body. I loved the set of his collar bone. It fascinated me and his chest. I touched the dog tags around his neck and his dimple and smiled. He smiled back and said, 'Now it's your turn.'

'What?' I said sleepily but he was already kissing my breasts and stomach. This time he wanted something from me and was constantly stopping to look at me, to stroke my face.

'I'm not going anywhere,' I told him jokingly. This seemed to fire him up because he began to kiss me more ardently, relentlessly until I became breathless. The tempo of the rain on the roof had slowed and it seemed to match Tom's movements as he plunged inside me.

Remembering now, listening to the rain, I could still recall the urgency in his voice as he begged me to tell him, 'More, more.' And, 'deeper.'

'Deeper,' I told him. He had never been so demanding and I was more than happy to comply, moving my hips hard against his.

I closed my eyes to try and block out the sharpness of the images that were playing through my mind. The sound of Tom's voice was resonant in the rain. Oh, how I want to relive that night, to feel that close to my husband again. But is it possible after nearly thirty years?

Now with the courage to telephone my husband, I discovered that it was too late to do so. Tom would be home from work. I am not ready yet to ring him at home because, what if I did, and Barbara answered? That would be the finish of us, I know. For this last month, secretly in some hidden part of my soul, I have been hoping that what Tom said was true. *That it was over between him and Barbara. Only the one time and I had caught them.* I couldn't bear the thought that he was still working with her but more unbearable was the reality of her sharing my husband's bed.

I would phone tomorrow morning. With the decision made I moved away from the window and sat down in the paisley print, wondering what I was going to do with myself for the rest of the day and dreading to think how long it would take me to get to sleep tonight.

The Island

As soon as I was out of bed I rang the operator for Wyoming but was told there were problems with the Sydney Telephone Exchange. The awful winds they had last night evidently, the telephonist told me. She suggested I try later. I said: *I can't. Later is tomorrow morning*. I spoke sharply from disappointment and immediately apologised. I shoved the phone down and paced the lounge room.

Slowly, but stealthily like a beautiful marmalade cat, the beauty of the spring day enveloped me. The sun was shining with both the softness and clarity that is only seen on very rare occasions. Maybe a trick of the light but it brought to mind school holidays, early mornings at the beach. And of course it was the school holidays. I needed to get out of the house and into the spring morning.

Yet I stood still, gazing at the sky. It was such a crisp pale blue, the colour of my car – the sky, the bay, my car. It was definitely the day to go to Swansea. To brace myself I looked through the photos on my mother's dressing table and on impulse gathered them together and put them in my bag.

Wearing my dark blue peasant dress, sunglasses and my favourite brown shoulder bag, I headed off in my beetle. I loved driving this car and the radio was a particularly good one. I tuned in to the local station and relaxed into the bucket seat. *Eagle Rock* was playing, after that *The Tracks of my Tears* and an oldie, *You Send Me*. I knew all the words to that one.

By Hexham I was singing the odd chorus to just a number of the songs playing. It surprised me how many songs I barely knew the words to. I felt like a medieval prisoner locked away for years and now finally seeing the sunshine after an interminable time. I wasn't blinded though, just joyful. And I knew that it wasn't a coincidence that on this morning music was accompanying me on my journey. I had shut music out of my life for a long time now and I didn't realise to what extent, until I was faced with song after song only vaguely familiar; a refrain in the background of my depression that I had not wished to acknowledge.

I acknowledged both things now: my depression and the music I had avoided, by never switching the radio on in my car and not putting the radio on at home because I missed Sarah's voice singing some of the songs. Her favourites at that time were the British bands, the *Animals* and *The Stones*. For five years, since Sarah left to go to College in the fall of 1967, I had blocked out music and more importantly Tom. Well now I am free, free to enjoy both. I would speak to Tom tomorrow and in the meantime I would sing all the way to Swansea. And I did just that, humming most of the time though, as of course, I didn't know the words. I knew the words however to *If I Can't Have You* by Yvonne Elliman and I sang it as I crossed Swansea bridge.

When was the last time I was here? Tom and I never got this far south, I'm sure. I think it was a picnic with Nancy, Sarah, Betsy and I. The memory was distant but the channel was familiar and the strip of land in the middle of the town dividing the traffic, although there was no traffic but there were a lot of cars parked near the shops, being Saturday. I hoped desperately that Maisie was living here, somewhere. The town seemed just the sort of place to be hiding an eccentric aunt.

Taking off my sunglasses, I walked into the nearest shop – a fruit and vegetable store. A middle-aged man with a moustache smiled at me. 'I was wondering if you could help me. I'm looking for...'

He cut in. 'American, are you? We don't get many international visitors.'

From his expression it was hard to tell whether he was joking or not but I found myself laughing anyway and told him, 'I was born in Australia.'

'Oh well, that's all right then. What can I do for you?'

Still smiling, I said, 'I'm looking for a Maisie Ashburn. She's my aunt.'

'Aunt, you say. I'm sure she's got no family. Not that I've heard her talk of anyway.'

'Well, she doesn't know about me. I want to meet her and introduce myself.'

'Well, well. That's exciting, isn't it?'

Studying his gleeful expression I was rather sorry I had provided so much detail. I was sure that by this afternoon most of Swansea would be informed. Brushing the thought aside I asked, 'Can you tell me where I can find her?'

'Oh yes,' he said, frowning for a moment. 'She's on the island. It's the white house with the blue windowsills.

'The island?'

'Coon Island.' He shook his head. 'You really aren't from around here are you?'

Coon Island. There was that feeling again: *Of course, of course*. Maisie lived on Coon Island. They had been staying with her. She was probably the other woman that appears in a number of the holiday photos and I hadn't realised, hadn't wondered who she was or spotted a resemblance to my father. Recalling my frustration and excitement on discovering the photos, I simply hadn't taken the time to look for any resemblances. My mind had rushed ahead with ridiculous speculations instead of quietly looking and really seeing what the photos revealed.

After he gave me the directions, I thanked him, bought a banana and set off. I only drove for a few minutes before I came to a small stretch of water separating the island from Swansea. There was a rickety wooden bridge ahead of me, only the width of one car and from it a gravel road ran behind the backyards of all the houses that were like white dots against the blue green of the channel. They were diamonds on the necklace of this green, low-lying point of land. I parked the car on a clear patch of ground to my right and got out to take in the view.

Most of the houses were just weekenders, small shacks that had obviously been added to over the years; holiday homes that had become permanent. Most had small slipways and rock walls against the tide and tiny gardens for front yards with Swansea Channel as the whole of their outlook. I could imagine myself fifty years ago coming to a rough shack, just one room, that had to be swept out every summer and then gradually, over the years, not wanting to leave. Who would, I thought, sweeping my gaze from the dark green islands to my left, to the opposite shore on my right. Across the aquamarine channel the shoreline was dotted with more weekenders, the windows of which were blinking in the sun.

I returned my gaze back to the island and began to walk towards the first of the houses. I could now see that some of the weekenders were in a dilapidated condition, not as pristine as they appeared from a distance. As I began to round the point, and the whole expanse of the waterfront gradually revealed itself, I noticed a gap in the sweep of houses, particularly towards the northwest. Some had presumably been recently demolished; the earth in places was littered with debris.

As I approached the front yard of the first of around fifteen odd houses, an elderly man came out and walked towards me.

'Looking for someone?'

'Maisie Ashburn.'

'Maisie will be pleased. She loves visitors. Hers is five houses down.'

I thanked him and walked on, feeling a little numb. The beauty was calming me but I knew deep down there was an undercurrent of doubt. As I listened to the water lapping against rocks and slipways, I struggled to remember what my worries were. How can I have any worries on a day like this? In this present moment there was nothing to worry about unless I wanted to drag in the past, haul forty seven year old regrets into this day, the 2nd September, 1972. Yet they must be addressed. I must explain my mother's behaviour, if I possibly can. I must apologise for the way my mother distanced herself figuratively and literally from the Ashburns. But it shouldn't be dwelt on to exclusion of this beautiful spring day. I mustn't let the past cloud Maisie's sunny afternoon. And mine too.

And then I saw her, sitting on a white kitchen chair on a small patch of grass in front of her home, a house that was just recognisable as the house from the photos. It appeared to have had another room added but the intricate woodwork scrolls under the eaves were unmistakable. This was where my mother holidayed with my father all those years ago. The very plump elderly woman looked up, shading her eyes against the midday sun. I was standing in her sunshine, my shadow falling on her. I carefully moved to crouch down beside her and let the sun fall on her again.

She had a shock of white curly hair, two missing teeth and a kindly face. She turned to me and said, 'I'd know that red hair anywhere. And the eyes,' she added, squinting to study my face. 'I heard about your mother's death but I just couldn't get to the funeral. I am sorry.'

'That's all right.'

'How about you just grab a chair from inside and sit with me for a while. Then we can go inside and talk.'

We did just as Maisie said. We sat for a while, I don't know how long, and looked at the expanse of water, which was sometimes aquamarine and when the wind whipped across the surface, pale jade. We stared at the shoreline opposite; watched boats pass and seagulls fly by. We sat, my aunt and me, and just contemplated the landscape around us; feeling the sun on our faces, listening to the soft flap of a pelican in flight, smelling and tasting the salt air.

Inside the small weekender while Maisie made us egg sandwiches for lunch, I finally found the courage to apologise for my mother's behaviour. Maisie waved this away.

'Not your fault, love. Mum and Dad were terrible to her and I just didn't know how to make things right. They blamed her, you see, for your father's death. Said he died because of little Tommy drowning. But it wasn't anybody's fault. To start with though, I blamed my mother.'

'Your mother?' I asked surprised.

'Yes, she was there when it happened. Decided to pop over and see how Helen was doing. You know, she just couldn't leave your mother alone and was always dropping into the little house around the corner from ours to interfere. I warned her, time and time again.' Maisie paused for a moment and stared into her cup of tea. 'It was around five o'clock in the afternoon, if I remember rightly, an awful time to call on a new mother. You were in your cot screaming for your feed and Tom was in the bath but there was my mother standing knocking on the door and standing on ceremony too.' Maisie paused again to wipe a tear from her eyes and I put my hand over hers. She grabbed it and held on tight.

'Your mother yelled out for her to come in, that she couldn't answer the door. She yelled out twice, I found out later. Tommy was mucking around with his boats. He called them "subarines". Finally when mother hadn't come in, your mother left him quickly to open the door. We think he must have hit his head. Immediately mum started talking about this and that. Your mother took her coat and spoke to her quickly and told her to sit down while she got Tommy out of the bath. By the time she went back it was too late.'

Maisie sobbed. 'It was terrible, Peggy, terrible for a long time afterwards. I blamed my mother. My mother blamed yours and no-one knew what to say to anyone. I tried to contact your mother, tried to meet up with her a few times. But it was hard for her with you so young, and when she left for Nelson Bay, I just didn't know how to make things right. I wrote for a year or two after that but never heard back. I did send you birthday cards but I think I stopped after about your fourth birthday. Should have kept going but I didn't know what was happening.'

'There was nothing you could have done, Maisie.'

'Oh yes there was,' she said rallying. 'I could have waited until you were say nine or ten and landed on her doorstep. Got to know you and then you would have known you had an aunt and could have come to see me as you got older. But by that time I was living in Sydney with a fella, Arnold, his name was. We ran a hotel in Surry Hills for a number of years till he died. After that, in '55, I came back to live in the old home. Mum and Dad had died and it seemed the time to come home. I sold that after a few years and came to live here. Always liked it here the best,' she said, looking out the windows to the view.

It was the time to pull out the photos. They brought a wonderful smile to Maisie's face. It seemed my parents came for a total of four summer holidays from 1920 to 1923, the last one nine months after Tom was born.

'These four photos are the ones from that year,' Maisie said, pushing the photos back towards me. 'They're the ones of the holiday after your brother was born.'

I am not surprised which ones she had singled out. I told

Maisie, 'When I first saw them under the dressing table I had the feeling she looked different. That maybe these were taken after I was born. But that was before I knew about Tom.'

'She worried about him that holiday, but as you can see she's still smiling.'

'Yes, she is,' I said, smiling now too.

'They were madly in love,' Maisie said.

I thought – just like me and Tom. 'I'm glad they had some happiness.'

'They did,' Maisie replied.

'And this one I said,' pointing to one of the three taken at her parent's house.

'I took all three because Mum and Dad didn't know how to use the camera. Henri was home that day and I wanted her in the photo but Tommy played up and she grabbed him and took him inside. You see she left his blanket on the grass. In one of the photos anyway.'

'Yes,' I said, everything falling into place.

'My sister Henrietta died from an epileptic fit in 1932. I'd love to talk about her, but not today,' Maisie said, getting up from the kitchen table.

It was obvious that our talk had drained my aunt so I just asked, 'Can I come next week?'

'Of course you can, love. Perhaps you can help me decide what to do about this house. They want me out but I feel I'm too old to move somewhere else.'

'I'll find you a new house. We'll go house hunting together.'

'Now why should you do that, Peggy?' Maisie said, in a matter of fact tone.

'Because you're family, Aunt Maisie,' I told her.

Maisie smiled and shook her head. 'Stubborn like your mother.' She paused. 'I've got money you know, quite a bit. I just don't have the energy to move.'

'I'll start looking in the papers.'

'Will you, love?' Maisie asked, moving to the door to see me out. As I was about to walk away, she told me, 'It was no one's fault, you know. Your mother coped the only way she knew how.'

'I understand that now,' I said, turning back and giving Maisie a hug.

'Well, you know where I am now, girl. Come any time you like.'

'I'll come next Wednesday morning, if that's all right.'

'Of course it is. I'm not going anywhere, love. Any time you want to come and see me.'

'I'm so glad we found each other,' I said, as I gave Maisie another hug.

'I sure am, Peggy,' Maisie said and waved goodbye. I waved back as I walked away. I felt like a child again with my whole life in front of me.

At Bobs Farm the Desiderata song came on the radio and this time I listened to the words, really listened. I arrived home very tired but also very happy, with a strange sense of feeling completely at home in my own heart. It had been helpful somehow to hear about Tom's death and to discuss with another person the difficulties of my mother's life. And before that, when Maisie and I just sat and looked at the lake and the sky, had been wonderfully calming. I realised now she was probably gathering strength for what she had to tell me, just sitting quietly and gathering strength. I hoped to sit with her again like that next week.

I decided she was an angel in disguise – wise too in a way that Joan was wise. I was looking forward to telling Joan about my trip and tomorrow morning ringing Tom.

Later after cooking, eating and washing up I walked over to Joan's on the small winding path that linked our backyards. Midway I came upon her. It was dark so I couldn't see her face clearly but when she spoke I knew something was wrong. She asked me how my day went. I said, 'I'll tell you later. How about you come back to my place and tell me what's wrong?'

Joan paused and after a deep breath said, 'I've had a letter from Angharad.'

'You've what?' I blurted out.

Quietly in the dark, Joan repeated, 'I've had a letter from Angharad.'

Orientation

Joan and I talked at my place for over an hour. Angharad's letter in an unstamped envelope was enclosed in one from Professor Thomas. It seemed that the professor had put off going through all Angharad's personal belongings from the hotel until just recently. 'I couldn't face the task straight away,' he wrote.

Joan remarked how pleased she had been when she read his honest statement and was very thankful for his letter. She had already read Angharad's more than five times when she gave it to me. As she handed it over I couldn't read her expression.

Earlier, outside, I guessed she was upset by her tone of voice but with the letter in my hands, her voice was steady and her face blank. It was impossible to tell whether she was distressed by the contents of the letter or pleased and that wasn't like Joan. She wasn't a closed book, just one with hidden depths. I was at a loss.

'Just read the letter,' she reassured me. She valued my opinion but didn't want to stay while I read it. I promised to read it by tomorrow morning. We didn't talk about Coon Island. I decided to save it for another day and then offer it to her as a gift, just as Maisie has accepted me without question, like a blessing.

Early in the morning I rang the operator and asked for Tom's work number. I was relieved that the phone was answered by Amy and asked her to put me through to my husband.

'Oh, he's in Wisconsin, Mrs Lockwood. He drove there yesterday.'

My heart was thudding in my chest and I began to feel sick. 'There's nothing wrong with Sarah? Has anything happened?'

'No, Mrs Lockwood,' Amy cut in quickly to put me out of my misery. 'Everything's fine. It's just a catch up trip. He's spending about a week there.'

'Thanks, Amy. I'll ring him there later tonight.'

I looked at my watch again. It was eight o'clock, about three o'clock Wyoming time. I would have to wait at least another five hours before I could safely catch them both at Sarah's. How I wish it wasn't the school holidays! A few hours helping at the school was exactly what I needed but it wasn't to be. Instead I must read Angharad's letter as I promised Joan. The fact that she wants my opinion of the letter worries me. But whatever the contents, I know I will have to tell Joan the truth of my response to it.

Sitting on the porch, just as I had when I read Angharad's first letter over a month ago, I unfolded the pages carefully.

Capel Curig
5th August, 1972

Dear Sis,

How are you, my dear? I have spent the last two days looking through church records and reading parish histories. I have decided to research our local church. I also want to see if I can find out anything about the strange stones nearby, the stones of our childhood at Cerrigydrudion. I can almost see you shaking your head as you read this. Another project! For later though. For now I am determined to begin work on my memoir as soon as I get back. I think it will do me good to actually have everything set out, year by year. I can then really evaluate all the choices I have made in my life.

I have begun to feel lately that I have actually chosen the right path, the one best suited to what I hold dear in my life. I am, where I was meant to be, I really believe that, Joan. In making notes for my memoir I have done some serious thinking about the two life choices that have haunted me: the ones that have caused me the most distress. And by those I mean Huw Williams, Professor Williams as he is now known and Dai Llewellyn-Jones.

*I didn't tell you but last January I decided to
find out about Professor Williams. He is teaching
in Cambridge now, almost retired. Gwen was
heading there for a lecture in the summer break
and on my request made some discreet enquiries.
It turns out he is 'still' a dreadful womaniser and
was almost dismissed from the English Department
ten years ago because of his dalliances with his
students. He is in his sixties now and has been
married for the last fifteen years; given his wife
more than her fair share of worries from what
Gwen could discover. So my very much regretted
refusal of the old rogue's marriage proposal,
twenty five years ago, evidently saved me a lot of
heartache.*

*That only left my other love Dai Llewellyn-
Jones. Sis, I bumped into him the other night at
the pub in Festiniog. He had a small cowed wife
with him, who he introduced as Nell. She was
pleasant enough but definitely appeared worn out
by him. I noticed that his eyes had become hard
and beady and he had a shifty manner as if was
about to be caught out at something. Caught out
bullying his wife I'm guessing. It was such a shock
Sis, to see the change in him. How had I ever
thought I loved such a person? But somehow I
must have sensed the arrogance in him and the
self-absorption in Huw. I have saved myself a lot of
heartache in both cases.*

*So what does that leave, as far as lost loves go?
Nothing really, only dream men that I never met,
that I might have met at the odd faculty meeting
I didn't attend; perhaps at one of the many
dances I never went to at Carmarthen University,
maybe at one or two parties in the early days at
Aberystwyth. But on each of those occasions I
stayed at home because I had something better to
do, research for one of my many projects or a novel*

I couldn't put down. It was my choice each time, my choice to stay at home. And now at this point in time I have no regrets at the way I have chosen to live my life.

The next day after seeing Dai, I visited our local church and placed flowers on our parent's graves. It was good to just stand there and look at our church, Sis. There was a gentle breeze blowing through the yew tree and I felt calm, almost happy. I stood looking at the church, the graves and began to see it all as if for the first time. Yes, the memories were there, but in their place.

With my recent discoveries concerning Dai and Huw, I no longer felt envious of all the brides that had married there. It was just not for me. I was not meant for that kind of life and luckily, I have been spared the type of crushing drudgery I glimpsed in Nell's eyes. Oh, but how I had been envious Sis, for many years, every time there was a wedding. There I'd be, working myself up into a state, worrying that I would spend my life alone; that I would never walk down the aisle with our Da giving me away. Well, I never did of course, but the only regret I have now is how many hours of my life I spent at our church consumed by envy at all the brides that have stepped smiling from its dim interior and disappointment at all the pointless and sometimes malicious gossip overheard in the grounds. And months too spent mourning our parents, which Mummy, particularly, wouldn't have been happy about. Well, somehow it all seemed to melt into the stonework and become part of the church.

Finally the church was just a church, a rather lovely building in all its bare simplicity. It was no longer a place where I felt let down by life. Life hasn't let me down at all. It has, quite simply, given me all that I have ever really wanted.

I have been thinking, too, about my career. All my working life I have made the past my present and it has troubled me sometimes. In many ways the present moment is the only moment but here am I living and breathing the teachings of philosophers that for the most part have been dead for thousands of years. However, I can see now, that in my vocation, I have brought their teachings to the present moment and their wisdom has helped me live my life.

Please excuse my ramblings but I have so much to say. I want you to know that I am proud of what I have done. All the philosophy classes I have taught over the years, bringing to young minds the great teachings of Plato, the Socratic method of thinking, Aquinas's cause and effect and so much more, I hope, leaving with at least a proportion of my students enough interest to spark their own quests for knowledge. Ask questions, that's the only way you'll find answers. I don't know how many times I've said that during the time I've been a teacher, and I've tried to make it a way of life, as well you know, Sis.

Well, it has been nice to come back to visit the old places but I am heading home tomorrow morning, stopping off at Portmeirion on the way. I am quite looking forward to writing my memoir and to putting everything in order. It has been interesting to say the least, to look back on my life and to begin assessing it as objectively as I can. (Not an easy thing to do!) However, I do feel that I have achieved a lot so far on my travels and I'm not talking geography here. It would have been nice though to have had some company. However, there we are as Mummy used to say. There we are! But my career Joan, I have had a lot of pleasure from that and my hobbies and you have been a joy to me, my darling Joan. I will leave you with one last quote.

'He who can no longer pause to wonder and stand rapt in awe, is as good as dead; his eyes are closed.' You know that one well I think, from Albert Einstein. I have found a lot to pause and wonder at in my life, not the least you, my wonderful sister. Wishing you were here to see the lake this morning at Capel Curig.

Your loving sister

Angharad

Carrying the letter, I ran faster than I have in years, and with me ran my younger self, in a yellow dress racing to meet Tom. I knocked frantically on Joan's door; sure I would die from frustration if she wasn't home. She was. Joan opened the door slowly and her face was transformed into an enormous smile when she saw mine. I was still panting with joy and excitement when she sat me down.

For a moment I struggled for words and then they all came pouring out. 'It's a wonderful letter Joan. She was in a state of harmony when she wrote it. All the forces in her life had come together. Everything made sense to her. She could see what was important and let go of the things that weren't. She felt proud of her achievements and of her hobbies too.'

'Oh, she did have some hobbies. Her projects,' Joan said.

We were sitting on Joan's brown velvet couch and when I noticed how pale and sad she looked, I moved closer.

After a moment Joan said, 'I never realised how much she minded never getting married or how much all the gossip about her strange ways bothered her. Oh, I knew that it worried her but not that much, Peggy. A few of the local girls used to talk about her in church. Cruel things, some of them said. She used to laugh it off. But it had hurt her and it had all stayed with her for a long time. I should have known how much these things bothered her.'

'We all keep things from others so that we can cope. And

maybe we shouldn't, but it's human nature.' I took Joan's hand. 'In the end though she let you know, didn't she?'

Joan nodded.

'And then she let these things go. She said it was as if they just melted into the stonework. She died completely at peace, Joan, and with her dreams realised: her wonderful teaching career and her passion about her projects, all the good she did for the local community groups.'

'Oh aye, and her research too,' Joan said. 'She was a very brave soul, wasn't she, Peggy?'

'She was, Joan, with a wonderful heart and mind and...' I paused. 'There's nothing to be sad about in that letter. Be proud of her.' I handed the letter back to Joan.

Joan smiled and when I smiled back, she nodded her head in agreement.

'But there's one thing. It's just a thought, a feeling from the letter,' I told Joan. 'I think if it's possible, she should be buried at Cerrigydrudion.' I struggled over the difficult name.

'Oh,' Joan said, brightening. 'That's in Professor Thomas's letter. Well, in Angharad's will actually. And she's left me her house and some money in a trust fund, a lot of money actually. So I thought when all the will business is finished I'll go over and hold a memorial to my sister and also establish some sort of scholarship to be offered at the university in her name.'

'That's a wonderful idea, Joan. And now you can go back to visit.'

'Yes, but not to see my sister.'

'No, that's true but to see that she's not forgotten.'

'Oh, aye, love, I can do that,' Joan said, wiping away a tear.

'And you can visit Portmeirion.'

'Oh, yes I can, can't I? I'd like to go there.' Joan was beginning to look like her old self. 'Thank you for reading my sister's letter.'

'It's a beautiful letter.'

'It is. I can see that now,' she said, looking at the letter. 'It's a beautiful, wonderful letter.'

Stand Wondering

And it *was* a beautiful wonderful letter, I thought, back home again after leaving Joan much happier, almost content. It was wonderful for Joan to have received and wonderful to be given the privilege to read – for in it Angharad had eloquently expressed what I had experienced yesterday during my reunion with Maisie; that everything had come together to bring me to a point in my life where I felt, that at least part of it, now had meaning. I had gained a greater understanding of the cruel blows life dealt my mother and I had forgiven her too, for cutting ties with the Ashburns. The situation had been intolerable and as Maisie had said – there was no way to put it right.

But I now had a chance to help my only surviving relative by finding her a house. Of course I don't know how much money she has to spend but I could at least work out what she might have to pay. I wondered if she would come and live in Port Stephens. I decided to ask her next Wednesday.

I know I'll learn a lot from my aunt. Already obvious was her quiet dignity and the way she handled all that life had thrown at her. I'm guessing that Maisie Ashburn had travelled far in her life and leant a lot on the way whereas for myself, I was only just starting to fathom things out. Joan had helped me, discovering more about my mother had helped and so had Maisie. Sitting on that chair in the sunshine, in silence gave me as much, I think, as our talk did later in the house. And lastly, so had Angharad's letters. But I had a fair way to go. There was Tom to sort out and hopefully there would always be Tom. Both Toms.

I spent an hour or two going through the Sunday papers looking at properties and around one o'clock I made myself a sandwich, sitting out on the porch again to eat it. It was a beautiful day, more beautiful than yesterday, if that was possible. There was more heat in the sun and a brighter glitter on the bay. How Tom used to love the bay and it was on a day like this thirty years ago that we met amongst the Christmas bush. In fact today was our anniversary.

I sat looking at the sparkling water trying to conjure up the calm I felt yesterday gazing at the channel with Maisie, but it was no use. My stomach was a mass of butterflies and I was sure my voice would falter when I spoke to him. But I would just have to get through the nervousness and cope with whatever happened. I would try to explain it all to him somehow.

When I called, Sarah answered. 'Hi, Mom, how are you? I haven't spoken to you since the funeral.'

'I'm fine, Darling. How's Richard?'

'He's fine. Work's going well.'

'That's good, Sarah. How about you? Anything on the job front?' I had been hoping for a while now that Sarah would be able to make use of her Economics degree from the University of Wisconsin but in the meantime she worked two days a week in a large department store not far from Richard's office.

'Not much, Mom.' There was a long pause. 'What's happening with you and Dad?'

'I've forgiven him.'

'Oh Mom, that's wonderful.'

I could hear the joy in her voice and my heart went out to her and then I thought she was about to say something but there was silence. She was waiting for me to speak. Nervously I said, 'Can I speak to him, Darling?'

'Oh, Mom,' Sarah spoke awkwardly. 'He's not here. Would you be able to ring him tomorrow night?'

Immediately I felt a wave of disappointment rush over me, so deep, so all encompassing that I was sure I would drown from distress. I believed so strongly that today was the day to speak to him; that now with the chance dashed I felt, inexplicably, the moment would never come again. Had I put the opportunity off just one too many times? It seemed so. I should have spoken to him weeks ago. I was not sure if I would have the courage to ring tomorrow. I was close to tears. I didn't know what to say to Sarah. Finally all I could come out with was, 'I'll see, Darling. I'll speak to you soon.'

I paced the house for nearly half an hour until eventually deciding to go for a walk, a long walk, and hours if necessary to help me sleep tonight. I would walk until my legs ached and I could hardly climb into bed. I paused for a moment in my bedroom, thinking about reading Tom's first letter but I knew it would make me cry again with regret and I was crying already.

I glanced at my face in the bathroom mirror. My red hair looked wild today. I brushed back unruly strands from my forehead, deciding to leave my hair out and wash my face. With a bit of lipstick on I was presentable but only just.

I was wearing one of my old favourite dresses, a brown crushed velvet but it was long sleeved and in an effort to cheer myself up and take on something of the beautiful spring morning, I grabbed my new green halter neck dress and tugged it on. It was a bit short but it was summery. On impulse I shoved Tom's letter in my bag. Closing the door behind me, I glanced up the street. Charlie's car was out the front of Nancy's, delivering an odd piece of furniture no doubt. I must call in and see her again and tell her about Maisie.

Feeling the sunshine on my shoulders, I took a deep breath and headed for the bay. My intention was to skirt the shops by keeping to the waterfront as much as possible and then head off towards Corlette, maybe even Salamander Bay, if I had the legs. A little while later, I was just walking up the small hill towards the old Post Office, now the Postmaster's residence, when Mrs Marley accosted me.

'Well, where have you been hiding? I haven't seen you for days. We've all been wondering where you've been. I was just saying to Ruth, that maybe you'd gone away for a while.'

'No, just to Swansea yesterday.'

'Nice day for it.'

'Yes it was.'

In that moment Mrs Marley's face brightened. 'Are you expecting any visitors?'

'Any visitors?' I asked, puzzled.

'Yes, visitors,' she repeated, a little annoyed with my vagueness.

'No, I'm not. Why do you ask?'

'Well there was a very good looking American gentleman asking after you yesterday. Evidently he went to the house but found it locked up. Merle told me. Merle's my friend who works at the chemist,' Mrs Marley explained. 'Well Merle said he was hoping to catch you today. He didn't say who he was but maybe Merle can find out his name.'

'No, that's okay. I'm sure I'll catch up with him,' I managed to say, my mind in turmoil and my heart pounding. I walked off without another word, unable, actually, to speak another word. I kept walking, increasing my pace past the church we were married in. I couldn't breathe and was light-headed with shock. I stopped for a moment to look at the bay through the surrounding trees. With my breathing under control, I began to walk fast and then near Thurlow Avenue I began to run. He wouldn't be waiting in the valley with the Christmas bush for they had all gone, replaced by a street and new houses. At Dutchies Beach I stopped for a moment and felt myself blush, remembering how we had made love here in the sand. Suddenly time had telescoped and the memory was intense and very close, almost tangible, as if our younger selves were actually there, now, on a blanket, our bodies entwined.

I slowed to a walk, my cheeks burning at the memory and then I laughed. Oh, we had had some fun together. The thought buoyed me on. I reached the rocks and clambered over them to the small grassy knoll but I couldn't see anybody on the spit. There was nothing for it but the long walk along Bagnalls Beach.

It was hot again like that other day and I could feel my shoulders burning. My leather bag was heavy and I had long ago kicked off my sandals and thrown them in my bag, uncaring about sand, about anything. Finally I came to the spit. It looked the same. At least I couldn't discern any change to the weekenders behind me. I sat down on the spit and closed my eyes for a moment wishing him here, and then I remembered the letter. I pulled it out of my handbag and read it again for the hundredth time. When I looked up towards Bagnalls he was there. Blue shirt and dark blue pants, against the white sand, encircled by the blue of the ocean. Funny he had worn almost the same thing the second time we met. Did he realise what day it was?

I stood up and shaded my eyes against the sun. I had a sudden urge to run to him, as on that other day, but I held off. It would be nice to watch him come to me. In the meantime as he walked ever nearer I was left to stand and wonder at this amazing second chance. I never once thought Tom would come to me here; that he would leave his business for a day, let alone for a week or more and arrive so suddenly like this. I underestimated him and his love for me.

Oh, the joy of seeing him again! He was closer but not close enough to speak. I kept looking at him, drinking in the sight of him after being apart for nearly three months. I was seventeen once more and revelled in the experience, vowing not to lose that part of me ever again. His letter was still in my hand as he came to stand in front of me, and just as on that other occasion he seemed nervous, and he was hardly ever nervous.

'You look just as nervous as you did that day. I remember you actually tripped over a log.'

He smiled. 'Yeah, I did. You see, I met this beautiful girl in the Christmas bush yesterday and today I saw her unbutton her blouse and let the breeze blow on her breasts.'

'You did!' I exclaimed. 'I'd forgotten that.'

'I never did.'

He was standing right in front of me, but studying me closely and looking anxious.

'All I knew was that I seemed to have this strange power over you. I don't think I've ever been aware of it since. But I felt it that day.'

'You've always had power over me. I'm here, aren't I?'

I could see the sadness in his eyes but I wasn't quite ready for an embrace. He seemed to sense this and after a moment glanced at the letter in my hands.

I wanted to tease him some more and following on his earlier banter of mixing the past with the present, I said, 'It's from my new boyfriend. I just met him the other day and he's written to me to explain how he feels.' This time he didn't smile. He thought I was serious. I could see the colour drain from his face and he stepped back from me. He said, 'I'm sorry. I should have known after…'

'After what happened with Barbara?'

'Yeah,' he replied, running his hands through his hair and beginning to move away from me.

This time I touched his arm and when he grabbed my hand I felt the yearning in his body. 'That's history. This is our anniversary,' I told him.

Tom relaxed a little. 'Not the day I tripped over the log though, that's tomorrow.'

'Yes, the day we first met is today but the Christmas bush is gone,' I explained.

'I know,' he said. 'I went there first.'

At that I threw myself into his arms. It was exhilarating to feel his embrace. A million years had passed since I've been in his arms. But he didn't kiss me. After a moment I looked up at him.

'What about this boyfriend?' he asked.

'You, silly.'

'But the letter…'

I pulled my arms from around his waist and showed him the letter. He stared at it in disbelief.

'I thought you lost it.'

'I never lost it. Mum took it. I just couldn't tell you that.'

'You knew she took it at the time?'

'Yes.' We both sat down on the sand. 'I mean, I was pretty sure.'

'Why?'

'Well, let's see…' I paused. 'I have so much to tell you. I don't know where to start.' I took a deep breath. 'Just the other week I discovered that I have a brother who died when he was a baby.' I paused and gazed into my husband's eyes. 'And his name was...'

'Tom,' he interrupted.

'You knew?' I said in disbelief.

'Not about your brother and I'm sorry to hear that, Peggy. But I knew all along there was something about my name. She went white, your Mom when I said my name.'

'You never mentioned it.'

'No, I don't think I did.' Tom hesitated. 'How did he die, Peg?'

'He drowned and it caused a terrible rift in my family. My dad died a week later, probably partly because of the stress. An accident at work,' I said after a moment.

'Peggy, I'm so sorry.'

'No, I'm sorry. I'm so sorry I didn't tell you a lot of things. I didn't tell you how much I minded leaving Mum or how disappointed I was that you couldn't come on both the trips.'

'I should have come both times, Peggy. I realise that now. If I had come I would have seen you with your mother and perhaps understood what you were going through with her.' Tom reached out and pushed aside a strand of hair from my face.

I closed my eyes at his touch. 'I'm sorry too that I didn't actually realise how withdrawn I had become when Sarah left for college. I mean, I didn't understand what was happening to me, I don't suppose most people do. But I didn't try to understand. I couldn't pull myself out of it and I've only just now realised how bad the depression was.'

'I couldn't reach you.'

'I know that now,' I said, trying to read his expression.

He returned my gaze and said, 'It was only the one time and she left the job the next day.'

'She's not your secretary anymore?'

'No. I have a new secretary now called Lola.'

'Lola?' I said in surprise. 'I used to love spending time with Lola in South Dakota. Do you remember her?'

Tom was laughing now and leaning against me. 'It's the same Lola. I've been negotiating with Larry this week to sell him half the business.'

'Sell the business?'

'Yes, it would give me more time to do other things, like maybe set up a business in Newcastle.'

'Why would you set up another business in Newcastle?'

'Newcastle, New South Wales, Australia.'

I threw myself into his arms again and we both fell back in the sand. After a moment we sat up laughing and for a while just gazed in silence at the beach.

'There's so much more I want to tell you and you have things to tell me,' I said after a few minutes, putting my hand over Tom's. He was quiet, studying the waterline and the shore opposite.

'Yes, we do. We have a lot to talk about.' Tom paused. 'My God, I'd forgotten how beautiful it is here,' Tom said finally.

The bay was the bluest I had ever seen it and the sky a wonderful clear, high dome above our heads. He turned to me with wonder in his eyes and I smiled back.

Acknowledgements

My deepest thanks go to so many people who helped make the past come alive. For details on life in Port Stephens during 1942/1943 and 1972: Josie Norburn, OAM, Dawn Tawse, Helen Roche, Audrey Blanch, Edna Thompson, Elaine Hall, Audrey Newtown, the late Kevin Patterson, the late Joyce Cohen, Joyce Keast, Marj McQualter, Jean and the late Elsie Diemar, the late Thelma Robinson, June and Jerry Fenwick, Jill MacKinnon, Danny Carroll, Beverley Rose, Des Muddle, Anne Simmonds, Jennifer Spruce, Mr and Mrs Randall, Joanne Smith, Betty Brickall, Barbara McKay, Cecily Haddock and Johno at Getaways Beach Fishing.

For details on Swansea and Lake Macquarie: Richard Okon and Gordon Humphreys. For North Wales, Jim Boys.

For military matters concerning HMAS Assault, the Joint Overseas Operational Training School and Port Stephens generally: Wayne Sampey, the late Jack Armstrong, Ernie Cox, Ellis Fuller, Fred Jackson, Ron Zeuschner, Commander Peter Shevlin, AM, RAN (RTD), James Hurst, Jack Clarke and Donald L. Bath. I would also like to add my thanks to the many people who responded to the Australia Remembers Campaign of 1995 with details of their memories of the war and civilian life. But for their efforts so much information would have been lost to future generations.

For details on the G.I. war experience and the divisions that trained in Australia: Karlene and Bud Schriner, Howard Kelley, Juan Gonzalez, Larry Gibson, Rich Heller and my wonderful old soldier CH McCormack.

For Wyoming and the South Dakota School of Mines and all things American: the very helpful Bill Hughes, Catherine Werner, Larry K Brown, Larry A. Simonson, Ellen Stuter, Judy West, Robert Nicholls, Lonnie Anderson and my angel in disguise of a GI war bride Betty Kijek.

I would also like to thank these people for their support and help generally: Rex Whiteside and the indomitable Margaret Lamb, the Port Stephens Historical Society and various other people. Keith, Wal and Hazel Green, Peter Bishop, Matthew Ward, Brian Joyce, Bryan Havenhand and Anna Kaemmerling, Catherine Milne, Cathy-Anne Townsend, Charmaine Clarke and Danuta Raine.